W9-BZU-290

Also by Jane Ashford

BLAME
IT ON
THE EARL

JANE
ASHFORD

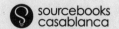
sourcebooks
casablanca

Published by Sourcebooks Casablanca, an imprint of Sourcebooks
P.O. Box 4410, Naperville, Illinois 60567-4410
(630) 961-3900
sourcebooks.com

Printed and bound in Canada.
MBP 10 9 8 7 6 5 4 3 2 1

One

THE RUIN OF TINTAGEL CASTLE WAS ONE OF HER FAVOR-
ite places in the world, thought Sarah Moran. It was a shame
she made it here so seldom, even though her family lived only
fifteen miles away. Today, however, she had convinced her
parents to bring their houseguests up the Cornish coast to
visit the ancient site, and she intended to make the most of
it. And so, while they looked over the remains of the medieval buildings, she walked the edges of the cliffs and searched
for secret nooks and crannies in this place where Uther
Pendragon came to Igraine and conceived the legendary King
Arthur. Sarah's mind filled with all the marvelous stories
she'd read as she wandered—quests and battles and love and
loss, not to mention several characters she had wished to give
a sound shake and some tart advice about their foolishness.

Rounding a tall stone outcropping, she noticed a long,
narrow shadow behind it. The slant of the sun was just right
to reveal a crevice, and when she went over to look, she
saw that the opening was wide enough to edge through.
She slipped in and followed some turns and twists, nearly
tripping once on the scatter of pebbles on the ground. The
boom of the sea echoed on the rocky walls, and the air was
damp with spray.

At last the space opened up a bit, and she could see the Atlantic waves breaking on the shore below. The currents here were fierce. On the left, a series of ledges descended. Could it be a rough-carved stair? Perhaps leading to some forgotten hideaway? Sarah leaned forward and peered down. No, the heights were too high to be steps, and they slanted the wrong way.

"Look out there," said a deep voice. "What are you doing?"

Sarah turned to find a figure emerging from the crevice. Outlined by sunlight that dazzled her eyes, it seemed at first that she had called up a knight of old, a magic guardian of secret ways perhaps. Then she saw his buckskin breeches and long-tailed coat. Only another visitor. "I thought there might be a stair down the cliff," she said.

He came up beside her and looked down. "Could it…" But when he took one further step, a slab of rock tilted under his foot and he lurched forward over thin air. Instinctively, Sarah reached out. Reflexively, he caught her hand. And then both of them were hurtling toward the sand in a rush of air and fear.

The man hit flat on his back with a thud. Sarah landed on top of him, drawing a huff of expelled breath from his chest. And then nothing. A wave roared in and sprayed them. Startled gulls screeched and flew off.

For a few moments, Sarah lay still, stunned, draped over a total stranger. Then she pushed up with her arms and twisted to sit beside him. From this angle, it was even clearer that the ledges weren't a stair. Indeed, from down here, the cliff seemed nearly sheer and much higher than it had appeared from above. There was no one in sight. The strolling visitors were hidden by the crag and piles of boulders.

Another wave hissed in over the sand, drenching Sarah's legs and spread skirts and the man's riding boots and breeches. She struggled to her knees. A third, larger wave broke over a boulder and showered them with spray. They were on a narrow strip of beach, barely two arms' span wide, and they'd been fortunate not to land on one of the large stones that dotted it. Sarah could see that the shore would be completely covered when the tide came in, as it was rapidly doing now. "Are you all right?" she asked the man.

He said nothing. Another wave washed up, slightly higher.

Sarah bent to examine her companion, putting her fingers to his wrist. His pulse beat evenly, but he was unresponsive. She could see no wound. Feeling the back of his head, she found no lump there. But he had hit the sand hard, with her weight atop him. A stunning blow apparently.

Another wave washed over them, cold and relentless. The tide was rushing in. They had to climb back up. Sarah stood, staggered to find her balance, and went over to the cliff. The rocks were overhung and slippery with damp. She tried a step up but her shoe didn't grip and she fell back. "Hello," she called. "Help! Someone help us!" Even at the top of her lungs, her voice was swallowed up by the roar of the sea.

A wave hissed in, soaking the man up to his chest. Receding, it pulled at Sarah's feet with worrisome power. She had to get him out of the way of the tide or it would drown him. But how? Even if she could climb the cliff by herself, she couldn't carry him. And the sea would engulf him before she made it up.

Frightened, Sarah looked around. She noticed an opening a little way along, the seaward end of a slender sea cave. She ran over to the cavern, which was lit by the lowering western sun. It went well into the cliff. The front part was full of water, but the sandy floor rose as it slanted inward. She thought there was a dry patch at the end.

She returned to the man, shook him a little in hopes he might revive. He groaned. "Please wake up," she said. He did not.

Sarah looked around. There was no rescue coming. There was no one but her to save them. She took a deep breath, gathered all her resolve, and stooped to take hold of the man's coat collar. She tugged. Though he wasn't a huge fellow, he didn't move. She dug in her heels, grasped his coat with both hands, and pulled with all her strength. A wave lifted his legs and hips, which was a help, and she managed to shift him a bit. Very slowly, she began to drag him toward the cave, her back protesting at the effort.

It was hideously hard work. It would have been impossible if not for the rising water, which began to float him on his back as they went. This was not all good news, however, because the strength of the current, coming and going, nearly knocked Sarah down every time. Incoming waves struck her legs like a blow, tripping her up and threatening to push her over. Going back out, they pulled at her skirts and made the sand shift under her feet until she nearly fell. Once she did, with a hard splash, losing her grip on the man's coat and only just catching it again before he was swept away. At this rate, she didn't see how she was going to save them. They had just made it inside the cave, where the water was deepening with each surge. She was shaken and tired and beginning to be terrified.

"Unnh," said her charge.

A bigger wave boomed in, hit an angle in the side wall of the cave, and sprayed Sarah with foaming salt water from head to foot. Some got into her mouth. She spat out the bitter liquid.

The man scrabbled at the sand, digging his fingers into the cave floor. He began to thrash in the water.

"Be careful!" exclaimed Sarah. She'd nearly lost hold of him again.

With a sudden lunge, he sat up. "Ow!"

"Are you hurt?" Sarah asked, keeping her grip on his coat.

He put a hand to his side, shaking his head as if to clear it. "What…what happened? Where are we?"

"We fell from the cliff," said Sarah. "Can you stand up, do you think?"

With her help, he struggled upright, only to be knocked down by the next wave, which tried very hard to pull him out to sea as it receded. Sarah gripped his coat collar again, leaning back against the current.

Coughing, the man scrabbled to hands and knees and then up. Still seeming dazed, he looked around.

"I couldn't see any way to climb back up," Sarah said. "You wouldn't wake. And the tide is coming in."

He staggered under the onslaught of another wave. The

water was well above Sarah's knees now, and the pull was fierce. "Come," she said, putting an arm around his waist as support for them both.

They went farther into the cave, much faster now that he was walking. His steps strengthened as they moved. The sandy floor rose a little. The water grew shallower. The crevice was narrowing. But Sarah could see that the small dryish patch at the end would not be enough to keep them from high tide.

"There," the man said. Following his pointing finger, Sarah saw a ledge in the rock, well above her head. And also far above the tidemark on the cavern walls. "Up there," he said. He bent, grunted with some discomfort, then laced his hands together, making a stirrup for her to step into.

Sarah put a hand to the rock and a foot in his hands. He flung her up, exclaiming in pain as he did so. She caught the ledge with both hands, boosted herself up, and rolled onto it. Fortunately it was several feet wide. She turned back at once to offer him a hand. He didn't take it but clambered up the uneven rock on his own.

And then they were huddled on the cold stone as the tide rose higher below, filling the cave with surging water.

Sarah realized that they were trapped. The tide would grow higher for hours and hours. "Perhaps we should have tried to swim," she said. "I didn't think."

"There are vicious currents all about here," the man replied. "And rocks to be dashed upon in the sea. No one could swim that. You did right to choose this place."

Sarah nodded. They were safe, she and a male stranger.

Who could be anybody. Inappropriately, scandalously safe. From the sea.

"I should not have grabbed your hand," her companion said. "I pulled you down. That was not chivalrous. I beg your pardon."

Not the sort of thing a blackguard would say surely. "It was only natural," said Sarah.

"But not honorable."

Sarah shrugged. She certainly would have done the same. Anyone would, falling suddenly. It was automatic.

"You saved my life," he said, his tone wondering. "How did you drag me so far?"

"The water took a good deal of your weight."

"And tried to pull you out to sea."

Sarah shuddered. "It was dreadful."

"And you were heroic."

The sun was shining directly into the cave now, illuminating the churning foam of the tide. The waves boomed in the mouth like thunder. Flying spray soaked the walls and ceiling. Soon the sun would go down and leave them in darkness. Sarah looked at the water hissing below her feet, irresistibly powerful. She didn't feel heroic just now. What were they going to do?

Though it had been a warm summer day, it was cool in this crevice, and her clothes were soaked. Sarah began to shiver. She drew up her knees and wrapped her arms around them. "It will be hours until the tide is out again," she said in a small voice.

"Yes." Her companion was pressing one hand to his side.

"I believe I have cracked a rib," he said in a distant, almost scientific tone. "More than one perhaps."

Sarah gazed at him. He was not a large man, but his frame was well muscled and his skin tanned from the outdoors. His hair was black, his eyes hazel under straight dark brows, his jaw square. He was, in fact, quite handsome, and his clothes and way of speaking suggested the gentleman. If you saw him in a ballroom, Sarah thought, you would hope he'd ask you to dance. But he probably wouldn't.

He was looking back at her. Sarah knew he was seeing a short, somewhat rounded young woman with sandy hair that made her brows and eyelashes indistinct and a sprinkling of freckles. She had received compliments on the sparkle in her light-blue eyes, but she knew they weren't sparkling now. Her bonnet was gone, though she didn't remember that happening. Her hair had come loose in wet, pathetic straggles. It wasn't fair. She was no raving beauty, but she could look so much better than a drowned rat.

"I am Kenver Pendrennon," he said.

Sarah thought there was something familiar about that name, but she couldn't think what. "Sarah Moran," she answered. It was hardly a moment to consider the proprieties of introductions.

"Ah. You were visiting Tintagel?"

Were they really going to make conversation? "With my parents and their friends," Sarah answered.

"I came alone. I often do. I love this place."

"So do I. It has such an atmosphere of antiquity."

"Exactly."

The stream of sunlight dimmed, a cloud on the horizon perhaps and a foretaste of the darkness that was coming. A larger wave crashed in, throwing up a wider spray, and Sarah flinched. "The water won't reach this ledge," he said.

"No, we are above the tide line on the rocks."

"You noticed that?"

She didn't see why he should sound surprised. The indications on the cave walls were quite obvious. "It was a rather important piece of information," Sarah replied.

"Yes, but... Yes."

Sarah shivered.

"You're cold."

"I expect you are as well."

He began to strip off his coat, wincing more than once as he jostled his injury.

"You mustn't give me your coat," said Sarah. Particularly with a cracked rib. He must have hit his head quite hard as well.

"I'm not going to," he replied. "We will both shelter under it." He beckoned as he scooted toward the back of their ledge. There wasn't room to stand up in this makeshift refuge, but he could lean back against the stone.

"I'll be all right," said Sarah, reluctant to go so close to a stranger.

"I'm in no condition to take liberties, even if I would," he said. "And I promise you I would not." He beckoned again.

She was cold. And would be more so. She had begun shivering. Throwing propriety to the winds, Sarah moved over to sit beside him. They both drew up their knees, and he spread his coat over them. Dissatisfied with the result, he shifted until their bodies touched from shoulder to ankle and adjusted the garment to mostly cover them.

Sarah blushed, which warmed her a little right away. She'd never been so close to any man, and he was a complete unknown. She sat very still. He made no move. Slowly, heat built up where they touched. The coat, even though wet, helped as well. But the situation was still horribly awkward. A wave crashed into the opening. The water had risen below.

"I don't suppose anything lives in here," said Sarah.

"No animals would den in a tidal cave," he replied. "There are far more comfortable spots."

"And nothing would come in from the sea, I suppose. With long grasping tentacles to reach up and…"

He jerked and muttered in pain. "What?"

"It's just that I've read about these great creatures that rise from the depths and pull sailing ships down to their doom."

"Doom?" He looked out over the surging water. "Tentacles."

"Like thick ropes that latch on and can scarcely be peeled away. Sailors have to chop them off."

"You have a vivid imagination."

"Yes, but these beasts are real."

"I really wish you hadn't thought of that."

"Me too," said Sarah in a small voice.

There was a short silence. "All right," her companion said then. "But you said 'the depths.' They wouldn't come near the shore. There wouldn't be room for them." He spoke as if partly reassuring himself. "We will be fine here."

"They wouldn't fit into this cave anyway," said Sarah.

"Exactly. The coastal water would be too shallow."

"That's true. Thank you."

"For what?"

"For being logically comforting."

He looked down at her with an arrested expression in his hazel eyes.

They sat on, growing warmer with shared heat. The sunlight dimmed and then disappeared. Darkness descended, with hardly a glimmer of starlight from the cave mouth. The rush of the sea echoed off the rock walls; the air was saturated with its briny scent.

The dark should have made it more frightening, but Sarah found herself feeling almost cozy. She'd never nestled close to another person for such a long time. Not since she was very small, at least. And although he was a man and a stranger, she felt safe and inexplicably connected to this Kenver Pendrennon. Perhaps it came from having saved each other from the terrible power of the sea. Or some shared way of looking at the world. Whatever it was, it had a tender quality, like nothing she'd felt before.

"Do you live nearby?" he asked out of the darkness.

"Yes, down toward Padstow."

"My home is east of here. So you've always lived in Cornwall?"

"Yes. Except when I went off to school."

"Oh, school." His tone was flat.

"You didn't like it?" Sarah asked.

"I never went. I studied at home." She felt him shrug. "My parents thought that best."

"Oh, I made my very best friends at school." Sarah realized that this was not a tactful response. "I liked learning about all sort of things," she added.

"Like gigantic sea creatures with tentacles." His tone was lightly teasing.

"Don't mention them!"

"We have established that they wouldn't come near shore," he said.

"I know, but…"

"You think a mention might summon them?"

"No, of course not." Sarah was severe. "They are animals, not magical beings."

"And we have no means of calling on *those*."

"I wish we did," replied Sarah wistfully. "Like Merlin. Haven't you always wished to meet him?"

"I'm not sure. I might prefer to see him from a distance perhaps."

"Why?"

"Well, he was rather ruthless," said her companion. "His actions here at Tintagel were not entirely admirable, for example."

It was true that Merlin had made Igraine see another man as her husband, Sarah thought. And thus welcome him to her bed. Which was scandalous. She flushed in the darkness. "So Arthur would be born," she pointed out.

"The end justifying deceitful means," he said. "And causing more trouble in the end."

"I suppose." He'd thought about it. Sarah was impressed. "Arthur was a hero," she ventured.

"Yes."

He sounded almost wistful.

"I always wished for a great chivalric quest," he added.

"Like the grail?"

"No. More like fighting villains and bringing justice." He gave a short laugh. "I know it sounds daft."

"No, it doesn't." Sarah noticed that his arm was around her and her head was resting on his shoulder. How had that happened? She ought to draw away, but she was so comfortable. "I hope you wouldn't go after dragons though. If there were dragons."

"What do you mean?"

"Well, it has often seemed to me that the dragons were just minding their own business. Devouring the occasional sheep or cow, yes. But what else are they to eat? Wolves do the same. And did the dragons demand that virgin sacrifices be left for them? How would they have done so? They don't seem to talk. Wasn't this an invention of frightened townsfolk?" Sarah bit her lip. She shouldn't have said *virgin*. That verged on the improper.

"Do you have some affinity for monstrous scaled creatures?" her companion asked, his tone amused.

Sarah's embarrassment dissolved into laughter. "I am fond of all sorts of animals."

"Some of which are more, er, cuddly? Kittens perhaps?"

"Of course kittens. Dogs. A teacher at my school had a pet crow. Very intelligent. I loved him."

They began to compare their varying histories of family pets. Gradually, the remarks grew further apart, and after another stretch of time, they drifted off to sleep.

The tide peaked and began to recede, sounding much the

same in both directions. In the depths of the night, the floor of the cavern started to clear, but the pair did not see it as they slept, nestled together like the illustration of a fairy tale.

The night passed. The water reached its low and started the endless cycle of returning. The salt-laden air brightened. Gulls cried in the distance.

Kenver woke with his arms around a young lady, her body pressed to his, her head on his shoulder. He'd opened his eyes in a willing woman's bed a few times in London, but this was different. It wasn't just that he was fully dressed in sodden clothing and was cramped from his curled position. It wasn't the odd surroundings or the pain of his injured rib. It was the girl. He looked down at the top of her head in the growing morning light. She was unprecedented in his experience, with an odd quirky charm. Last night, they'd talked so easily and openly. Not like acquaintances or even friends; more like… kindred spirits. And the warmth of her against his side in the murmuring darkness had been so comforting. It was as if, with the talk and the silences and the shared warmth, a bond had knit between them. He still felt its sturdy strands. He couldn't even see her face, yet the connection remained strong.

There was a glimmer of sun on the water below them. The low water. The tide had turned and receded. In fact, it was starting to come in again. They had to hurry. He sat straighter, suppressing a grunt at the twinge in his side, and pulled his coat off the two of them.

His companion—Miss Sarah Moran, he remembered— blinked and looked around as if wondering where on earth she was.

"The sea has gone down," he told her. "We must leave at once."

"Oh." She pushed away from the stone wall. "Oh, yes!"

Kenver put on his coat, ignoring the pain that came with each movement, and scooted over to slide off the ledge. Landing in ankle-deep water, he reached up and caught Miss Moran by the waist as she followed him. For a moment, they stood chest to chest on the sand, her curvaceous body pressed against his. A hint of desire passed through him. That was unacceptable. He turned and moved away.

They waded out of the cave to the place where they'd fallen, and Kenver examined the cliff in the growing light. A wave splashed against the rocks, wetting them again. There were cracks and crevices visible all the way up. He should be able to climb even with his injury. "I'll go and find help," he said.

He was about halfway up when he realized that Miss Moran was clinging to the rock face just below him. "What are you doing?"

"I can get up this," she replied. "Now that I see where to step." She'd knotted her skirts and petticoats about her mid-section, leaving her lower legs bare. Her very shapely legs. A little shocked, Kenver looked away and climbed on.

He scrambled over the top of the cliff, avoiding the slab that had teetered under him yesterday, and turned to help his intrepid companion up the last few feet. She blushed as she untied her skirts and let them fall. He felt he ought to say something about the curiously tender night they'd shared, but he couldn't think what.

They made their way through the winding crevice, Kenver

wondering how he was to get her home. He supposed his horse was still here. The poor beast would have been tied to a bush all night. Unless someone had stolen him.

They emerged into an open space beside the ruined medieval castle. Despite the early hour, it was not empty. In fact, there seemed to be quite a crowd of people milling about. Briefly, they all turned and stared at them. "Sarah!" an older woman cried. She rushed forward, started to enfold Miss Moran in her arms, and hesitated at the wet and sandy state of Sarah's garments. "What has happened to you?"

In that instant, Kenver saw his companion with a parent's eyes. Miss Moran's dress was torn in several places and streaked with dirt and green algae. The wet cloth clung to her form quite improperly. There was a green smudge on her cheek as well. Her hair straggled about her shoulders with no sign of a bonnet. She was wet and disheveled. She looked…ravaged. The other people here were eyeing her, and him, with sly speculation.

"What have you done to my daughter, you blackguard?" A middle-aged gentleman ran toward Kenver with his walking stick raised to strike.

"Papa, don't," Miss Moran responded, fending off the lady who must be her mother. "We fell over the cliff and the tide rose…"

"We?" the man interrupted. "What we? Where did you meet this man? How did he lure you away from us?"

"He didn't…"

"It was a chance encounter," Kenver began. "An accident."

"Accident! You call my daughter's ruin an accident?" The older man—Mr. Moran, without doubt—looked furious.

"We did nothing wrong," said Miss Moran. "The tide cut us off. We had to wait until it ebbed."

There was a murmured comment among the onlookers. Someone tittered in response. Looking over the rows of staring eyes, Kenver realized that this story would spread like wildfire through the neighborhood. Miss Moran's disheveled appearance would be detailed. There would be rampant speculation and salacious jokes. He knew there were people who could not imagine a young couple being alone together without succumbing to desire. Mr. Moran, still shaking his walking stick over Kenver's head, might well be one of them. "You will not get away with this," he said.

Mrs. Moran began wringing her hands. "Oh dear, oh dear," she moaned and burst into tears.

"Please stop, Mama," said Miss Moran. She looked distressed, whether over her parents' behavior or her own plight Kenver didn't know. Both, probably.

A different sort of couple might have smoothed this over. Possibly. Or perhaps not, Kenver acknowledged, seeing the whispers spreading among the crowd. In any case, Mr. Moran said, "You will make this right, you cur. I'll have the law on you. Make no mistake about that."

"Papa!"

Miss Moran was near tears. Kenver hated to see it. Out of all the hubbub, this was the thing that made him say, "I will, of course, do the right thing."

This brought proceedings to a brief halt. Miss Moran made a gesture of denial.

"And who the devil are you?" asked Mr. Moran.

"My name is Kenver Pendrennon."

The older man went still. "Pendrennon?" he repeated.

It was obvious that he recognized the name. "Yes," said Kenver.

"Ha."

"You don't have to do anything," began Miss Moran.

"I would be delighted if you would be my wife," he interrupted. Somewhat surprisingly, it was not untrue. Exactly. He couldn't decide whether it was precisely true either. The circumstances were too confusing.

"I won't let you…"

"Be quiet, Sarah," snapped her father. "We accept your offer. And we expect you to honor it."

Kenver stiffened. "No one has ever impugned my honor. And no one ever shall!"

There was a bit more talk after that and an agreement that Kenver would call at the Morans' home the following day to discuss arrangements. Then his horse was found, and the crowd dispersed. Sarah Moran was led away from him by her parents. The look she gave him over her shoulder tore at his heart.

An hour later, Kenver stood before his own parents at Poldene Hall and explained where he had been overnight, along with the outcome.

"Marriage!" exclaimed his mother. "Out of the question. No."

"Surely that is not necessary," put in his father. "You say you did not…interfere with the girl."

He said this as if he didn't quite believe it, Kenver noted. Even his father, who should be most likely to trust his word, doubted his tale. Were some men really so venal? "I must do the honorable thing," he replied.

"Your head is stuffed full of legends and antiquated non-sense," replied his mother.

"It is not a legend that I put a young lady in a perilous position."

"Or she did you. It's known that you often visit Tintagel. Her parents probably stationed her there to accost you. And now they're gloating over their success."

"They did no such thing," Kenver answered. "This was purely an accident."

"And as such, it should not ruin your life," said his mother, pouncing on the idea. "I have bigger plans for you. A splen-did match. Not a hasty marriage to some local nobody."

"They are not nobodies. Her father has an estate near Padstow." Hadn't she mentioned that? Or was he assuming more than he knew?

"It can't be much of an estate if I've never heard of him," said his father.

"He is a gentleman of property, and Miss Moran is a fine young lady." Kenver was certain of the latter, at least. And her parents had looked prosperous. This was more of a deduc-tion than a lie. "I offered for her before a crowd of people," he added, in hopes of ending the argument. "Everyone heard."

"No, this can't be happening," moaned his mother.

"We forbid it," declared his father.

"I am of age," Kenver said. They both glared at him.

Kenver's upbringing had emphasized obedience above all other values. He'd begun to notice that more as he grew older, particularly after being away for a time on a visit to his uncle in London. Recently he'd suspected this focus had something to do with the disappearance of his older sister. He'd been a small child when that occurred, and he didn't really understand the circumstances. He knew only that her name was never to be mentioned.

The few times he'd tried to fight his mother and father, it had been extremely unpleasant. The truth was, he was just a little…not afraid of them. Not that. Wary perhaps. No, careful, that was the word. He didn't enjoy disputes.

Now, his mother looked grim. "You cannot expect us to welcome an…interloper," she said.

"No, indeed," said his father. He always agreed with Mama.

"You must forget all about this rash impulse," she added.

Kenver bent his head. The best thing to do when they scolded was diversion. After they met Sarah Moran… Well, somehow they'd all make it right. "I believe I cracked a rib in the fall," he said.

This worked, as he'd known it would. His mother fluttered around him. "What? Why didn't you say so? We must send for the doctor."

Kenver decided that was not a bad idea as it ended this conversation. He left her to send the messenger and retreated to his room to finally shed his wet, sandy clothes.

Two

THE MORAN FAMILY'S DRIVE HOME WAS NEARLY SILENT, and very awkward. The houseguests riding with them—a pleasant couple, friends of Sarah's mother from Devon—seemed not to know what to say. They did not spare the sidelong glances, however. Sarah saw that she had become an object of pitying curiosity. And this was from friends. What would strangers think? The older four were also exhausted after a night spent searching the crags of Tintagel. Everyone simply wanted to be home.

Sarah fled to her bedchamber as soon as they reached the house and was met by a horrifying image in the long cheval glass. Her gown was torn and filthy, literally encrusted with dirt. It clung to her body most improperly. Her undergarments showed through one long tear. There were streaks of green algae in her hair, on her face, and down the back of one arm. The thought of Kenver Pendrennon seeing her this way was horrifying. Drowned rat was a charitable description. She looked like something that had crawled out of the sea to die.

A knock on the door revealed that her mother had ordered her a bath. Sarah had never been more grateful.

It would have been lovely to fall into bed when she was clean, but Sarah didn't feel that she could. Instead, freshly dressed and coiffed, she went to find her parents. "You mustn't try to force Mr. Pendrennon to marry me," she said when she found them with their heads together in her father's study. They looked at her and then back at each other.

"He offered freely," said her mother.

Sarah didn't see it that way. He had been chivalrous, not willing. How could he be when she'd looked like a dripping gargoyle? The memory made her shudder again.

"How do you expect to weather the scandal?" asked her father, in the tone he used with stubborn, unreasonable people.

"Perhaps it won't be such a..."

"Mrs. Chine was there," interrupted her mother.

Sarah's heart sank. Mrs. Chine was known for spreading stories full of sly innuendo. What she didn't know for certain, she made up. And she never stopped.

"She'd heard you were missing, somehow."

"And rushed to discover what was happening," said her father.

"So quickly." Sarah hadn't thought the tale would spread so fast. "Well, I daresay people will forget all about it very soon."

"Talk will die down eventually," agreed her father. "But no one will forget."

"Certainly no eligible marriage prospects," said her mother.

Sarah gazed at her parents. They looked solemnly back.

"You are our only child," her father said. As if she didn't know. "We made sure you went to a fine school. Very well thought of."

And expensive, Sarah knew. She'd loved it.

"We wanted you to have a season in London. You enjoyed that, I think?"

She had, even though she'd attracted no special attention among the *haut ton*. Certainly nothing approaching an offer of marriage. She'd known that the cost was a stretch for her family. Her father had carefully put money aside to provide her season. There would not be another.

"We had thought to take some time to consider your future," he went on. "But matters have been taken out of our hands."

It wasn't fair. A slip on a rocky cliff should not overturn her entire life. "I'm happy here at home," she said. But this was only partly true. Sarah hadn't spent a full year at home since she was thirteen. And during the weeks she'd been back, she'd begun to feel its limitations. There were hardly any books here, for one thing. At school, she'd had shelves and shelves to browse through, and London had offered a circulating library. Here at home, she had only a few volumes from childhood, which she'd read over and over. She could purchase new books now and then. But they were a luxury. She missed libraries terribly, as she also missed her school friends.

"This estate will come to you," her father said.

Sarah made a gesture of protest. Her father was very healthy.

"But you are not interested in running it," he added.

It was true. Though Sarah loved to learn about all sorts of topics, and she didn't doubt her own intelligence, crop yield percentages and return on investment and tenancy agreements did not inspire her. They jumbled together in her head after a while. Her father had offered her many opportunities to join him in his work on the estate, but this had not gone well. Her mind had wandered. She'd wished to be elsewhere, preferably with a new book, and hadn't always been able to hide it. Her father had been disappointed, and that had hurt them both. Sarah knew that Papa had inherited a small, run-down estate and then worked all his life to improve and expand it. With great success. He was very proud of his achievements—and rightly so. She was too. He wanted to put his legacy into competent hands, which hers…actually were not, difficult as it was to admit this.

"So I don't think you would wish to retreat here and avoid all society," he continued.

Of course she didn't wish to do that. Some of her happiest times had been with her circle of school friends.

"A good husband and a happy marriage are best for you," said her mother.

It was actually what she wanted.

"And now a prospect has…come along," said her father. "Not as I would have wished, but…"

"You didn't seem to dislike him," interrupted her mother. "Whatever may have passed between you." Both her parents looked away.

Even they, even *they*, believed that something improper had happened in that sea cave, Sarah thought. Her heart sank. She felt as if a trap was closing on her. "He only offered out of obligation," she murmured. "He didn't want to." No man could have, after a mere few hours in dire circumstances.

"He didn't seem so *very* reluctant," said her mother.

Sarah heard doubt in her tone. So Mama couldn't really believe it either.

There was a short silence as the Moran family contemplated the situation.

"As I said, it is not as I would have wished," said her father. "The situation is unfortunate. But the match is acceptable."

"Outstanding, in fact," said her mother.

"What?" Sarah didn't see how they could know anything about this.

Her parents gazed at her. "The Pendrennons are one of the most prominent families in this part of the country," her father said.

"His father is the Earl of Trestan," added her mother.

"What?" repeated Sarah, trying to take this in.

"We've never met the family," her father went on. "A bit too far away for visiting. But we knew the name, of course."

Why had Sarah not recognized it? Because she didn't pay attention to such things, of course. Because she navigated society like a wide-eyed tourist rather than a canny sophisticate, or so her friend Charlotte always said.

A blush scalded Sarah's cheeks. Last night's companion was the son of an earl! Someone, probably Mrs. Chine, would certainly claim that Sarah had set out to entrap him. She'd have Sarah lying in wait like a hunting cat, ready to pounce, drag him into that cave, and do *whatever* was necessary to keep him there. When, in fact, she'd never heard of him or his noble line. Sarah gritted her teeth. Mr. Pendrennon would never believe that. Noblemen thought everyone knew who they were. She'd seen that in London. Was he even a mister? And not some kind of lord?

Sarah's father was thoughtful. "My land, which would be no great matter to a Londoner, say, will be a worthy dowry here, because it is near the Pendrennon holdings, you see. They will be glad to add it to the estate."

"And you will be living not more than fifteen miles away," said her mother happily.

They spoke as if the marriage was certain. Sarah shook her head. The earl's son was probably regretting his hasty words. He must be. She would never hear from him again.

There was a knock on the study door, and a maid came in. "Mrs. Chine has called to see you, ma'am," she said to Sarah's mother.

"Tell her we aren't in," said Papa.

"No." Sarah's mother rose. "I will talk to her. It's best to stay ahead of the gossips when one can. She should spread *our* story, not one she concocts from flying rumors."

Sarah sprang up. "I will go and tell her it's all a misunderstanding," she declared.

"No," said her parents at the same moment.

"You're worn out from your ordeal," said her mother. "You should go and lie down on your bed."

"I refuse to marry a man who does not really wish to marry me," Sarah replied. She meant to speak forcefully, but her voice wavered a little.

"You don't know that he does not…"

"How could he?" she wailed. In that moment, she felt she had nothing to offer a handsome, high-born, prosperous gentleman. London society had certainly thought as much.

Her parents exchanged a long glance. "Take a rest," said her father. "We will talk of this again when you are recovered."

Her mother went off to receive Mrs. Chine.

Sarah felt she ought to keep fighting. But she was tired and befuddled by this sudden change in her life. Surely nothing more would happen today. She allowed herself to be persuaded to go to her room.

———————

Kenver rode out to call on the Morans early the next morning. He'd had to consult the Poldene estate manager, who knew every inch of the countryside for miles around, to discover where they lived. The Moran estate was just far enough away to be out of Poldene's main area. But it was close enough that he could visit and return the same day.

He left before his parents were up and was glad to escape his home. They had not stopped trying to persuade him not to marry. Not for a moment. They'd hammered at him through the evening, making the same points over and over, insisting that he draw back from his impulsive offer and never considering that he was old enough to make his own judgments. They were expert at rousing doubts, especially his mother, full of stinging criticisms of Miss Moran. Kenver told himself that they knew nothing about her. He set aside the thought that he didn't really either.

It was true that he hadn't been contemplating marriage just yet. He was only twenty-three. He'd planned to enjoy several more London seasons as he looked about for a bride.

The marriage mart was full of lovely, aristocratic, wealthy young ladies, and his mother never tired of enumerating their charms, or arguing that he could reach as high as he pleased. She made these girls sound dazzling. The polar opposite of the small, bedraggled Sarah Moran.

But with that thought came the memory of a soft, sodden form nestled confidingly against him, talking of tentacles and dragons in the most nonsensical way. Kenver smiled as he rode along. He'd never felt as…at home as he had in that cave. It made no sense, but there it was.

And then there was the matter of honor. From his earliest youth, Kenver had devoured tales of chivalry and knightly quests. He'd often imagined the exultation one must feel on achieving such a task. He had not been encouraged to formulate many tangible goals. But he was determined to be an honorable man.

After two hours riding, he came upon a substantial house situated on a small rise that ran down to the River Camel. He was conducted to a pleasant parlor where Miss Moran was sitting with her mother and received with some surprise. Had they not been expecting him? Had they imagined he wouldn't come?

His companion from the cave looked far better today in a fresh blue cambric gown with floral embroidery, her sandy hair artfully dressed. Yet she appeared much more conventional too. Kenver found he missed the dauntless adventurer streaked with green algae.

They exchanged commonplaces for a time, and then Kenver said, "I had thought to discuss our plans."

Miss Moran stood up. "We can walk in the garden," she said.

"Surely we are comfortable here," objected her mother.

"Mr. Pendrennon and I should have a private conversation."

"It's not proper that you…"

"If we have an *understanding*, Mama, then there can be no objection to a stroll. You will be able to see us through the windows the whole time."

Kenver admired the way her light-blue eyes flashed when she said this. Here was the spirited creature he'd met the other night. Miss Moran was far prettier when she was animated. In repose, her face seemed to retreat into the background.

Mrs. Moran had no reply to this statement, and her daughter went out briefly, leaving them to make stilted conversation. She returned in a bonnet. He followed her outside into a pleasant terraced garden with the river flowing below.

"How is your rib?" she asked him.

Even Kenver's mother had not remembered to ask about it. "Better," he replied. "The doctor bound it up."

"Oh, good."

They walked down three steps, across a narrow swath of flowers, and down three more to a wider terrace with a small gazebo at one end.

Miss Moran looked out over the vista. "Obviously I will not hold you to your offer," she said, her voice trembling a bit. "The circumstances were unfortunate, with people crowding around. I could not force you into marriage over something that was not your fault."

"But it was," Kenver replied. "I grabbed for your hand and

pulled you down. If I'd been more careful, you wouldn't have fallen. You could have run for help."

"And none of it would have happened at all," she replied.

He felt a pang of regret at the idea. "We would never even have spoken, I suppose. We'd have remained strangers all our lives."

She looked up at him, and Kenver felt that she too was remembering how they'd huddled together under his coat and nestled close to sleep. Their talk in the darkness had felt so sweetly intimate, more so than any other connection he could recall, even though there had been no caresses.

"But we're still strangers, aren't we?" she asked.

"No," he answered without thought.

She gazed up at him.

"Don't you feel we formed a connection?"

She flushed and looked away.

"I meant nothing improper…" Kenver began and broke off. The things his parents had been saying about Miss Moran told him what kind of gossip must be spreading. Vulgar people would be even worse than his family. He'd heard that sort of talk where men gathered to drink and gamble. They not only assumed a man and woman caught alone would behave shamefully but enjoyed imagining each licentious detail. And somehow, inevitably, it was all the female's fault.

Sarah Moran must know something of this. Yet she didn't moan or weep or complain. She never had through all their trials. She was…intrepid. That was the word for her.

A spatter of rain hit the flagstones. Kenver took her hand and drew them into the shelter of the little gazebo. A rush of wind drove the rain after them. It was the kind of squall that could capsize small sailboats on the sea. They backed into the driest corner, close together in the tiny space. "Do you think we have offended Poseidon somehow?" asked Miss Moran.

Kenver looked down at her, once again startled and delighted. "No one but you would think of Greek gods at this moment. Poseidon rules the oceans, doesn't he? I believe Zeus is responsible for rain."

"And thunder and lightning. Oh dear." She leaned over to peer at the sky.

This pressed her against his uninjured side, her body warm and soft and lithe. A wave of physical attraction shivered through Kenver even as she quickly pulled back.

"And Zeus is so…unseemly," she added.

Kenver laughed. "A bit of a blackguard, in fact."

She nodded self-consciously.

"But perhaps our adventure was a gift from some kinder gods," he said.

She turned to stare up at him, lovely blue eyes wide. "A gift?"

"Why not?"

"They say one should beware of the Greeks bearing gifts."

"I assure you I am not a Trojan horse," he answered. She laughed, and Kenver felt a surge of triumph. "And we needn't think of Greeks. What about our own Celtic gods?"

"The spirits of Lyonnesse?"

"Why not?"

Miss Moran turned to gaze out over the river. "This summer, a fortune-teller promised me an adventure," she said. "I didn't know it would be…"

"Cold and uncomfortable and frightening?" he suggested.

"Touched by magic," she replied, turning back to look at him.

A man could get lost in those eyes, Kenver realized. They didn't only sparkle. They had depths and…layers— intelligence, kindness, determination, a sense of honor he recognized. Her lips parted as if to speak. But she didn't. Kenver's head bent, and then he was kissing her.

He shouldn't be. This was presuming. He ought to draw away at once. He started to, but she put an arm around his neck and pulled him back. An awkward embrace shifted into a soft, exploratory, then dizzying kiss. Kenver was very sorry when it ended, not to mention aflame with desire. Should he beg pardon? But she had seemed eager.

Miss Moran blinked as if returning from a far distance. "I always wondered what it felt like," she murmured.

Had that been her first kiss? "And what did it feel like?" he wondered.

"Odd and then…sweet." Her voice was uneven. "And after that, a bit like those riptides in the sea. As if I could be swept off and never find my way back."

Kenver felt a rush of aroused exultation. It was perhaps the headiest emotion he'd ever experienced, making his head spin. "You really must marry me," he said.

"But you never intended to…"

"Doesn't Shakespeare say something about taking advantage of the tide in one's affairs. Tide, ha! That's apropos."

"'There is a tide in the affairs of men which, taken at the flood, leads on to fortune,'" Miss Moran recited. "'Omitted, all the voyage of their life is bound in shallows and in miseries. On such a full sea are we now afloat. And we must take the current when it serves, or lose our ventures.'"

Kenver sorted through this sudden spate of eloquence, with partial success. "That's it," he replied. "Take the current, avoid the shallows and miseries. How do you remember it all?"

"I read it." Miss Moran gazed up at him, tempting him toward another kiss. "But that's Brutus," she added.

"Who?"

She continued examining his face.

"I should know," Kenver said. "I don't. You can tell me such things."

"Brutus stabbed Julius Caesar in the middle of the Roman Senate."

"Ah, yes. I remember. 'Et tu, Brute,' eh?"

"And he committed suicide in the end."

"Not a very good model for us then." He was half teasing by this time.

"I found him sneaking and peevish," said the adorable Miss Moran.

"I believe your unique opinions will never grow stale."

Her breath caught. "My opinions?"

"And your apparently vast store of knowledge," he said.

"Ada said I would find someone who thought so." She looked desolate suddenly.

"Who is Ada?"

"One of my school friends. She's married now."

He squeezed her hand in an attempt at consolation, though he wasn't quite clear what for. "And so shall you be. Won't you?"

She gazed at him searchingly again. "Are you sure? Truly?"

Kenver nodded. "It's a bit surprising. But I am." He held that conviction in his eyes. Because he meant it.

"All...all right," she said.

He kissed her again. It was even better this time, and it went on for a tantalizing stretch of time.

They returned to the house with the matter settled between them. Her parents received the news with what looked like relief, shifting into a warm welcome to their family. Kenver knew that this was more than Miss Moran—Sarah—could expect at Poldene. At first. But he was sure now that his parents would warm to this surprising girl. How could they resist her?

He went on his way in the early afternoon, when the rain had passed off and streams of cloud scudded across the sky. He was nearly to the edge of Poldene land when a male acquaintance, also out riding, hailed him. "Pendrennon! Heigh-ho!"

Kenver pulled up to await him.

"Everyone's chattering about you today," the fellow said.

"Are they?"

"Like magpies. I heard you'd fallen into a sweet little honeytrap."

"I beg your pardon?"

"But your mother told mine that you'll wiggle out of the girl's clutches all right and tight." He grinned. "Not that Mama put it just that way."

Kenver felt a flash of anger. He hated to hear that people were speaking of Sarah in this disrespectful way. If he'd had the least lingering doubt about his course of action, it dissolved. "Rumors are so often incorrect," he said. "I am, in fact, about to be married to an exemplary young lady."

"Huh? But it was your mother..."

"You may wish me happy," Kenver interrupted.

"Are you though?" His friend peered at him.

"Thoroughly." It was nearly true. More or less true. It would be, later on, when he'd scotched these insulting rumors and surmounted some of the other difficulties that lay ahead. He did wish his mother had been slower to speak. She clearly meant to fight this marriage, which was a lowering reflection.

"Well, that's...good then," said the fellow.

With a nod, Kenver turned his horse's head and rode away.

Sarah went back to the gazebo after Kenver had gone. She sat there with bowed head and folded hands, outwardly quiet but swept by a welter of feelings. It *was* almost like being carried away by the riptides at Tintagel. In the course of two days, her life had been snatched and tossed like flotsam on the waves.

Should she have said no? The gossip would be hateful and humiliating, but she could have weathered it somehow. Probably. The thing was, she'd *wanted* to say yes. When she gazed into Kenver Pendrennon's entrancing hazel eyes, she saw the handsome, earnest suitor she'd dreamt of from the edges of ballrooms while the young men in London barely noticed her. She'd been swept up in his chivalrous notions, his apparent enjoyment of her conversation, which society had found awkward and odd. And those kisses! She felt dizzy when she thought of *them*.

Very soon, though, wouldn't he notice that she was ordinary-looking and unpolished? In her group of four dear friends from school, Ada and Harriet were the pretty ones. Charlotte was striking and witty, always ready with a comeback to any conversational sally. Sarah, on the other hand, was…quiet and bookish, practically a bluestocking. She preferred reading to almost anything else.

In school, that had brought her success. She'd been praised and admired. Even later, when she and her friends had solved a mystery, her abilities were prized. But a London season had shown Sarah that such skills meant nothing to the larger world. She said unusual things. People stared and sometimes tittered. The young men who'd approached her, making her heart beat a little faster, had wanted to know how to interest Harriet, who was an heiress. Kenver—the son of an earl!—would soon discover that he'd engaged himself to a social failure. That would be dreadful in his elevated circle.

But she had said a great many odd things to him, Sarah remembered, and he hadn't seemed to mind. He'd wanted to hear more. He'd held her so tenderly through that night in the cave. And he'd kissed her as if…as if he liked it, as far as Sarah was able to judge. Which wasn't very far at all with her utter lack of experience. Reading about passion was *not* the same. That had been made crystal clear this morning.

Still, Sarah's heart yearned toward Kenver Pendrennon. It

shouldn't, she told herself. She scarcely knew him. Actually, she didn't know him at all, even if part of her insisted that she *did*.

He was the son of an earl, her brain repeated. They hadn't talked about that. Or how his wife would move in the highest ranks of society and be expected to shine there. This was a far better match than Sarah had imagined making. His family must think the same. Yet they must be kind people to have reared such a wonderful son.

This sent her off in a reverie about resting in his arms through the night with many more of those astonishing kisses. It might be wrong of her, but she *did* want to marry him. She could observe and learn how to go on. She was good at learning. His family would help her. She could become the sort of wife he deserved. Resolve made her sit straighter and raise her chin.

Was this really the adventure the Irish Traveler had seen in her cards? It was nothing like what Sarah had imagined. She'd thought of solving a mystery as momentous as their discovery of the Rathbone treasure or going on an expedition to a far-off land or uncovering a priceless ancient manuscript in a dusty attic and deciphering it. And yet, Sarah suddenly thought that under certain circumstances, marriage could be every bit as amazing as these pipe dreams.

―――――――

Sarah's father had no patience for banns. He pointed out that the weeks they required simply extended the opportunities for talk and speculation. The sooner the marriage took place, the sooner these would die down. And so a marriage license was procured. One of Sarah's London gowns was embellished for the occasion, and she stood up beside Kenver in her local church on a misty August morning less than ten days after she'd met him.

The timing of the ceremony had been kept quite private. They had not wanted curious neighbors "happening by" to stare. Sarah had agreed that was best. But she was unhappy that Kenver's parents did not attend. He'd made excuses, murmuring about the smallness of the occasion and the length of the drive, which did not seem such great obstacles to Sarah. She still had not met them. It kept being put off for one reason or another, and that made her uneasy.

As she spoke her vows, she couldn't help but compare this subdued event to the recent weddings of her friends Ada and Harriet. They'd been surrounded by rejoicing family and a crowd of friends. Even Harriet's irascible grandfather had been celebratory. Sarah had only her parents, the bland vicar, and the creeping damp of the mist. Her fingers curled tighter on Kenver's coat sleeve, wrinkling it under her hand, and she watched his face as he made his promises. He looked and sounded determined. Which was good—he showed no sign of doubt—and bad—he evinced no visible joy. Sarah told herself that weddings were serious, anxiety-provoking occasions. But she found her spirits sinking as the ceremony proceeded. Only Kenver's smile as they signed the register lightened her mood.

The wedding breakfast at Sarah's old home afterward

was also a small affair. Her parents had invited a few local friends and some mere acquaintances like Mrs. Chine. Her less-than-delightful presence would ensure that news of the wedding would spread quickly, be marveled over if necessary, and pass into history. Seeing the neighborhood gossip interrogating the vicar, Sarah thought they'd accomplished their purpose. Later, as Mrs. Chine wondered loudly about the absence of Kenver's family, she hoped they had not made a mistake.

The newlyweds stayed only an hour before setting off on the drive to Poldene Hall, Sarah's unknown new home. As Kenver handed her into the carriage, she searched his face for doubts or regrets. He smiled at her and squeezed her hand. "Nearly done," he said.

Aware of the driver's curious gaze, she stepped up and in. Kenver followed, shutting the door, and the vehicle started off. Sarah leaned out to wave at her parents and wondered if her expression was as uncertain as theirs. She watched them until the carriage turned a corner and headed northeast. They would pass by the road to Tintagel on their way to Kenver's home, which lay beyond it. "I suppose there must be a lake at Poldene," Sarah said.

"Yes, how did you know?"

"*Pol*, lake, and *dene*, valley," she added.

"You know Cornish?" he asked.

"Only a few words."

He nodded. "I am the same. I don't think anyone really speaks it anymore."

"No. Not like Welsh."

"Welsh?"

"They are related languages."

"Are they?"

He looked amused. Might she say fondly amused? Sarah almost dared to think so. "Along with Breton," she added. "All three are remnants of the old Celts. According to what…"

"You have read," he interrupted.

She hunched a little, self-consciously, and then saw the twinkle in his hazel eyes. Heartened, she added, "They would have spoken something like it at King Arthur's court."

"Really?"

"Yes. Nobody spoke the way we do. Back then."

"Because English is a mixture of Saxon and Norman tongues," Kenver said. "I read occasionally too."

Sarah was delighted to hear it.

Kenver was glad to see his new wife—still such an unfamiliar word!—smile. He pointed out various attractive views, and Sarah admired them. But all the while, he was brooding about the reception they would receive at Poldene. Kenver wished again, as he had been doing since the marriage was decided, that they could take a honeymoon trip. Preferably a long one, lasting for some months—plenty of time to settle in together. That would be ideal. But his personal allowance was too small to allow for such travels, and when he'd hinted that a boost was customary upon an heir's marriage, his parents had ignored him. They had an uncanny ability to make one feel that words were simply dropping into an icy void, echoing and ineffectual. He couldn't quite imagine the heat it would take to break through that barrier.

"There is the road to Tintagel," Sarah said.

He followed her gaze to the lane that led out to the ruin. Where all this had begun. Tintagel had long been one of his favorite places, and now it was imbued with tender memories of their night in the cave. Had he ever felt such a magical weaving of connection before? He couldn't recall another. "We will have to go back there one day soon," he murmured.

"We could lower a rope and climb down to see the cavern."

Kenver looked at her. Sarah was such a bright presence, with a mind full of ideas no one else would have. "And search for traces of giant tentacles?"

"We agreed that the monsters of the deep would not venture so close to shore," she replied with mock severity.

"Very true."

She laced an arm through his and leaned against him. She felt soft and delightfully rounded and very sweet at his side. Kenver bent for a kiss. This one was just as satisfying as the one in her gazebo garden, rousing a heady mixture of affection and urgent desire. He turned to slip his arms around her and pull her closer. Sarah fit just right in his embrace. He let his hands roam over a shape that promised myriad delights. He was afire to show her what that meant. If this endless drive would only finish and he could get her alone.

Her bonnet was in the way, and he nearly tore it off and threw it aside. But then a pulse of warning shot through him. They shouldn't arrive at Poldene panting and disheveled. That would be a serious mistake. He pulled away and was happy to see that Sarah looked disappointed. "We will have a suite of our own at Poldene," he told her breathlessly. He straightened his neckcloth and pulled his coat back into place. Sarah put her hands to her bonnet and righted it. Clearly she grasped his meaning.

Since a trip was not possible, nor an establishment of their own for now, Kenver had concentrated on preparing spacious rooms for them in the wing opposite his parents' quarters. The suite was unused, and he could ask the servants to pay special attention to it without involving his mother. Poldene was a large house. He and Sarah would make their own place within it. There would be long stretches of time when they need not see his family. Not to mention all the delicious nights that lay ahead.

After more than two hours, the carriage turned sharply left and entered the head of a valley that gradually widened as they descended. The vegetation grew lusher in this sheltered landscape. Sarah caught glimpses of the sea far ahead. They passed a small lake, its dark-blue surface reflecting the sky. "There is the lake," she said. She was torn between observing the landscape and gazing at Kenver with thwarted desire. She decided not looking at him was best, lest she throw herself into his arms again. She mustn't be drooling when she met the in-laws she had yet to set eyes on.

They moved farther downhill, into heavier woods. Sarah lost sight of the ocean. And then, Kenver said, "Here we are."

Sarah leaned out to look. At the end of a tree-lined drive, Poldene Hall was massive, a stone pile that had clearly been built over several centuries. It loomed over the landscape, meant to impress, if not cow, visitors. Somehow, on this drive, she'd forgotten about the earldom and the weight of history and obligation that accompanied such a position. She'd forgotten that this marriage came with a host of expectations, none of which she knew how to fulfill. Poldene didn't look like a place where she belonged, and Sarah was assailed by a sudden attack of nerves.

Three

THE DRIVER BROUGHT THE CARRIAGE EVEN WITH THE pillared entrance and stopped. Kenver opened the carriage door, jumped down, and offered his hand. Sarah slowly alighted, her eyes on the ranks of uncommunicative windows. They seemed like lidded eyes that might open at any moment to condemn her.

Poldene's heavy front door swung open without any visible hand. Then three huge dogs lunged through and loped toward them.

Kenver stepped in front of her. "They won't hurt you," he said. "Don't run away though. They'll chase you."

As if she would. Sarah moved to his side and waited for the dogs to reach her. They raced up, bumped against their legs, and capered around in circles. They didn't jump on her, which was fortunate since their russet-furred shoulders were at the level of Sarah's hip. They could easily have knocked her over. The larger male probably outweighed her. "Friend," said Kenver in a commanding voice. "Friend."

The dogs seemed to recognize the word. They crouched playfully, tails wagging.

"Hello," Sarah said, holding out her hand to be sniffed. She loved dogs, and these were magnificent. "How beautiful you are." When they had satisfied themselves as to her scent, she set a hand on one's shaggy, crimped fur. A few tendrils stood up straight on top of their heads and some fell over their eyes, giving them a jaunty look despite their size. "Are they deerhounds?" she asked, stroking the big animal.

"Yes," Kenver replied, looking at her with raised brows. "Most people are frightened of them at first."

"But they're perfectly behaved. What are their names?"

"Fingal, Ranger, and Tess," replied a cool, dry masculine voice above her.

Sarah raised her eyes to find a man and woman standing at the top of the three steps that led up to Poldene. They seemed very tall, but that might be the angle. Sarah had thought she was reconciled to being loomed over. At her height, it happened quite often. But their expressions added to the feeling—unsmiling, superior. They must be Kenver's parents, the earl and countess, Peter and Alice Pendrennon. Sarah could see some resemblance to her new husband. Kenver had their dark hair and slender frame. He'd inherited his father's square jaw and his mother's hazel eyes. She'd never seen him look so stern, however.

The Pendrennons appeared to be older than Sarah's parents—perhaps in their midfifties. Their hair showed touches of gray. The earl was spare; he didn't seem to have an ounce of extra flesh anywhere on his frame, and his cheekbones were sharp as blades. He looked like a disgruntled hawk. His wife was more solidly built, in straight lines, not curves. No one, taking in their closed expressions, would have imagined that they were pleased to see Sarah.

"There was no need to send the dogs out," said Kenver.

"They are a good test of character," replied his father.

The female dog—Tess, it must be—licked Sarah's hand, so she assumed she'd passed. That brought no sign of thawing in Kenver's parents' faces, however. "I suppose Fingal is the older one," she said. It was the first thing that came into her head.

"How did you guess that?" asked Lord Trestan.

She'd surprised him. That was something anyway. Whether good or bad, Sarah couldn't tell. "It's a different sort of name, perhaps for a progenitor."

"Progenitor," murmured Kenver's mother. The word seemed to have offended her even further.

"Shall we go in?" her son asked.

The earl and countess turned and walked away from them. Kenver went up the steps, the dogs at his heels. Sarah followed, passing through a small vestibule into a lofty chamber with a huge fireplace at one end and an oaken stair at the other. Darkness pooled in the corners of the high ceiling. Kenver performed the official introductions. His mother visibly winced at the words *my wife*.

There was no invitation to a more comfortable room. This one was clearly an ancient showpiece, not a place one sat to get acquainted. They stood in an uneasy group on the flagstone floor while Sarah's spirits sank lower and lower. Why hadn't Kenver told her that his parents weren't happy about their marriage? He hadn't dropped a single hint. She glanced at him. He looked stiff and rather…blank.

Lady Trestan's eyes bored into Sarah. Sarah couldn't help but think she was searching for flaws. And finding them.

"Your father has some land down toward Padstow, I understand," said Kenver's father. He made it sound like a few paltry fields.

"Yes."

"Has he been there long?" Lord Trestan asked with languid disdain.

Did he imagine they were parvenus? Sarah rallied in defense of her father. "All his life," she replied. "My family has lived there for more than five hundred years." It hadn't been an estate for all that time. Indeed the holding had probably started out as some sort of hovel. But she didn't see any need to mention that.

"Indeed?" The earl's dark eyebrows could not have gone any higher. "I would have thought the name was Irish."

"It is derived from the Anglo-Saxon *mor ende*," Sarah said. A forebear of hers had traced their bloodline. His findings might even be accurate. "Later corrupted to the Irish usage," she added.

The earl looked nonplussed. Sarah felt a thread of triumph, which died a quick death as she wondered if it would have been better not to answer back. But he'd hit at her father. She couldn't just ignore that. She waited for Kenver to say something. He did not.

"Is your mother's family also so…venerable?" asked the countess. Her tone was cold.

Sarah's heart sank further even as she raised her chin. This was wretched. Kenver's parents were clearly *not* the kindly couple she'd imagined. She was reminded of the worst gathering she'd ever attended, an evening party during the London season, where cruel quips and crushing snubs had been the order of the night. None of her friends had been there, and she'd ended up half behind a wall hanging to escape notice. "Mama was a Fairley," she answered.

"A connection of the Hampshire Fairleys?"

"Not that I am aware of. She grew up in Devon. Her father's circumstances were similar to mine." Sarah pushed on. If she was to be interrogated, she might as well get it over. "I was educated near Bath." She was happy to name her school. No one could fault that. It was one of the best in the country. Immediately, she found she was mistaken.

"Young ladies are better taught at home," said Kenver's mother. "I suppose you have no training in managing a large household." She gestured at the grand room.

"I'm sure you will have much to teach me," dared Sarah.

The older woman's eyes flashed like a duelist ready to fire.

"I will show you our quarters," put in Kenver, speaking at last. He offered his arm and turned toward the stair. Sarah took it like a lifeline.

"Sarah will be in the room across from mine," said his mother behind them.

Kenver turned back and looked at her. "But we were to take the state suite. I gave orders..."

"I heard," interrupted Lady Trestan, so dryly that Sarah had to suppress a wince. "But when I looked into preparing it for you, I discovered a great patch of damp in the ceiling."

"I didn't see anything like that," Kenver said.

"You must learn to be more observant." His mother spoke as if she was addressing someone far younger than twenty-three. "We've had to bring workmen in to tear it down. They are looking over the whole wing actually. That part of the house has not been tended in some time."

"As I had mentioned last spring," Kenver said.

"Always ready to throw money about," muttered his father.

"We didn't know the suite would be required any time *soon*," added his mother.

"The room next to mine would do then," Kenver said, his cheek reddening slightly at the implication.

"The fireplace smokes," replied his mother.

"It does?"

"Oh, yes. Dreadfully."

Sarah didn't believe her. But she could see it was no use arguing. *Her* opinion was worthless here. She waited for Kenver to respond. What excuse would Lady Trestan find if they suggested she share Kenver's bedchamber? Not that she could imagine making such a request of these icy aristocrats.

Instead of fighting on, Kenver turned away and led her over to the stairs and up them. Sarah felt hostile eyes on her back all the way. When she was certain they were out of earshot, she said, "You didn't tell me your parents were so opposed to our marriage."

"They were not entirely in favor," he began.

"Kenver, they obviously hate everything about it. And me."

"Of course they don't." He frowned as they walked down one corridor and turned into another. "I didn't know they would be so…"

"Repelling?" It seemed the right word. They had so clearly wanted to eject her, like castellans fighting off an invader.

"I've never seen them so…impolite."

"You never married against their wishes before."

He looked down at her. "They'll come around once they get to know you better."

Sarah thought the opposite was more likely. "I would never wish to come between you and your parents." Clearly she had, unknowing. "Oh, what are we to do?"

"It will be fine."

"What makes you think so?"

"You'll charm them." He smiled.

"I? Charm them? That is my task?" Sarah hadn't thought her spirits could sink any further. Now they did. She wasn't charming. Her friend Ada was charming. Just as Charlotte was acerbic and Harriet unflappable. Sarah was intelligent and thoughtful and a mistress of arcane facts. Those were her talents. People either enjoyed them or they didn't. Her new in-laws were obviously going to fall in the second category—those who found Sarah odd and annoying. She couldn't imagine them "coming around." And she didn't know how to be any different. She would be herself, and things would get worse and worse. Was this what a nervous spasm felt like? she wondered.

"They always cool down," Kenver said. "That's the way they are. They make a great fuss, and then after a while, it's all right."

For him, perhaps. But Sarah was not a beloved only son. She was, clearly, a massive disappointment, an enemy to be vanquished. She didn't think the word was too strong.

Kenver stopped and opened a door on the right. He walked in like an advance scout checking for ambushes.

Sarah paused to look at the closed door opposite. Lady Trestan's bedchamber sat there, a sentry to be passed each time she entered. And she would have no password to give her safe conduct.

"Come in."

She stepped forward. It was not a grand room, given Poldene's size and state. There was space for a bed, a wardrobe, a washstand, and a small dressing table with a mirror. There was no writing desk or shelves for the books she'd brought along. One of her two trunks held mostly books. And there were her trunks, back in a corner. The hangings and coverlet were blue. Lemon and beeswax scented the air. Yet it was not welcoming.

"This won't be for long," Kenver said. "I'll oversee the work, and we'll move into the state suite as soon as may be."

"What is that?" she asked, wondering where he had hoped to establish them.

"A sitting room and two bedchambers in the other wing," said Kenver. "They say Prince Henry stayed there in 1611 when he was Duke of Cornwall."

Sarah's mind automatically supplied facts. "He was the Stuart prince who died young."

"Trust you to know that. Many people have never heard of him."

"Historical sources suggest that he would have made a better king than Charles the First."

"Do they?"

"It's the sort of things they would say, of course."

"It is?" Kenver looked amused and perhaps even interested.

"Well, a dead prince is all hopes and potential, isn't he? Chroniclers can admire him all they like. Theorize and postulate far more than they can over an inept, beheaded king."

"Ha." He smiled at her, and Sarah felt a tiny bit better. "There is a library downstairs," he went on. At her look, he said, "I thought that might interest you. You are free to use it, of course."

"Is it much…frequented?" Sarah asked.

He didn't misunderstand. "My parents don't often go there. I have always found it…peaceful."

Perhaps they could retreat there together. Perhaps it could be a haven.

"This room is yours," Kenver added. "Feel free to change whatever you like."

There seemed little room for changes. And how was she to make any on his—their—small allowance? He *had* told her about that. It seemed they were wholly in the power of his parents. Would it be a terrible scandal if she stole a horse from the stables and rode home again? Yes, it would. It would also be an act of cowardice. Sarah tried to feel braver.

There was a knock at the door. Sarah braced herself as Kenver bade the person come in.

An older servant entered. "I've come to see to the unpacking," she said. She eyed Sarah without enthusiasm. Perhaps fifty, with streaks of gray in her tightly coiled brown hair, she wore a black dress that did not flatter her sallow complexion. Sarah took in her downturned lips and flat brown eyes and understood that this woman would never be her friend.

"Cranston?" said Kenver. "I had thought Gwen would…"

"Her ladyship sent *me*," was the flat reply.

"Ah."

Sarah wanted to object. She wanted Kenver to object more strenuously. Cranston so obviously followed Lady Trestan's lead in disapproving of their marriage. The entire Poldene staff would be loyal to their mistress, Sarah realized, but Cranston obviously took that position very seriously.

She could unpack her own trunks. Sarah nearly said so, before realizing that this would be seen as a sign of her unfitness for her new position. A proper Poldene bride would have had a personal maid to bring with her from home. Sarah knew that. But her mother's lady's maid attended to both of them, and there was no one to spare. For the London season, they had hired an experienced abigail familiar with all the latest fashions. That superior servant hadn't wished to come with them to the country, even had they been able to afford her continuing services.

Cranston moved toward the trunks. The room felt crowded with three people in it. Kenver stepped away. "You are going?" Sarah asked.

"Not for long."

She couldn't beg him to stay with Cranston listening. "Where is your bedchamber?" Sarah flushed. Was this question still improper now that he was her husband?

"At the end of this corridor," Kenver answered, gesturing to the right. "Two doors beyond my father's."

So both his parents would be between them. How very apt. "I could go with you," Sarah said.

Cranston harrumphed as if shocked.

Sarah's flush deepened. She hadn't meant she could go to his room. It had just come out that way.

"I want to check on the workmen." Kenver moved toward the door, somehow looking younger than he had standing up at the church beside her. "I won't be long." He departed, leaving Sarah feeling very much alone in a strange, unwelcoming house. Except for Lady Trestan's spy, of course. Cranston opened her trunks and began to examine her belongings. Her disapproval flowed out to fill the chamber.

Sarah walked over to the single window and looked out. There was a stretch of garden below, running up to the crags that edged the valley. She opened the casement and leaned out. The sea was to her left, the road by which they'd entered on the right. The scent of flowers rose from the plantings below.

Sarah was suddenly reminded of her first day at school. She hadn't known that building either, or anyone in it. And yet she'd found friends and a great deal of happiness. But no one at school had been prejudiced against her from the beginning, a dry inner voice commented. Thinking of her old friends reminded Sarah that she had to write them about her marriage. What was she going to say? A sigh escaped her.

"What are all these books for?" asked Cranston.

"They are just some old favorites of mine."

"Do you have any clothes?" the older woman inquired, without a trace of respect.

"In the other trunk."

Cranston's sniff of disapproval made Sarah glad she had the fashionable dresses from her London season. "Have you been at Poldene long?" she asked.

"More than thirty years. I came with Lady Trestan when she married."

"Oh, how nice."

"For a bit. I was her ladyship's maid until she hired her hoity-toity London dresser." Cranston's tone was sour and bitter.

Perhaps she wasn't completely Lady Trestan's creature then, Sarah thought. "Well, you will be able to introduce me to the staff."

"I don't see that it's my place to be introducing you." Cranston held up a gown that Sarah adored and eyed it with disdain before putting it into the wardrobe.

Feeling that she couldn't bear to stay in this small room with this surly person for a moment longer, Sarah said, "Could you tell me how to find the library?"

"What would you be wanting that for?"

"There are no shelves in here. I will look for a place to put my books."

"I don't know that you'll be allowed…"

"I'll ask permission first, of course," Sarah interrupted. She met Cranston's sullen gaze and waited.

Finally, grudgingly, the woman gave her directions. Sarah slipped out and made her quick, furtive way downstairs. Cranston might have steered her wrong, she knew. But if she had, she would simply search on her own.

This turned out to be unnecessary. Sarah found the double doors Cranston had mentioned and walked into a large parlor fitted out with bookshelves. It was not a grand library with soaring ceilings and upper galleries, but there were books, a small desk, and some comfortable armchairs arranged around the fireplace. Like all the rooms she'd seen at Poldene, it was well kept. The furniture gleamed with polish; the air was fresh. Yet the space felt untenanted, and Sarah believed Kenver's assertion that the family rarely came here.

She went to gaze out one of the tall windows and found that it overlooked the back terrace and the sea in the distance—a potential escape route should one be needed. The ground was only a few feet below. Feeling as if an escape route was exactly what she wanted just now, Sarah sank into an armchair and clasped her trembling hands. She hoped she'd at least discovered a refuge in this unwelcoming place.

Four

CRANSTON REALLY WOULD NOT DO, KENVER THOUGHT when he'd left his hat and gloves in his chamber. The woman had a sour disposition, and she always treated him as if he was still five years old and had tracked mud across a priceless carpet. He preferred to avoid her. His mother never noticed Cranston's ill temper, of course. The maid didn't show it before *her*. Mama thought of her former maid as a valued old family retainer.

Kenver brightened a little at this thought, even as Sarah's forlorn look came back to him, a cutting reproach. Perhaps his mother thought Cranston was a sort of…gift. A mark of respect even, assigning Sarah a senior servant. If he explained that a younger attendant would be easier for Sarah to manage, that would make sense surely. It was a logical argument. And it would be easier to speak to Mama without Sarah present. He squared his shoulders and went to look for his mother.

He found both his parents in her sitting room, seated on either side of the fireplace, leaning a little forward. They swiveled and sat back as he walked in, almost as if they'd been plotting mischief. Which was ridiculous, of course. They looked at him without speaking. There was no convenient chair near theirs. Kenver put his hands behind his back and stood before them. "I, ah, wanted to speak to you about Sarah," he began.

"We can't pretend to be happy about this match," snapped his father.

"You pretend to be glad to receive my great-aunt Cora, when I know you are not," Kenver pointed out. "And there was that fishermen's delegation about the old dock."

"Not the same," declared his father.

"No, Sarah is…"

"We have gone to great lengths to prepare for her," interrupted his mother. "The north wing is crawling with workmen."

"Lord knows what it's going to cost," complained his father.

Kenver's mother gave him a speaking glance. Papa hated spending money, and they had sometimes conspired together to promote needed expenditures. It was a sort of game between them. As allies, Kenver thought. "I don't understand about this damage." Of course he had looked over the state suite before bringing Sarah home, and he'd seen no sign of it. He tried to envision where the patches of damp had been found.

"Takes an experienced eye to spot these problems," said his father.

"In the *normal* course of things, we would have had plenty of time to make ready for your bride," put in his mother. "Months probably between an engagement and the wedding."

"Huh," huffed his father.

They gave Kenver the look that said he'd been foolish, but that of course they would forgive him if he did better in future. It was not unfamiliar. It tended to put Kenver off his stride. "The room where you have put Sarah…" he began. He didn't know how to point out that its placement was awkward for the wedding night. This was not a topic he could discuss with his parents.

They simply waited for him to go on.

"It is a bit cramped."

"I put her right across from me," said his mother. "I thought that a respectful placement."

"But the rooms on that side of the corridor are much smaller than the front ones." It was an odd quirk of Poldene's architecture, and Kenver had never known them to use the rear rank.

"You think I should give up my chamber to her?" asked his mother.

"What?" He hadn't meant any such thing. It would never have occurred to him. "Of course not, Mama."

"I should think not indeed," grumbled his father. "Outrageous suggestion."

Which he had not made! "But the chamber next to mine, are you certain about the fireplace? I didn't know it smoked."

"As you never go in there," replied his mother with an indulgent smile.

"No, but…"

"So how should you know?"

"Yes, but…it is August." That seemed a telling point. "We aren't likely to need fires."

"With the way the sea mists sweep in?" asked his mother.

"Gets right down into your bones," his father said with a shiver.

"Surely you would not wish to subject Sarah to that sort of biting damp," added his mother.

The sense of fighting a losing battle crept over Kenver. He knew it rather well. "Perhaps we could have the chimney cleaned?"

"And cover the place in soot," objected his father. "It was everywhere the last time."

Kenver couldn't deny it. The chimneys at Poldene were a tangled maze seemingly. They needed to be sorted out at some point. But not now. "Ah, Cranston. I don't think she is the best choice to wait on Sarah. I had thought Gwen could attend her. I did mention it." He was certain that he had, though all the conversations about his approaching marriage had been fraught.

"Gwen?" replied his mother, looking surprised. "She's only been with us for a year. Or a bit less, I think."

"She is near Sarah in age." She also seemed cheerful whenever Kenver encountered her. He'd thought they would get on.

"But Cranston has far more experience as a lady's maid," his mother went on. "She waited on me before I hired Gireau."

"I know, Mama, but…"

"She knows what's proper and will be able to tell Sarah how to go on in a larger household. Sarah will benefit from her advice."

Kenver doubted that. "I just don't think…"

"You cannot expect me to give Sarah my dresser?" interrupted his mother.

"No. I…" The idea had never entered his mind.

"You dare!" exclaimed his father.

"No!" snapped Kenver. "Why would I? I never suggested that. I simply think that Cranston is not the best choice."

"What would I tell Cranston?" asked his mother. "How am I to dismiss her? After all these years. It would be quite humiliating."

"I'm not asking you to throw her out of the house."

"Don't speak to your mother in that tone," ordered his father.

His mother gazed mournfully at him. "I only want what is best for you," she half moaned. "You were meant for much greater things."

"Greater how?" Kenver asked. "You expect me to live here at Poldene and look after the estate, do you not?"

"Of course," said his father. He sat straighter as if ready to fight for this point.

"And so I shall," Kenver assured him. "How would some other marriage make any difference to that?" If he could take them through the steps of a logical argument, surely they would see.

"A match that brought money and grand connections—" began his mother.

"I am satisfied with the income from our land," Kenver interrupted. "I will increase it as I can, of course, while caring for our people."

His mother shook her head. "A bride no one has ever heard of, with no distinction."

"So you wished my marriage to be admired by other people. Society, I suppose."

"She won't be respected, Kenver." Mama looked down her nose, eyes half-lidded. "Nor will you be, for choosing her. Not to mention the very…irregular circumstances of the marriage."

"Respect can be earned. And my personal happiness…"

"Happiness," snorted his father. "You scarcely know this girl. In fact, you do not know her at all. You cannot tell whether she will make you happy."

And yet it seemed to Kenver that she would. Might very well.

"She doesn't know how to run a household of this size or be a hostess to the neighborhood," his mother said.

"Sarah is extremely intelligent." This at least he was sure of. "She would be glad to learn from you, Mama."

The look he got in return did not suggest this would be forthcoming.

Kenver turned away and left the room. Everyone needed time to adjust to the sudden change, he told himself. Tempers would cool. People would become better acquainted. All would be well in the end.

Returning to Sarah's bedchamber, Kenver found only Cranston there. The woman stared at him as if he was intruding. What had she been doing? Sarah's clothes must be in order by now. Actually, what did Cranston *usually* do at Poldene? He had no idea. "Where is my wife?" he asked her, his tone more clipped than usual.

"She inquired about the library," said the older woman.

Of course she had. He ought to have guessed and gone there at once. Kenver turned, then hesitated and looked back. He met Cranston's hard gaze and held it until the woman's eyes dropped.

Kenver found Sarah sitting by one of the library windows with a book. When she raised her eyes, he was sad to see that she looked anxious. "How is the work going?" she asked.

"What?"

"You went to check on the workmen? That is, I thought you said you were going to do that."

"I am just on my way there. I wanted to be sure you were…comfortable. What are you reading?"

"I found a history of your family. I thought it would be good to…"

Brushing past the way her voice trailed off, Kenver asked, "Is it the one written by the first earl?"

She consulted the title page. "Yes."

"That is more legend than history. He wrote it to promote his interests with Queen Elizabeth. I believe he thought amusing her was the best way to do so."

"It did seem a little…imaginative."

"I expect he would be pleased to hear you say so. Taking it as a compliment, of course. Have you come to the story of his miraculous descent from Tristan and Iseult?"

"No." She looked at the book. "He didn't really claim that?"

"Oh yes."

"But, in the stories, they never had any children."

"Well, as the first earl would put it, how do you know? It was all a very long time ago. And he had the documents to prove it."

She smiled. Kenver was very happy to see it. "Did he? Have documents?"

"Not that he would ever show anyone. So I would think, no."

"I don't see how Tristan and Iseult would have had time, with all the fateful magic potions and escaping execution and their tragic deaths."

Kenver laughed. "Indeed."

"They would have been terrible parents," she added. "Always enacting desperate emotional scenes."

"Mmm." With nothing to say to this, Kenver held out his hand. "Come. I will give you a tour of the house."

Sarah set aside the now more intriguing volume, stood, and clasped his hand. His fingers were warm and strong around hers. She'd never been happier to see anyone than when he walked in. His appearance had lightened a room that had begun to feel oppressive despite the rows of books. She'd never felt forlorn in a library before, which could not be a good sign.

"You should become acclimated, so that you can find your way around and not feel lost," he added.

She did feel lost, and she didn't think a better understanding of the geography was going to help. But she walked with him toward the door. His mother might have been the one to show her around her new home, but clearly she would not be doing so. "May I bring my books here?" she asked.

Kenver looked down at her. "What?"

"I brought some favorite books with me. There are no shelves in my bedchamber." She did not add, *and no room for any.* That must be obvious. "May I put them here, do you think?"

"Of course you can. This is your home." He went to a partly filled shelf and pulled the books from it. He found a vacant space on another and shoved the volumes into it.

"Don't disarrange anything," protested Sarah.

"I would be astonished to find that there is any order here. This shall be your shelf. I'll have your books brought here."

"Should we ask…"

"There will be no objection." He didn't actually intend to mention it. "Come." He offered his arm. Sarah took it, tucking her fingers into the crook of his elbow.

"Poldene is shaped like a capital H," Kenver went on as he led her out into the corridor. "With the middle a bit stretched out, facing southwest toward the sea. The public reception rooms are in that central section with our bedchambers above them. The south wing holds the kitchens and estate offices and servants quarters in the back half and a dining room and ballroom in the front. It is actually the newest part of the house. My grandmother fancied the idea of grand balls. Our…future rooms in the north wing are part of the older guest accommodations. That wing also has a series of parlors on the lower floor, the gallery and the nursery above."

Kenver opened a door at the end of the hall. When they stepped through into a long narrow room hung with portraits, Sarah got the sense of age and…not neglect, but the natural wear and tear of centuries.

"This is the gallery. We may as well begin with ancestors, eh?"

"Is the first earl here?" She was interested in the face of the man who'd claimed descent from Tristan and Iseult.

"He is, toward the middle." Kenver led her down the chamber, the parquet floor creaking under their feet, and stopped at the far end. "Our history begins with this fellow," he added.

Sarah looked up at an undistinguished painting of a man in medieval garb hung in the center of the narrow wall. It was not very well executed. The colors were muddy.

"This is Rafe Pendrennon," said Kenver. "An enterprising Cornishman. He was knighted by King Henry I in 1131 because he married Adeliza, er…"

"Was she one of King Henry's illegitimate children? He had a great many, I believe."

"That is the rumor." He smiled down at her. "Should you know such things?"

"I read," replied Sarah. "And people tend not to ask what one is learning from thick historical tomes. They think such books must be boring, you see. And they are afraid you will tell them. At length."

His smile widened. "Ah. Perhaps these are people who have suffered boredom at some point? When they did ask?"

Sarah smiled impishly back. "Possibly."

"Have you ever been called devious, my lady?"

"Only by my good friends." A familiar pang struck Sarah. Ada and Charlotte and Harriet had been constant companions all through school and into her London season. She missed them acutely now when a friend would have been so welcome.

"Ha."

She'd amused him. Sarah enjoyed that. Poldene felt lighter, possible, when it was just the two of them. "So Rafe Pendrennon and his half-royal wife held onto their position in the fighting that followed King Henry's death?"

"They did, oh mistress of all things historical. They seem to have kept their heads down and stayed out of the dynastic disputes. That became rather a tradition in our family. 'Avoid politics and add acres whenever you can' might be our motto."

And now they would have her father's land to add. Years and years from now. "Instead of what?" Sarah asked.

"Oh, we have no actual motto. That might attract attention."

Sarah laughed. "There is no portrait of Adeliza?"

"No. We have very little information about her."

"Because she wasn't important for herself," observed Sarah. "But only for her grand connections."

"I…suppose," he replied, looking uncomfortable.

They moved down the room, Kenver naming his ancestors running up to the present time. "There is the first earl," he said at one point.

Sarah examined a man in Elizabethan dress, his hand on the hilt of a sword hanging at his side. He had a gleam in his eyes and a small neat beard. "He looks a bit like Sir Walter Raleigh," she noted.

"From all I have heard, he would have relished the

comparison. He was the exception to the Pendrennon rule of avoiding politics. He haunted Queen Elizabeth's court, looking for ways to please her."

"I wonder what he tried," said Sarah. Their eyes met. For some reason, she thought of searing kisses. A flush heated her cheeks. She swallowed. "He was made an earl for his efforts?"

Kenver nodded, his gaze holding hers. "We were mere barons before him."

"Mere," Sarah echoed. They had rather different views of rank.

He showed her the line of earls since the first, men in the finest dress of their eras, sometimes with wives and children posed around them. And in one case a horse. "Here we come to the present," he finished.

They had reached the other end of the gallery. Sarah looked up at a portrait of four people. She recognized a much younger Kenver and his more youthful parents. "How beautiful your mother looks," she said. Lady Trestan was smiling, too, an expression Sarah hadn't yet observed.

"She was admired."

"And the girl is just like her. Do you have an older sister? I didn't know." How could she know so little about her new husband?

"Much older, yes. Twelve years."

"Twelve!"

Kenver nodded. "I think… No one has said precisely. Some infants died between us. I believe three."

"How terrible." Sarah felt her first twinge of sympathy

for her new in-laws. "What is your sister's name? She is married?"

"Tamara. Yes, married."

Sarah wondered at his stilted tone. "Does she live far away?"

"Quite far away. I believe."

Sarah couldn't understand his stiff attitude. "That makes it difficult to visit, I suppose."

"We don't. There was a...falling-out."

"About what?" Sarah worried that she was prying. But she was joining this family. And she was curious.

"I'm not certain," said Kenver. "I was very young when she left."

"Well, but..."

"My parents do not mention her. You shouldn't... They don't care to hear her name."

"Don't..." Sarah's voice trailed off in astonishment. How could anyone feel that way about their own child? Had Tamara committed some dreadful crime? Looking at the girl's face in the portrait, Sarah doubted that. Appearances could be deceptive, of course, but the icy reception Sarah had received at Poldene made her tend to champion Tamara over Kenver's parents.

"Does your family really go back to the Anglo-Saxons?" Kenver asked.

It was a clear signal not to probe the mystery about his sister. Sarah gave in, without giving up. "Well, my great-grandfather looked into all the old records, and he said so."

"You aren't sure?"

"It seemed to me that he made some…unwarranted leaps of logic."

"Because you have gone over the documents yourself."

Did he look fond? Sarah thought he might. The idea warmed her through and through. "Well…"

"Of course you did. So your great-grandfather was a neck-or-nothing historian?"

Sarah laughed, enjoying the phrase. "Yes. And I don't think he made all his jumps. But the Morans have lived here for a long time."

Kenver nodded, smiling. "Shall we go on?"

"Yes, I love old houses." Sarah's enthusiasm was reviving as she relaxed. "My friend Ada and her husband are restoring a half-ruined castle in Shropshire."

"Perhaps we could go and visit her," Kenver said as he led her out of the gallery into another corridor.

Sarah's spirits suddenly soared. "Could we?"

"Why not? If she will invite us, of course."

"She would!" With a thrill, Sarah realized that such things might be possible now. She could go places and see things. Staying with friends was not expensive. Of course, she would first have to tell her friends about her marriage and how it came about. Those letters were proving a challenge.

Kenver set his hand on a doorknob. "These are the rooms we will eventually use," he said. "We can both see how the work is going." He opened the door, and Sarah stepped into a spacious sitting room with three long windows on the oppo-site side. Faded floral wallpaper in buff and peach gave it an airy feel. The furnishings she could see looked comfortable, though most had been pushed off into a corner, and some were covered by dust sheets. There were older sofas and armchairs in complementary colors, a delicate writing desk with its chair turned upside down on top, a half-empty bookshelf. Open doors at each end led into large bedchambers. She could see through to another door into a dressing room on the far side of the one on the left. Compared to the cramped room she'd been given, it looked marvelous, except for the sizable hole in the ceiling beside the windows.

A young workman who had been sitting beneath the cavity had sprung to his feet when they entered, setting aside a hunk of bread and cheese. "Milord," he said to Kenver.

"Is this where you found the damp?" Kenver asked, walking over to gaze upward into the hole. "I didn't notice anything when I was in here last week."

"Damp." The man nodded.

"What is being done to fix it? And is it only you?"

"No, milord. Mr. Hicks took Jem and went to fetch some cured oak."

"Oh, is Hicks handling the repairs?" Kenver turned to Sarah. "He's very good. He has done a great deal of work for my father. He knows his craft."

Sarah nodded. She saw no sign of damp in the ceiling plaster. They would have ripped that part out, of course, if it existed. She gave herself an inner shake. The Pendrennons would not dismantle their house just to make her less comfortable.

"I suppose you are having to attend to the attics as well," Kenver said to him. "There is a leak in the roof?"

"I, er, I'm not sure, milord. Mr. Hicks would know all about it."

Kenver nodded. "When he returns, tell him I'd like to speak to him."

"Yes, milord."

They walked through the two bedchambers and glanced into the attached dressing rooms. Sarah found the suite appealing and, more importantly, quite private. "Couldn't we move in here now?" she wondered. "There is just that hole in the ceiling."

"It does seem minor. I'll consult with Hicks. We could stay out of his way during the day."

"Oh yes." Sarah was ready to do whatever was necessary to secure these pleasant quarters. Established here, she would be able to find her feet and make a place for herself. "What are my duties at Poldene?" she asked as they moved on to the lower floor.

"Oh, ah, just to get settled for now."

"So I am like a visitor here?"

"No, you are a member of the family," said Kenver forcefully.

Sarah wondered if he was trying to convince himself. "My family works together to keep the estate running smoothly," she said.

He nodded in appreciation of this. "Let us just leave it for a while, until everyone becomes accustomed to the new arrangement."

"Do you think they will?"

"Of course."

His tone had gone hearty, but Sarah was not convinced. And she noticed that in the rest of their tour, they avoided areas of the house that must be the haunt of his parents.

"Come outside," he said. "Having seen your old home, I know you will like the gardens."

Her old home. This was her home now. But the word did not seem apt.

He led her through a door that put them at the end of one of the legs of Poldene's H shape. They were at the back of the building. A terrace with a low stone railing ran across the central portion. From there, a wave of flowers and shrubs spread out like a glorious multicolored carpet. Blooms of blue and yellow and red and white dotted the greenery. Sarah could hear the sea off to the right but couldn't see it from here.

"Come," said Kenver again, extending a hand.

They walked together along a path with flowers bending over it like courtiers bowing to passersby. The August air was so heavy with sweet scents that it was dizzying.

A thumping rhythm announced the arrival of the three deerhounds, bounding along, tongues hanging out. They came to dance around Kenver and Sarah, making a game of eeling under the leaning stems that lined the way.

"Fingal, Ranger, Tess," called Kenver. And he began to romp with them, running and jumping, holding a hand high to urge them on, stopping suddenly to make them twist past him. Grinning, he beckoned.

Sarah was much more likely to be curled up with a book than racing through a warm garden. But she couldn't resist. She skipped along behind and then among them. The dogs seemed delighted. They fawned on her. Tess licked her hand. They crouched and wiggled their haunches, inviting her to join their revels. And so she did, cavorting as she hadn't since she was much younger.

When the path opened out into an oval of lawn, they raced around it. Fingal, the eldest, with a touch of gray in his muzzle, led the way. The two younger dogs seemed to take their cues from him, deferring to his age. So while Ranger and Tess tumbled over each other with mock growls, they did not pounce on Fingal. If dogs loved a place, Sarah thought, it couldn't be all bad.

Laughing, Kenver caught her by the waist and whirled her round and round. When he set her down again, he bent to claim a kiss that seared through Sarah, leaving her weak in the knees. She clung to him, senses reeling, intoxicated by the garden perfumes, the exuberance of their run, the touch of his hands. He pulled her closer and kissed her again, slowly, lingeringly. Sarah melted in his arms.

He held her, his body tight against her, muttering, "Where can we go?"

The question brought back the realities of their situation. A gauntlet of guardians waited inside the house. Sarah looked over his shoulder at the looming building and saw a face at an upper window, staring down at them. She could only make out a pale oval before the drapery twitched and the watcher was invisible. She stiffened. That gaze had not seemed kindly.

Kenver felt her reaction. "What?" he asked. He had to pull back to look down at her.

His hazel eyes burned into Sarah. This was her wedding day. It should belong to them. "Nothing," she answered. There was no one to see now.

His hands tightened on her. "It will be all right," he said. He took her lips in another kiss.

Sarah tried to fall into it as she had before. But the sense of hostile eyes above them was too strong. She couldn't let go. When Kenver drew away again, a bit puzzled, she said, "Someone may...come along."

He met her eyes. Sarah braced for irritation or impatience, such as any man might feel in these circumstances. She wouldn't blame him. She felt some of that herself, beneath the uneasiness. But Kenver put a hand to her cheek, gently caressed, and nodded.

They moved apart, walking on with only clasped hands.

Sarah noticed that while Ranger and Tess were still frolicking over the lawn, Fingal was looking up at the house as if the older dog also had noticed the watcher.

Five

SARAH WOULD GLADLY HAVE SKIPPED DINNER THAT evening. Briefly, she imagined pleading illness and then sneaking down to the pantry in the middle of the night to assuage her hunger. But that was ridiculous, and cowardly as well. She would not be a coward. Also, she did not know where the pantry *was*.

"I thought this would be suitable," said Cranston, holding up the gown she'd chosen for Sarah to wear for the meal. It was an ancient green muslin Sarah had brought along for gardening or other such chores she might find here. A dreadful choice. Sarah would have thought it stupid if she hadn't been certain Cranston wanted her to look like a country dowdy on her first evening at Poldene. If she'd had any doubt that Cranston was the countess's creature, it withered away in that moment.

"I'd prefer to wear the pink with the lace trim," said Sarah, naming one of her favorite dresses from her London season. She knew it looked well on her.

Cranston's lip curled at this criticism of her taste. Sarah ignored her.

Disputes over jewelry and the arrangement of her hair followed. They were exhausting and left Sarah with a hovering sense of failure even when she prevailed. Cranston's manner convinced her that the elder Pendrennons would disapprove of anything she wore, no matter how fashionable.

"You look splendid," said Kenver when she emerged from her bedchamber. He was waiting for her in the hall as she had made him promise to do.

"Thank you." Sarah was aware of her limitations. She might look pleasant or even rather pretty; she did not rise to splendid. Especially now when her face must show the strain of the last half hour.

"Is something wrong?"

The door was closed behind her. Sarah spoke quietly so as not to be overheard. "Is Cranston the only... That is, you had mentioned another attendant. I would prefer that." Anyone else would be better, Sarah decided. Or no one. But she knew the latter choice would rouse an argument, and she would be despised for suggesting it.

"I did speak to Mama," Kenver said. "She thought Cranston was better suited to...show you how things are done at Poldene."

Aware of his uneasy expression, Sarah bowed her head. He didn't need her complaints. They both knew that Cranston was an adversary. She would just have to find some way of dealing with her.

Kenver led Sarah directly to the dining room. There was no gathering beforehand for cordial chatter. His parents were already there and seated opposite each other at an oblong table. Kenver and Sarah took their places on the empty sides—just too far apart for easy conversation, in Sarah's opinion.

Soup was served, eaten in silence, and removed. The first course was set out. Kenver reached across to help Sarah to a variety of probably delicious dishes. She was finding it hard to taste anything.

"I have just received some splendid news," said the countess. "We are to welcome two illustrious guests."

"The Newsomes?" asked Kenver.

"No. It isn't anyone you've met. They are acquaintances of your uncle." She glanced at Sarah. "My brother," she added, as if Sarah couldn't have worked this out for herself. "He wrote from London that they had departed for Cornwall and required a proper place to stay. I sent my acceptance by fast courier along the route to be sure to find them. They are the absolute cream of the *haut ton*."

She withheld the names, clearly hoping that her listeners would beg to know. Sarah thought she would try complying. "Who is it?"

"No one *you* would be acquainted with," replied Kenver's mother repressively.

So it was no good trying to defer, Sarah concluded. These newcomers would probably take their cue from the elder Pendrennons and treat her the same way. "I look forward to meeting them," she lied.

She watched Lady Trestan realize that she would have to present the daughter-in-law she found so entirely inadequate to her fashionable visitors. Unless she locked Sarah in a storeroom until they were gone. She looked as if she'd bitten into something sour. Sarah almost enjoyed her chagrin. If this hadn't been her new family, where she *wished* to be at home, she would have.

"I see you have Hicks at work on the state suite," Kenver said to his father.

"How do you know that?"

"The fellow there told me so when I showed Sarah the rooms. Is the attic much involved? Must we replace any roofing?"

"I'm leaving it to Hicks," replied his father. "He knows his craft."

"Yes, but..."

"Are you saying he doesn't?"

"No, Father, I just wondered..."

"I haven't gone feeble just yet. I am still able to manage a group of workmen."

"Of course," said Kenver. "I never imagined anything else."

Sarah wondered at Lord Trestan's attitude. Had Kenver questioned his father's competence at some point? That didn't sound like him. It seemed Lord Trestan was naturally a bad-tempered man. The earl and countess seemed well matched.

Silence returned. No one seemed inclined to break it. The clink of silverware was loud in the room, and the meal felt endless to Sarah. At last, however, it was over. The countess rose. Sarah quailed at the thought of retreating with her to an emotionally glacial drawing room while the men drank their port. It was one thing to confront Lady Trestan in a group. A hand-to-hand duel would be much harder. But Kenver stood as well, came to her side, took her arm, and said, "Good night, Mama, Papa." Before they could reply, he whisked Sarah out.

The return to her room was a relief. Sarah breathed a sigh when they closed the door behind them. She wondered if there was a key to the lock. Unsurprisingly, no one had given her one.

"I hope you…" Kenver began.

There was a brisk knock on the door. Cranston came in without waiting for an invitation. "Are you ready to retire?" she asked, even though it was still quite early.

Once again, the small room felt very full with the addition of a third person. Sarah's patience came to an end. "No," she said. "You may go."

Cranston did not move. "When shall I come back then?"

"I don't need you anymore tonight."

"Who is to help you out of your gown?"

Sarah thought that Kenver might do that. Though the day had seemed endless, this was just their wedding night. From the flush on his cheeks, the idea had occurred to him too. "You needn't worry about that," she said. She met Cranston's stare and waited. Finally, the maid went out. But there was no sound of retreating footsteps. Sarah was certain that Cranston was standing just outside the door, probably with her ear against the panels.

From the angry look on his face, Kenver thought the same. "There is no need for us to…hurry anything."

Everything about their union had been hurried. "If I am going to be married, I should like to be really married," said Sarah quietly.

There was a furtive sound outside the door. Kenver grimaced.

"I suppose we couldn't lock Cranston in a storeroom somewhere," said Sarah, remembering her thoughts at dinner.

Kenver blinked.

"We would let her out in the morning."

A laugh escaped him. "That would mean a great deal of shouting."

Which he preferred to avoid, Sarah had gathered, even in their short time together. There were families who enjoyed a rousing verbal scrap, like her friend Charlotte's. Neither hers nor Kenver's was that sort. Cranston would bring his mother down on them as well. And the scene would confirm all of Lady Trestan's doubts about her suitability.

"Only joking," said Sarah. Which she had been, mostly. Partly. "Of course we can't." Thinking of the tenderness as they huddled together in the cave and their frolic in the garden, she felt tears prick her eyelids.

"We just need a little time," said Kenver.

A thought floated up in Sarah's brain. She could not ask too much of him. His parents were doing everything they could to make him regret his choice. She didn't think he'd expected the level of friction that her arrival had roused. If her family had been doing that... Well, she couldn't imagine them in the role, but it would be an enormous pressure. "Time. Of course," she said.

He took both her hands, squeezed them. "I will make things right," he said.

Sarah took in his determined expression, the resolute set of his shoulders. She nodded.

Kenver bent to kiss her quickly, turned, and went out. Sarah braced herself for Cranston's return, and she was not mistaken. The maid came right back in, uninvited.

Sarah allowed Cranston to prepare her for bed as that meant she would go away until tomorrow. Through the silent process, Sarah's throat was tight with emotion, fiercely repressed as long as Cranston remained in her room. Afterward, a few tears escaped.

———

Kenver didn't go to bed. It wasn't late, and he wasn't the least bit sleepy. On the contrary, he was seething with irritation and frustrated desire. Hatless, in evening dress, he went downstairs and out into the soft summer night. Shoving his hands into his pockets, he walked the grounds of Poldene, every path familiar under his feet. Fingal slipped up to join him, a light-footed shadow under the stars. The deerhounds roamed the gardens at night and kept the place safe. Kenver let his hand drop in a brief caress of the dog's head. He had to think what to do, and walking often helped. It would also calm him.

He'd expected some difficulties with this impulsive marriage. He wasn't a fool. He and Sarah were barely acquainted after all. His parents weren't pleased. Of course he'd known that. But he hadn't expected such...open opposition from them.

And why not, he asked himself now. He'd never had much luck changing his parents' opinions. They saw him as young and foolish, making no allowance for his increasing age and experience. In their minds, they would always know better. He'd adjusted to that as a…fact of life, he realized. He had ways around it. He was out on the land a good deal and had many places inside Poldene where he could hole up. He'd learned to want what was possible. A good deal *was* possible. He understood the advantages of his position.

And so their managing ways hadn't mattered too much when it was just him. But now there was Sarah. She deserved better. Changes would have to be made. He would have to find a way.

Kenver walked across the oval of lawn where Sarah had set him afire this afternoon. He wanted his wife!

Fingal gave a soft woof, as if he too remembered their earlier frolic.

It would be best if they could go away, Kenver thought. But his father had a firm grip on the purse strings. Even a post chaise to go and visit the friend Sarah had mentioned was out of Kenver's reach right now. This quarter's allowance was mostly gone, and Papa could withhold payment of the next if he wished to. As for the costs of their own establishment— Kenver was well aware of how much that would require. It was out of the question. Also, he loved Poldene. It had always been his home. He'd expected it always would be.

He stood in the dark garden, breathed in the scents of roses and the sea. With an instinct to comfort, Fingal thrust a wet nose into his hand. Fingal had been part of Kenver's life since he was a boy of thirteen. The dog had grown from a tumbling puppy to the patriarch of his own line, and now into venerable old age. If he could speak, he might have useful advice. But of course he could not.

In her nightdress, with her hair braided down her back, Sarah gathered her courage and opened her bedroom door just a little. The corridor was empty. She held out her candlestick to throw more light. Nothing. She heard no sounds. The candle flame wavered only slightly in the still air. Taking a deep breath, she stepped out and scuttled along the hallway to knock on her husband's bedchamber door. There was no answer. Afraid that someone would come along and see her, Sarah turned the knob and went in, closing the door with a soft click.

The room was empty. There was no sign that he had been in it since dinnertime. She walked across and looked into the adjoining dressing room. It was also empty. Cupid and Psyche, she thought, the foolish girl who married an invisible lover and was tyrannized by her vindictive goddess/mother-in-law. "Idiot," Sarah murmured. "Kenver is not invisible, and the countess is *not* Aphrodite." That very inapt comparison actually made her smile.

Suppressing further wild ideas of enchanted castles and hollow hills, Sarah gazed around the room. Kenver's quarters were richer and more spacious than what she'd been given, which did not surprise her. Signs of him were everywhere—a discarded neckcloth, a pair of gloves, silver-backed brushes. She picked up a glove and held it to her cheek. She breathed in his scent, familiar from their embraces in the garden.

In her voracious consumption of any book she could get her hands on, Sarah had encountered quite a few concepts that a proper young lady was not expected to know. She'd read about the pleasures of the marital bed—in annoyingly vague terms for the most part, so that the topic remained tantalizing and mysterious. Kenver's kisses had confirmed some bits. Sarah knew now what it was to be wildly aroused. She was eager to explore the rest.

Could she climb into his bed and wait for him there? The idea thrilled and scandalized her. What would he say, think? It *was* their wedding night. He would be startled though. And what if he was not glad to see her when he returned?

A muted sound from beyond the small door on the other side of Kenver's dressing room made Sarah freeze. Kenver must have a valet, she realized, as she had the lamentable Cranston. Another of Lady Trestan's loyal staff. If the man came in and found her here…

Sarah's nerve broke. Checking the corridor and finding the coast clear, she retreated to her own room. Standing beside the bed, the candlestick wavering in her hand, she caught her breath.

Sadness threatened. She refused to cry! It was stupid to feel that all was lost. This was only the first day of her marriage, though it felt like an eternity. She needed a plan.

The shadows danced around her in the candlelight.

For now, she would pretend to be contented, Sarah decided. That would annoy Lady Trestan. Which she should not want to do. But she did. The elder Pendrennons must not know how lost she felt.

Her friend Charlotte always said that Sarah was the worst liar in the world. In their schoolgirl schemes, Sarah was never given the role of dissembler. Well, she could learn, Sarah thought. She'd always been very good at *that*. She would learn whatever was required to make her marriage succeed. Kenver deserved happiness too. Indeed, as she saw it, their happiness was intertwined, a braid of two strands. And she didn't think his parents cared much about either. Her jaw set with determination. She would be glad to find she was wrong about that, but she didn't think she was.

Sarah went to the half-full trunk, retrieved a favorite book, a reliable friend, and crawled into bed with it rather than her new husband.

———————

The next morning, Kenver lay in wait until Sarah appeared from her room. Thankfully, it wasn't late. He was an early riser and didn't care to dawdle away the day. When she hesitated at the door of the breakfast room, he said, "Mama takes a tray in her room. And Papa will not be down for a little while."

They went in and rang for tea.

"Do you ride?" Kenver asked her as they ate. He had a moment's worry. If she didn't, his plans would have to change.

But Sarah said, "Yes. Not as well as my friend Charlotte. I don't care for jumping."

He smiled at her. "Noted. I've none of that planned. But I usually spend part of each day out on the estate. I wondered if you would care to come along."

"Yes," said Sarah at once.

They were both aware that she didn't wish to stay at Poldene alone, and Kenver realized that he didn't much like that himself. In recent years, he'd formed a habit of roaming the countryside for hours with just a packet of bread and cheese in his saddlebag. That habit had taken him to Tintagel on one fateful day, as a matter of fact, and changed his life.

"I'll go and put on my riding habit," she added. "Shall I meet you in the stables?"

"Unless you wish me to come and wait." In the corridor outside his mother's chamber, which would be uncomfortable.

Sarah seemed to read his mind. She shook her head. "I won't be long."

She was such a sensitive creature, Kenver thought. It was remarkable. "I'll go and choose a horse for you."

"It needn't be a slug, as Charlotte would say. I ride fairly well."

"A mount with some spirit but no tendency to sudden leaps."

She smiled at him. Such an easy, open smile. Kenver felt a tug in the region of his heart. Among all the other things he longed for, he wanted to inspire that smile as often as he possibly could.

They rode down the drive before Poldene side by side. If anyone was watching from the windows, Sarah didn't see them. Kenver had given her a lovely little mare who frisked with joy at the outing. Her good-tempered capering made Sarah laugh. "All right?" asked Kenver.

"Perfect," she replied.

The day was overcast. Fat clouds drifted across the sky on a cool breeze from the sea. The scent of fresh-mown hay came from fields inland. Sarah breathed it in and felt her spirits lift in freedom. When they turned into the lane outside the grounds, she leaned forward and let the mare have her head for a run. Kenver pounded along beside her, grinning.

Reaching the village at the head of the valley, they slowed. Kenver nodded greetings to an old woman and a young mother holding a baby. Most of the people would be out helping with the harvest at this time of year, Sarah knew. One middle-aged man was not, however. He stood by a thatched cottage leaning on a tall staff. When he raised a hand, Kenver turned toward him. "No, don't get down," the man said when Kenver started to dismount.

"I don't want to keep you standing."

"I can easily do so," was the reply. In the accents of an educated man, not a rural villager.

This seemed to be a sore point, Sarah noted as Kenver let it go. "This is Ralph Stovell," he said to her. "The village schoolmaster. Stovell, my wife."

As she thrilled a little to the new label, Sarah saw awareness of their story in the man's blue eyes, with no sign of condemnation. She also thought she saw lingering pain in their depths.

"I had a letter from Dellings," Stovell said. "He's pleased with John's enthusiasm and application. Predicts great things for him. Says the lad's growing out of all his clothes, however."

Kenver took a leather pouch from his coat pocket,

unlaced the strings, and extracted a guinea coin. He handed it to Stovell. The man nodded in acknowledgment, then stepped back as if he had no more to say. Kenver put the pouch away, and they rode on.

"It's unusual to have a trained schoolmaster in a small village," Sarah said when they had left the cottages behind.

"He appreciates a quiet life. He was hurt rather badly in the war."

"His leg?" She'd noticed how he leaned on the staff.

"And other wounds that are less visible."

Perhaps that was what she'd seen in his eyes.

"He doesn't care to talk about it," Kenver added.

"I could see that."

He gave her a quick glance. "I found him on the cliff path, nearly three years ago now. He was trying to tramp cross country as he used to do as a student. But he'd fallen and couldn't go on. He was lying at the edge, looking over."

Sarah met his hazel eyes and understood that Stovell had been thinking of throwing himself into the sea. "So you found him a place as schoolmaster."

"We…discussed matters and came up with the idea together." He looked at her again. "We don't mention exactly how it came about."

She nodded a promise. "And who is John?"

"A village boy apprenticed to a solicitor down in Truro."

That was also quite unusual.

"Stovell and I have an arrangement," Kenver continued before she could ask. "Most children learn trades from their parents, as you know. A smith's son becomes a smith. The daughter of a skilled seamstress is taught that art. Farm laborers bring their offspring into the fields. And so on. But now and then, a child is different."

"Good at their books," Sarah suggested.

"Partly that. But perhaps just not suited to their parents' work. Or inspired by some other. Stovell keeps an eye out, and a sympathetic ear, and when we're certain they mean it and are determined, we find them an apprenticeship or position. Schooling sometimes."

"That is splendid," said Sarah, full of admiration.

He shrugged as if it was no great thing.

They rode on. All along the way, Kenver was greeted by workers in the fields and residents of tenant cottages. He seemed to know every detail of their families and situations and was pelted with news of more. Many of them came over with quiet questions or requests for him. Now and then, he retrieved his pouch of coins and handed some over. Sarah didn't hear what they said, but the transactions were clear. Kenver was supplementing actions by the Poldene estate manager, or perhaps even circumventing some decisions. He was woven into the fabric of this place, needed and admired and obviously respected. "This is how you spend your days?" she asked when they had left one of these groups behind.

"Mostly."

"You said you wanted a knightly quest, but you already have one. Tending your own countryside."

"It's not the same," he objected.

"Yes, it is. What else were those ancient knights doing?"

"Important things. Battles. Missions. Righting wrongs."

"I suspect you are doing that," Sarah said quietly.

Kenver stared. She looked utterly sincere. And appreciative. She was not mocking him. This intelligent, perceptive young lady really thought he was the equal of those old questers. The idea was too revolutionary to take in all at once.

A gust of wind caught at his hat. The vagaries of local weather were in his bones. "It's going to rain. Come. There's a place to shelter not far ahead."

He increased the pace and brought them to a barn at the edge of a stubble field before the first drops fell.

"Are you tired?" he asked as he helped her down from the saddle.

"A little. I don't usually ride so long."

"We'll have a good rest." He began to empty his saddlebags. He'd made sure to bring more than bread and cheese today, and he was pleased when Sarah exclaimed over the waxed packet of thinly sliced chicken, crusty bread, peaches, and tightly corked bottles of cider.

He added several cloth napkins to the pile and left her to arrange them as he tended the horses, loosening their girths and bringing them water from a trough outside the doors. There was fodder stored here, and no one would grudge him a bit. Then he joined Sarah on an aged bench to eat.

Hunger kept them quiet for a while. Kenver used his pocketknife to pry the corks from the cider. The tart, sweet liquid tasted like harvest bounty. He cut the fruit into quarters, discarding the pits.

"This is rather like the sea cave," Sarah said when he offered her a section.

"We're not soaked with brine," Kenver responded.

"No. And we have food."

"We're not trapped," he pointed out.

She laughed. "So it's not really like it at all. It just…feels similar somehow." She bit into the peach.

She was right. Here they were, alone, far from the press of humanity, with talk and silences, close together side by side. And there was that bond knit between them, palpable, mysteriously sturdy. He used a corner of his napkin to catch a trickle of juice running down her chin.

Sarah looked up at him, her blue eyes soft. He bent to kiss her, tasting peaches on her willing lips.

Matters went from tender to fiery in a flash of desire. Kenver didn't notice the thud of cider bottles dropping to the dirt floor. He pulled her against him and let their kisses go urgent. His hands moved over her, impatient with the barriers of cloth, finding the buttons of her riding habit.

He had undone two of them when caution nagged. He could tumble her here in the hay, as other couples had no doubt done before. The place was well-known. Which is why some might arrive to shelter from the rain. To find them… It was…not respectful. She was his wife. Stifling a groan, Kenver drew back. Napkins lay in the dust with spilled cider and fragments of peach. "People use this barn," he said.

Sarah blinked. She looked adorably disheveled. Her hair curled about her flushed cheeks, and her hat had fallen off. He could see the quick rise and fall of her chest. He wanted her unbearably.

Aching, Kenver bent to pick up the bottles. There was

only a bit of cider left. He drank it. Then he rose to tidy away the rest of their picnic. "Check the horses," he managed, taking the remains to his saddlebags.

He stayed there for a while, regaining his composure. When he came back, Sarah had restored her hair and put on her hat. Somewhere in this whirl, the rain had tapered off. "If you're rested, we should go on," Kenver said. Should because his control really only went so far.

She nodded. He brought their mounts and helped her up, then led her down toward the coast. "We are circling back toward Poldene now," he said.

Sarah heard him but scarcely took it in. Her senses were still reeling; her skin burned with a thwarted wish to be touched. It would have been horribly embarrassing if they had been caught…indulging in the hay. Of course she knew that. The gossip, on top of the story of their match, would have been dreadful. Lady Trestan… She wasn't going to think about that! But there was no one about. Except… Two laborers carrying shovels rounded the corner of the lane ahead. They saluted Kenver as they passed. A cottage on the hill to the right probably overlooked that barn. A boy swung down from a tree farther off and slipped through the bushes like a lad avoiding chores. So Kenver was right. He knew his lands. Obviously. She must stop thinking about his hands and his lips and…everything.

She took a deep breath, and another. The sound of the sea grew ahead, with its salt scent. They came to a cluster of fishermen's homes on a cliff above a small cove. Sarah was surprised when Kenver stopped before one of these, dismounted, and came to help her do the same. "I need to speak to a man down at the boats," he said, indicating the flotilla below. "Mrs. Vine will take care of you."

She turned to find a stocky woman of perhaps fifty coming from the cottage, wiping her hands on a pristine cloth. She bobbed a small curtsy when Kenver introduced Sarah. "I've some of that currant cake you like," she said to him.

"I thought you would," replied Kenver. He smiled at Sarah and turned toward the path leading down to the water.

Mrs. Vine ushered her into a front room that held two small tables and chairs. "Travelers have started coming along the coast," the woman said. "To look at the sea." She shook her head as if mystified by this. "They like a place to stop and have a cup of tea and a bit of cake. I'm a baker, so I spoke to his lordship and…" She gestured at the tables. "Sit you down."

Sarah did. A few minutes later, Mrs. Vine returned with a tray holding a teapot and cups and a splendid-looking cake. "What a lovely pattern," Sarah said of the porcelain.

Mrs. Vine gave her a sidelong look. "His lordship 'found' them in the back of a cupboard. Someplace. So he said." When Sarah smiled, Mrs. Vine grinned and cut a large slice of the cake to set before her.

Sarah picked up a delicate fork, wondering if it too had come from some storage nook at Poldene, and ate a bite. "Oh, that's wonderful." A medley of marvelous flavors melted on her tongue. "I think it's the best currant cake I've ever had."

Mrs. Vine beamed. "My daughter has a post making pastries and such at a fine London hotel. That's not common, you know."

Sarah nodded. It certainly wasn't for a young woman. Or any child of such a small place really.

"His lordship helped her to it. She's growing famous because of *my* recipes."

"I can see why." Sarah took another luscious bite.

Kenver returned soon after to devour his own huge slice and chat with Mrs. Vine about her daughter. Soon after, Sarah and Kenver mounted up and rode back toward Poldene. "People call you 'your lordship,'" Sarah observed as they went.

"I can use the title Viscount Otterham," he replied. "But I don't care to. It belongs to the earldom—my father—and is granted as a courtesy to the heir. Seems unnecessary."

Sarah took this in and decided she rather liked his attitude.

It had been a lovely day, she thought, one of the best she could remember. If only dinner could be the same.

Six

MESSAGES HAD FLOWN WITH UNUSUAL SPEED UP AND down the London road, and two days later, the mysterious, illustrious guests were due to arrive at Poldene. Sarah and Kenver had not been told what time they were expected, but as it chanced, they were out walking in the gardens when carriage wheels sounded on the gravel drive. Curious, Kenver turned their steps toward the front courtyard, in time to see a vehicle with a crest on the door pull up with a flourish of the coachman's whip. "What a cracking team!" Kenver couldn't help but exclaim. The four grays were perfectly matched.

The carriage door opened, and a handsome man with dark hair and an athletic figure descended. Kenver had spent enough time in London to recognize a Corinthian in the first stare of fashion. The fellow turned and offered his hand to a dazzling blond lady, another example of sartorial perfection. Kenver wondered how his uncle had come to know such a polished pair.

"Oh," said Sarah at his side.

Kenver didn't blame her. He couldn't remember ever seeing such stylish visitors at Poldene. The front door opened, and his parents emerged to greet the newcomers.

Kenver noticed that the dogs did *not* come rushing out ahead of them to overwhelm these new arrivals. He led Sarah forward, curious to discover who this might be.

His mother looked disgruntled to see them approaching. Kenver ignored her frown and joined the group.

"Sarah!" cried the lovely blond visitor. She looked startled.

"Cecelia, hello," his wife most surprisingly replied. "Are you the houseguests?"

"Yes, we have kindly been invited to stay at Poldene."

"Oh, how lovely." Sarah sounded surprised and relieved in equal measure. Kenver was simply amazed.

"You know each other?" asked his mother. Her tone was astonished, edging toward disbelief. The look she gave Sarah was acrid.

Kenver saw both the guests notice her attitude. The fashionable lady raked them all with blue eyes that seemed as astute as they were lovely. "We are very good friends," she replied. "I'm delighted to see you, Sarah."

There was the slightest hint of a question at the end of that sentence. "This is my husband, Kenver Pendrennon," Sarah replied.

More surprise, Kenver noted. It seemed a morning for it.

"Our son," said his mother as if Sarah had usurped her prerogatives. Which she had, rather.

"Kenver, these are my friends the Duke and Duchess of Tereford," Sarah added.

And enjoyed saying it, Kenver thought. He couldn't blame her, after days of his mother's snubs. "Pleasure to meet you," he said.

"I really can't think how you came to be acquainted," said his mother. Her chagrin was all too evident. It was embarrassing.

"We enjoyed each other's company during the season," answered the duchess.

"You. And Miss...*her*?" Mama's tone suggested that she thought some trick was being played on her.

Both guests turned to look at her with slightly raised brows. Their gazes combined interrogation and censure in such a finely tuned mixture that Kenver filed it away for future reference. And a time when he might need to commit exquisitely polite annihilation.

"We should go in," said his father.

His mother blinked. She took an instant to recover from those looks, then said, "Yes. Of course." She stepped between her guests and her son. "Do come in," she added, clearly not to Kenver and Sarah.

The guests followed her without looking back. They weren't the sort to give in to such impulses, Kenver judged. He decided not to follow. Let his mother play lady of the manor and calm down. He wondered where she intended to house them. "Well, that was a surprise," he said.

"I knew they were coming down to Cornwall to see about one of the Tereford properties here," Sarah replied. "It is quite run-down, I believe. We'd spoken of meeting during their visit. I thought there might be a letter soon. But this seems..." She paused, considering. "I suppose Poldene is the only house in the neighborhood grand enough to host the Terefords." She shook her head, murmuring, "But it feels like the hand of providence."

He gave her a questioning look.

"To have a friend arrive," Sarah said.

Was he not a friend? Perhaps he wasn't really. Yet. He certainly intended to be. One of the gardeners rounded a shrub and began pruning its branches. Unnecessarily in Kenver's opinion. Some member of the Poldene staff always seemed to pop up when he and Sarah were together. His mother's tactics were becoming wearisome.

"I will ask Cecelia's advice," Sarah added, as if speaking to herself. Noticing Kenver's raised brows, she said, "Cecelia is up to anything."

Kenver's observation of the duchess had been brief, but he had no trouble believing this.

"And the duke is very pleasant company," she added.

"Clearly top of the trees," said Kenver.

"Oh yes."

"Mama was…" He wasn't certain how to finish that sentence.

"Astounded to find that I was friends with a duchess?"

"Well." He couldn't deny it.

"I suppose this will make things with her all the harder."

"Or she might come to appreciate you. As I do."

"You've scarcely had the opportunity," Sarah answered in an acid tone he hadn't heard from her before. Her expression was strangely set too. The phrase "cat among the pigeons" floated into Kenver's consciousness. But who was the cat?

Another carriage, laden with luggage, came down the drive. Kenver stepped forward to direct the driver, and the superior valet and dresser inside, around to the stables.

Sarah was not surprised by the knock on her door in the hour before dinner, nor to find Cecelia awaiting entry when she opened it. She had made sure to be ready well before time and send Cranston on her way. "Oh good, you're alone," Cecelia said. She walked in, surveying the room. "Not a mean, dusty garret then," she added. "Only rather cramped."

There was no need to ask how Cecelia had found her in a strange house, Sarah thought. She just did such things. As she clearly had understood the attitude of Kenver's mother without being told. "And directly across from my mother-in-law," Sarah said dryly.

Cecelia laughed.

It was a lovely, musical sound. And Cecelia was a bright, assured presence in the room. She lightened the whole atmosphere of the place. "I've never been more glad to see someone in my life," Sarah told her.

"Yes, but, Sarah, what are you doing here? And married without a word to anyone? I had letters not two days ago. Harriet and Charlotte said nothing about this."

"I haven't had time to write. It was rather sudden."

Cecelia raised her golden brows and waited.

"Not time," Sarah admitted. "Courage." She poured out the whole story—Tintagel, cave, whispers, Kenver's gallant offer.

"My goodness, what an adventure."

Sarah couldn't help a hollow laugh. "I so often wished for adventures. It turns out they are quite uncomfortable. And then they go on and on. I was thinking about rescue last night."

"And what would rescue be, Sarah?" Cecelia's look was searching. "Are you sorry to have married?"

"No. Yes. Not Kenver, although we… It's his parents."

Cecelia nodded.

"I didn't know until I came here how angry they were about the match. We'd had no time to get acquainted." Sarah broke off. That had sounded daft. Of course they hadn't.

The duchess considered. "Arranged marriages can work. I have seen it."

"When the people arranging them try to be certain they go well?"

She acknowledged this with a nod.

"Will you help me, Cecelia?"

"Of course. When I know what you would wish me to do."

"Make Kenver's parents like me?"

"I'm not certain…"

"No, that was a joke. A poor one. Can you observe and give me advice?"

"Of course I will do that." Cecelia reached over and squeezed Sarah's hand.

It was immensely comforting. "Thank you."

———

When they went in to dinner, Kenver saw that his mother had put Sarah and her duchess friend as far from each other as possible at table. But there were not enough of them in the party to make that more than a small slight. Then Mama began discussing people who might be mutual friends but were unknown to the rest of them. She seemed prepared to spend the entire meal reviewing their family history and connections. The guests were affable, but they didn't look very interested. "I hope your rooms are comfortable," he said to the duchess at the first lull in the conversation.

She smiled at him, and Kenver was briefly dazzled. "Yes," she said. "Your mother told us a prince once stayed in them."

"A…" It took Kenver a moment to assimilate this information. "You are in the state suite?" he asked, thinking he could not have heard her correctly.

"I believe that was the name. Which prince was it?" asked the duchess.

"One who died young before taking the throne," put in Sarah drily.

Kenver met Sarah's crackling gaze. But he still couldn't quite believe it. He turned to his father. "What about the repairs?"

"Hicks got more workmen in and managed to finish," was the reply.

"There was a hole in the ceiling." Kenver had checked on the irritatingly slow progress yesterday. No, it had been the day before. He and Sarah had ridden out on the estate again yesterday.

"Ah, I thought there was a smell of fresh plaster," said the duke. "Didn't I say so, my dear?" He had the air of a spectator at a mildly amusing play.

The duchess threw him an admonishing smile.

"Never mind, Kenver," said Mama, frowning. "Our guests don't care about such things."

"Oh, my wife is fascinated by estate management," said the duke.

"On our own properties," replied the duchess, her tone suggesting that he had gone far enough. He appeared to accept this with unimpaired amiability.

"What property have you come to Cornwall to inspect?" asked his father.

"It is a house called Tresigan," answered the duchess.

"But that's haunted." The words slipped out before Kenver thought. His brain was still fixed on the state suite.

"Of course it is," replied the duke with a wry glance at his wife.

"Don't be ridiculous," said Kenver's mother. She waved this aside. "People tell the stupidest stories."

"Do you know the place?" the duchess asked Kenver.

"I have never been there. I've only heard tales now and then."

"About the haunting?" asked Sarah, looking intrigued.

"There is no such thing." Kenver's mother frowned at her.

"I suppose we shall see," said the duke, his tone suggesting he agreed. "We are driving over tomorrow to take a look."

His wife smiled at Kenver. "You and Sarah should come with us. We could use some local guides."

Seeing Sarah's brightness at the thought, Kenver readily agreed. His mother huffed her disapproval, but she didn't quite dare to object.

The rest of the evening passed more pleasantly than previous ones. The houseguests exerted themselves to be charming, at which they were obviously expert. Kenver's parents responded like wilting plants given water. He wondered at first if Sarah might feel slighted, but she clearly did not. In fact, she seemed to be watching the duchess with a kind of gleeful admiration. It was almost as if they were plotting something. He started to ask when he escorted her back to her room later, but Sarah opened the door of her bedchamber, looked inside, and closed it again. "Cranston is inside," she said.

"Of course she is," said Kenver, trying to match the Duke of Tereford's masterful intonation. Cranston also had the ears of a bat. "I'm sorry about the state suite," he said.

"Are you?"

"They rushed the work for the guests," Kenver told himself. "My mother would do a great deal to impress a duke."

Sarah nodded.

"I hope it was competently done."

"Your mother probably stood over Hicks and made sure of it," Sarah said.

Kenver snorted a laugh. The picture was all too plausible.

"Now that there was someone *worthy* to stay there," she added drily.

He shifted uneasily. "As soon as this visit is over, we will move in there."

"Shift our things in the dead of night?" she asked. "Perform a fait accompli? It sounds like a ballet leap, doesn't it?"

"What?" It was a joke. Dry humor lurked in her blue eyes. The arrival of her friends had enlivened her. He felt a wave of affection for this girl he had taken as his wife, followed by a burst of desire.

It was maddening that he couldn't take her in his arms

and cover her with kisses. If he swept her up and carried her off to his room... He would find his valet there, and that extremely correct, aging gentleman's gentleman would be overcome with embarrassment. Kenver could so easily visualize the aghast expression, the fumbling apologies, the small items dropped in hasty retreat. Snatched up, dropped again, muttered chagrin. Not a romantic scene.

Footsteps sounded at the end of the corridor. His mother appeared, coming to her bedchamber. She stopped and stared at them as if they were doing something revolting.

"Good night," Sarah said and disappeared into her room.

Kenver nodded to his mother, wished for a font of wisdom to consult, and headed out to walk the grounds again.

———

The Terefords' traveling carriage was brought round early the next morning, and the duke and duchess, Sarah and Kenver climbed aboard as an ample picnic hamper was tied onto the back. One of the Poldene stable boys sat next to the coachman on the box ready to direct him. Kenver had said that although the distance was not long to Tresigan, the tangle of lanes could be confusing.

It was a golden late-summer day, and Sarah felt a giddy relief at being on an outing with friends, away from the disapproving gaze of the countess. For hours! She and Cecelia exchanged news. The duke offered tidbits about doings in London. And if Kenver looked surprised at their easy chatter, Sarah didn't mind showing him that she was more than a country nobody.

Less than an hour later, they turned from the country lane into a weed-grown drive. It didn't look as if any vehicle had passed along it in months. Blackthorn thickets reared up on both sides, threatening to engulf them. They had to slow for a series of deep ruts. "This does not bode well," said the duke.

A length of briar, tossed by the breeze, latched onto the coachman's hat and pulled it off. He grabbed for it and missed, with an angry exclamation. The groom from Poldene jumped down, retrieved it, and climbed nimbly to the box again.

"Not well at all," added the duke.

They edged around the rampant bushes, thorns scraping on both sides of the carriage. Sarah heard the coachman mutter about paintwork as they emerged into a clearer space, only to confront a positive riot of vegetation.

"My God, it really is covered in ivy," said the duke.

"It looks like a fairy mound," said Sarah.

Vines flowed from the top of a fifty-foot cliff some distance away. The ivy snaked across a few yards of garden and up over a building, wrapping around it like a mottled green scarf. The ivy leaves, stirring in a soft breeze, obscured details, but Sarah could just make out a blocky two-story house. Bits of a peaked roof poked through here and there. Ivy tendrils reached out as if waving at them, looking for further supports.

The driver pulled up, and they got down from the carriage. The duke discovered a line of overgrown flagstones that led toward the front of the mound. And the door, Sarah assumed. They picked their way along it, tall weeds catching at their skirts and coattails.

"We should have brought a scythe," said the duchess.

"And someone to wield it," replied her husband. "In fact, I begin to wonder why I travel anywhere these days without a full crew of workmen at my back."

Sarah started to suggest that there were plenty of local people looking for work. Just in time, she realized he'd been joking.

"I don't suppose we have anything like a key?" the duke asked his wife.

"Oh, have you found a door?"

"No, but…"

"No key."

The duke accepted this with resignation. "Uncle Percival really was a tiresome old fellow," he commented.

"The previous duke," Cecelia told Kenver. "He didn't pay much attention to his estates."

Her husband gave an elegant snort. "For fifty years," he added. "He was a connoisseur of rack and ruin."

There was a sound of tearing stems and creaking wood above their heads. Looking up, Sarah saw that a casement window was being pushed open on the upper story, fighting the entwined vines for every inch. Finally a man's head emerged, and he looked down at them. Sarah took in his long, tangled black hair, rampant beard, and beetling eyebrows with amazement. He was as covered by hair as the house was by its cloak of ivy. "Go away," ordered this apparition. His voice was creaky, as if he seldom used it. "No trespassing, by the order of the Duke of Tereford."

They all stared up at him. He glared back. Sarah thought his glittering eyes might be green.

"I am the Duke of Tereford," said Cecelia's husband. "And I don't recall giving any such order."

"No, you ain't," replied the man. "He's up in London. Never comes near here."

"I have driven down from London to look over this house."

"The duke's an old man, older than me."

Sarah wondered how old he was. It was impossible to tell, though there was no sign of gray in all that hair, she noted.

"My great-uncle died last year, and I inherited the title. Would you care to see my visiting card?" Cecelia's husband held one up, a small rectangle of pasteboard in his immaculate glove. Cecelia hid a smile.

"Anybody could have cards made up," growled the man. But he sounded less sure.

There was a stir at Sarah's side. "I am Kenver Pendrennon," said her husband. "From Poldene. Perhaps you know it? This is definitely the Duke of Tereford."

"Pendrennon." The name clearly meant something to the man. He stared at Kenver from under his bushy brows.

"We are coming inside," declared the duke. "We would prefer not to have to subdue you first." His tone suggested no doubt of his ability to do so.

"Eh," said the man. He seemed to chew something over. "You'd best come around back then. The front door don't open any longer. Well, not without a deal of clearing, and mebbe an ax, it won't." His head disappeared before anyone could reply.

They trooped around the house through the knee-high

weeds. The coachman came along in case additional persuasion was required, while the stable boy stayed with the horses. It was quite a distance. The house was wider than it had looked from the front.

"I didn't think it would be so large," said Cecelia.

"I fancy there may be a courtyard in the center," the duke replied.

They rounded the back corner of the building and discovered that the ivy had been chopped away for a vegetable garden here. It had also been trimmed back from two windows and a door on the ground floor. The latter opened as they reached it.

The hirsute man stood just within. He wore a loose shirt that had once been white, buff trousers, and wooden clogs of the sort that country people carved for themselves. The clothes were worn but not ragged, and Sarah thought that they, and he, looked clean.

"Who are you?" asked the duke.

"Merlin," he replied.

Sarah met Kenver's hazel eyes. They were twinkling. Hers probably were too. No, they certainly were. "Merlin the magician?" she couldn't help asking. This earned her sidelong looks from her ducal companions.

"Mayhap," the man answered.

Kenver laughed.

"Ha," said the duke, acknowledging the humor without indulging in it. "What are you doing here? Were you installed as caretaker?"

"Eh."

"Because if so, you are doing a wretched job."

"Wasn't," the man mumbled. "Ain't. Place was left empty."

"So you broke in."

"It wasn't hardly locked up."

The duke sighed. "By which you mean the lock was poor, and you were able to get through it."

"I don't see why a house should go to waste."

Sarah had some sympathy with this point. She also noted that the man's rural accent had gone crisp and more cultured with that last sentence.

"Are you behind all the tales of haunting?" asked Kenver.

The sly grin was enough of a reply. Merlin's teeth looked very white against the mass of black hair. "Those as snoop may find more than they was looking for," he said.

Sarah appreciated Kenver's cleverness in realizing this right away.

"Let's look through the house," said Cecelia, ever practical.

Her tone made the man step back. Sending the coachman back to his team, they entered a long, narrow room that had once been the manor's kitchen. It was now obviously the man's entire living space. He clearly cooked over the large fireplace with an oven at one end. A few pots and dishes sat on a shelf beside it. A pallet lay in the front corner at the other end. And a table and chair occupied the middle of the space. Sarah noted that the place was sparse and shabby but not dirty. Doors leading into other parts of the house were shut. Greenish light filtered through ivy leaves came through high windows on the side wall. These had not been trimmed like those in the rear.

The duke went to one of the inner doors and pushed. It did not open. "Are these locked?" he asked their inadvertent host.

"Nah. Warped."

"I see." The duke put his shoulder to the door and shoved. With a screech of dry hinges and scraping of wood, it yielded.

They walked through Tresigan's empty rooms, moving around the ground floor and then testing the stairs before doing the same on the upper level. They found nothing but dust, a bit of debris, and one patch of damp. A broken window upstairs had allowed birds to enter and nest. The floor of that room was spattered with droppings.

Back downstairs, they forced open an inner door and revealed the central courtyard the duke had suspected. Cascades of ivy had grown down from the roof and pooled in this open space, humped and mounded over what might have been small trees. Sarah started to step through the doorway. "Don't go out there," said the duke. "We can't tell if there are broken pavements or even holes to trip you up."

She pulled back.

"This is unusual construction for this area," said Kenver. "It's almost like an atrium."

"Do you think the house might have begun as a Roman villa?" Sarah asked. "There was trade from Cornwall to the empire."

"It can't be that old." But Kenver looked intrigued. He edged over and pulled at the ivy, exposing a section of wall. "It's built of brick. Not ancient." He smiled at Sarah. "Too bad."

Sarah nodded, the Romans briefly forgotten in the allure of that smile. Her pulse speeded up. Kenver held her gaze as if he could tell.

"It looks as if no one has tended to Tresigan for a century or so," said the duke.

"Many years at least," replied Cecelia. "It is a shame."

They returned to the kitchen. The man who called himself Merlin was sitting at the table, hands folded as if awaiting his fate.

"Where do you come from?" asked the duchess. "Who is your family?"

"I am Merlin from the hollow hills," he answered, gesturing at the cliff behind the house. "I sprang from the realm of faery, and I rule this place."

The duke sighed. Sarah again noted the change in the man's accent.

"We've brought a picnic," Cecelia said. "Would you like a cup of tea?"

"You've got tea?"

"Yes. And cakes."

Merlin's eyes lit. Sarah revised her idea of his age downward. His hands were not gnarled with years, she noticed, though they were work worn and the nails bitten down.

"And I see you have a teapot," Cecelia said.

"With naught to put in it but well water."

"We can remedy that."

Sarah admired the way Cecelia spoke to him, as if he was a morning caller or newly met neighbor instead of…whatever he was. Of course he couldn't be Merlin the legendary wizard. Though how marvelous it would be if he *was*. Catching Kenver's look, she was certain he was thinking exactly the same thing.

The hamper was fetched. The blankets they'd brought were spread beside the luxuriant vegetable garden. The tea was brewed at the kitchen fireplace and brought out. Food was spread before them. Sarah half expected Merlin to eat like a starving animal. He was certainly skinny. But his manners were avid but acceptable.

The duke was surveying the house. "The first thing to do is to pull off all this ivy," he said. "Then we can see whether the roof is sound and so on."

"You can't take it off," said Merlin.

He received a haughty look with raised eyebrows.

"Place'll fall down without it," he claimed.

"Indeed? Have you tried?" The duke's tone was very dry. Sarah wouldn't have cared to be its target.

"The aerial roots might have damaged the old mortar," said Kenver. "Which is all the more reason for it to be removed. As they will go on doing so." He rose and went over to pull a handful of vines off the house.

"Is there damage?" asked Cecelia.

"It doesn't look bad that I can see. Not here, at least."

"Ivy works its way into any cracks though," said Cecelia. Kenver nodded.

Sarah was watching Merlin's face through this exchange. He must be afraid of losing his home, even though the house wasn't actually his. But she didn't see much fear. "How long have you been living here?" she asked him.

He turned to look at her.

Realizing that she hadn't been introduced, Sarah added, "I am Sarah M…Pendrennon." Her new name still sounded foreign in her ears.

"Eh? Pendrennon?" Merlin frowned at her.

"Kenver's wife."

Now he looked thoroughly startled, though she couldn't imagine why. His eyes—they *were* green—drilled into her before he dropped them. "Been here a while," he said.

He didn't wish to say, she concluded. In fact, he didn't want them to know anything about him. It made sense. Sarah supposed he could be brought to book for trespassing. She glanced at the duke. What did he mean to do about Merlin? And if he ordered the man to leave, would he go?

"Sarah." She turned to find Kenver gazing at her. "Care for a stroll? Take a look at the garden?" he asked.

"That's mine, that is," said Merlin.

"We won't disturb it."

Sarah stood up at once and took Kenver's offered arm. He led her over to the tidy rows of vegetables. "Peas," he said in a bland tone. "Past it now. Carrots. Potatoes, I believe."

"Very well kept," Sarah replied, equally impassive.

They looked at each other, silently came to an agreement, and moved on around the ivy-covered corner of the house. A path in the vines led somewhere. Sarah didn't care where.

"We are actually alone," Kenver said.

"And Cecelia won't 'happen by' and discover us."

"No?"

"She never would."

With one impulse, they stepped into each other's arms and came together in a searing kiss. The balmy afternoon suddenly felt even warmer, heady with green scents and the burr of crickets. Kenver's hands moved urgently over Sarah's body. She arched up against him, eager for more. They kissed, paused, kissed again. She grew dizzy with desire.

"If only I had one of those blankets," Kenver panted.

They could fall onto it amongst the ivy. "Like maenads," she breathed.

"What?"

"The worshippers of Dionysus. They wore wreaths of ivy and held orgies in the forest."

Kenver gazed down at her. "Not quite orgies. They were known for tearing animals to pieces with their bare hands."

"Animals?" Sarah blinked. "Bare?"

"Maenad translates as 'raving ones,'" he added.

"It does?" Sarah shook her head. "I never managed to learn Greek." She sighed with regret. "I did so like the idea of woodland orgies."

He looked around. "Would you call that clump of trees a woodland?"

Sarah examined the ivy-draped straggle of saplings, looked at Kenver, looked back at the trees. "I hadn't really considered... Rocks. And insects."

He snorted a laugh.

And Sarah heard her name called from the other side of the house. She sighed more deeply. "That's Cecelia."

"It is," Kenver acknowledged.

"Time to go."

He nodded.

Sarah reached up to straighten her bonnet. "I suppose they will know what we were doing."

"I suppose I don't care," he replied.

The call came again, though no one appeared to search for them. They turned and went.

In the end, no decision was made about Merlin, except that Sarah noticed Cecelia left the extra food when the hamper and blankets were gathered up. The duke saw it too, she was certain, but though he looked sardonic, he made no remark.

Kenver asked Sarah's question as the carriage pulled away. "What are you going to do about that fellow?"

"Do you know of a lunatic asylum nearby?" responded the duke.

"James," said Cecelia.

"Joking, my dear."

"He didn't seem deranged exactly," Sarah said.

"The hollow hills?" murmured the duke.

"Oh." She sighed. "I wish it was true."

Kenver smiled at her. "Don't the old stories say that time runs differently inside faery mounds?"

"Centuries passing like weeks?" Sarah replied.

"And the wanderer comes out to find everything changed." Kenver's hazel eyes gleamed, as if he shared her wish for a brush with magic.

"So he could be an ancient wizard!"

"Who moves into a derelict house and plants a vegetable garden?" asked the duke.

His wife smiled. "Where is your love of the fantastic?"

"Overwhelmed by the mare's nest Uncle Percival left behind." He looked across at Sarah and Kenver. "The previous duke created more chaos than I could ever have imagined."

"An odd sort of legacy," said Kenver.

"Indeed."

"We will find a place for Merlin," said the duchess. "Some employment perhaps."

"Enchanting the cabbages?" the duke murmured.

"I might be able to help," said Kenver. "I know the people hereabouts."

Cecelia gave him an approving nod, and Sarah glowed at this additional evidence of his kindness. Sitting next to him in the carriage, their legs pressing together when the vehicle hit a bump in the lane, she could think of nothing but his kisses. Surely there was a way to make theirs a proper marriage? Poldene had many rooms. If they just insisted on having their own—together. But Lady Trestan turned the least hint of opposition into war. And she was ruthlessly good at it, sharp as a swarm of stinging wasps. With years ahead of them in the same household—Sarah suppressed a shudder—it was best to move carefully. Assuming she didn't go mad in the process.

The conversation shifted to estate management. Kenver showed his sure grasp of the topic, and Sarah watched him and Cecelia impress each other with their ideas. The duke seemed to enjoy the spectacle as well.

Kenver was summoned by his father when they returned to Poldene. Sarah retreated to her room. The duke and duchess went arm in arm to their own quarters. "Do you intend to keep feeding that trespasser?" he asked her when they reached their suite.

"Did you see how thin he is?"

"Yes."

"So you can't object…"

"I am not objecting, Cecelia. I simply like to know what's in your mind." He drew her to the small settee before the fireplace and pulled her down beside him. "It seems we are in for another tedious visit."

"Isn't that what you always do in the summer? Make country visits? When you are not in Brighton, of course."

"I went to house parties where the hostess took care to gather lively, interesting people. And to arrange all sorts of original entertainments to keep us busy. It was rather a competition."

"It sounds as if they spoiled you."

"That was the point."

"I never went to any of those," Cecelia said.

He looked surprised. "Surely you were invited?"

"Papa may have been. I suppose? He would have refused. Aunt Valeria? No, I don't think so."

"Since she makes no bones about despising society. And pretends to be deaf."

Cecelia nodded. "Neither of them would be interested in house parties certainly."

"So you were trapped in London all summer? I didn't notice. I beg your pardon."

"I wasn't 'trapped.' I remained in our comfortable house. And there was always a great deal to do."

"For other people." He put an arm around her shoulders and pulled her close. "We could simply abandon Tresigan, you know. It may not be worth saving."

She started to object.

"Or hire a crew of workmen to set it to rights and leave them to it. I could take you to a perfectly delightful house party."

"Where?"

"I would find one."

"You are so certain of invitations?"

His smile was assured rather than smug.

"Of course you are, oh nonpareil. But I can't go away now. I have to charm the elder Pendrennons."

The duke raised dark brows. "Why? They seem rather dull people."

"So that they will welcome Sarah into their family."

"Does that actually follow?"

"I don't know. But I must see what I can do."

"For your friend." His smile warmed with understanding. "I see. Another mission of mercy. Very well. I'll lend a hand. Just don't drag in that strange fellow at Tresigan."

Cecelia's kiss was more of a distraction than an answer, and they both knew it.

Seven

THERE WAS NO DOUBT THAT THE DUCHESS OF TEREFORD was delightful, Kenver thought at dinner that evening. And anyone could see why the duke was a darling of society. He kept up an easy flow of conversation and anecdotes without dominating the group. He drew interesting tidbits out of the others. Even Papa. Kenver couldn't remember a livelier dinner at Poldene. What he didn't understand was why this glittering pair was making such an effort with his parents. Yes, houseguests were expected to be pleasant and contribute to the entertainment of their hosts. But Mama and Papa had offered none of the attractions of a fashionable house party. The Terefords might be grateful for a comfortable place to stay, since Tresigan was practically a ruin. But their efforts far exceeded the value they'd received in return. Perhaps social graces were simply so engrained in them that charm had become automatic.

Then he began to notice that the duchess was steering the conversation in a particular way. First she mentioned Sarah's dear friend the Duchess of Compton. The details of her society wedding were reviewed, making it obvious that Sarah had attended. She shifted to Sarah's stay with another school chum, the Countess of Ferrington, earlier this summer. She

drew Sarah out with questions about these notables, famil-
iarly Ada and Harriet, making clear that they had a long history together and were truly close.

Kenver could see that his mother was startled by these
elevated connections, hardly those of a countrified nobody.
And after a while, he realized that he was a bit surprised
himself. He'd been thinking of Sarah—desirable, adorable
Sarah—as his sweet little wife. Full of amusing ideas, tender
and kind, but not the confidante of duchesses. He was happy
to learn more about her.

Looking up, Kenver found his mother staring balefully
at him, as if he'd arranged her humiliation by the Duchess
of Tereford. Which of course he hadn't. And in any case, it
wasn't humiliation. Or only if she insisted on seeing it so.
With this, Kenver acknowledged that the repairs in the state
suite had been pure fabrication. There'd been no patch of
damp. He hadn't missed seeing it. He felt a flash of anger.

Sarah burst out laughing at a clever quip from the duke.
Thank God the fellow was married already, Kenver thought.
One wouldn't want to compete with *him*.

He watched Sarah in sidelong glances. She looked happier now with her friends than she ever had at Poldene.
Laughter lit her features. He was glad to see her so. But the
addition of the duchess to their little society also put a bit of
distance between them. Sarah had someone else to turn to, a
companion she was much better acquainted with. He heard
them making plans for the following day and understood
that he was no part of them. Neither was the duke apparently, but that seemed small consolation.

Though the evening seemed endless, it did finally end. The houseguests retired to their controversial suite. Sarah went as well. Before his parents could say anything to him, Kenver also escaped, heading for the side entrance into the gardens.

"Where are you going?"

Kenver started and turned to find Sarah in a dim corner behind him. Had she been waiting for him? His heart leapt at the thought. "Out for a walk," he replied.

"In the dark?"

"I know the grounds very well, and there's a half-moon."

"May I come? I'm not sleepy."

Her wistful tone touched him. "Of course. You will want a shawl."

"I don't need it."

"The sea wind is cool in the evening."

"I don't want to go back to my room."

Because Cranston would be hovering there. Couldn't he replace the woman? That much at least? He would!

They slipped out the door and into a soft August evening. The air was drenched with the scents of lavender, roses, and the sea. Waves murmured in the distance. He took her arm to lead her along well-known pathways.

"It's strange to be outside in the night," Sarah said.

Not something that young ladies generally did, Kenver supposed. "It's quite safe here."

"I'm not afraid." She looked up at the stars. "I like it. It feels...like a secret world revealed."

But when a dark shadow slipped out of a side path and approached them, she jumped.

"It's only Fingal," said Kenver. "He walks with me."

Sarah put out a hand to caress the animal's curly head. "The dogs patrol the gardens at night?"

"Yes."

"That's a comfort, Fingal," she said to the dog. "I'm sure you are very good at it too."

The deerhound gave a soft woof, the sort of sound he only offered his official friends.

"Where are Tess and Ranger?" Sarah asked.

"They range wider. Fingal stays close to the house." There was no need to speak of his age. "Come and see," Kenver said. He led her along a path to the lookout point that jutted from the cliff where Poldene stood. The half-moon hung over the sea, making a shimmering silver pathway on the water. On this promontory, with the rocks receding behind them, they seemed to hang above it like birds.

Fingal whined briefly, not liking to see his charges so close to the edge. He sat down to wait for them to come to their senses.

"Oh," said Sarah. "I feel as if we could step out and walk across the sea."

"To the isles of the blessed," Kenver replied to this echo of his own imaginings.

"Where the Greek heroes went when they died."

He looked down at her. Moonlight silvered her face as she gazed over the water. "Of course you would know. Are you ever caught out?"

"I read a great deal. Too much perhaps."

She sounded apologetic. He didn't want that. "Not at all. I appreciate the...compendium."

"Do you really mean that?"

"I do."

The words seemed to shimmer over the sound of the waves, like an echo of their marriage vows.

"I'd like to live in a world of myth and legend," said Sarah then. "A sorceress like Morgan le Fey or the Lady of the Lake."

"Weren't they evil?"

"They were complicated. There was more to them than could be seen from the surface. And they faced some thorny dilemmas."

"Didn't one of them betray Merlin and lock him away?"

"That depends on which tale you read," Sarah replied. "And apparently he's escaped and gone to live at Tresigan anyway."

Kenver laughed. "When you say such things, I can almost believe them. I *want* to believe them."

She turned to him. A pulse of yearning passed between them. The damp air and the rhythm of the tide were the same as that night in the sea cave. Kenver bent and kissed her.

Her arms came up around his neck in eager response. Her mouth softened and yielded, following his lead. He pulled her closer, pressing their bodies together, letting his hands go where they would. Desire burned through Kenver's veins. Clothing seemed an intolerable barrier. His pulse pounded.

Kenver pulled back, breathing hard. She was his wife. They had a right to all the dizzying delights of passion. With ample time, in comfort. He was not going to pull her down into dew-laden bushes under Fingal's puzzled gaze. This was his home. By God, he would take her to his room and deuce take anyone who tried to interfere.

He wrapped an arm around her waist and swept her along, striding so fast that he lifted her from the ground once or twice. Sarah made no objection. She seemed as eager as he.

Kenver rushed her through the door and up a side stair. But when they reached his bedchamber, they found the door open and Cranston standing inside. "What are you doing here?" Kenver demanded.

"I came to inquire about my lady. No one seemed to know where she'd gone."

The woman's gaze ran over them, making Kenver keenly aware of their flushed faces and disheveled garments. Cranston clearly dared to disapprove. As if this was any of her affair. Rage at this unconscionable interference, fired by thwarted desire, burned through him. "You overstep," he said. "Get out."

"I believe I know my duties," Cranston answered.

"Obviously you do not, as I have told you to leave. Entirely. My wife no longer requires your services."

"I take my orders from Lady Trestan."

"Well, you may go and tell her what I said," Kenver answered.

"Lady Trestan has retired for the night," the woman replied without a trace of deference. "She will be quite annoyed if I disturb her."

"I said go, Cranston!" He glared at her.

Cranston held his gaze for much too long. Then she turned and walked slowly out of the room. Kenver had no doubt she was lingering just around the corner to overhear anything they said. Or did. He felt a keen desire to throttle something.

"I'd best go to my room," Sarah said.

The romantic mood had certainly been squashed. Sarah looked strained and unhappy. "We will move into the state suite as soon as the guests depart," Kenver said. "Our own private quarters where no one will disturb us."

"Yes."

She didn't sound as if she believed him. "I will make sure of it," he added.

Sarah nodded and moved away. The set of her shoulders looked defeated.

Kenver ground his teeth.

———

When Sarah climbed into the Tereford carriage with Cecelia after breakfast the next day, she felt the muscles in her neck and back ease. The relief was amazing. She could almost pretend that she was still just Sarah Moran and none of the events of the last few weeks had happened. If she wished to. Did she? Swinging from burning desire to frozen contempt, and back again, was wretched.

A brush of the dizzy arousal from Kenver's kisses came back to her. She couldn't wish him away. But why couldn't she have met him in the usual way, at a ball or an evening party, and become acquainted with him before they were married?

That was to assume he would have approached her at such an event, a dry inner voice pointed out. She hadn't attracted that sort of attention in London. And his family would have discouraged any connection between them.

"Are you all right, Sarah?" Cecelia asked as they drove.

She was shaken and uneasy. Last night, in the soft sea air, she'd been whirled to the heights. And then, outside Kenver's bedchamber, she'd been pulled to the depths. Sarah wasn't accustomed to such swings. She was even-tempered, calm. At least, she always had been.

"This marriage, are you happy with it?" Cecelia continued. "I can't tell. You are such a quiet person."

"When Kenver and I are alone, all seems...very well." And could be much more, if they had time together, Sarah thought.

"Yes?" Cecelia nodded. "That is the most important part."

"But not the only one. Particularly because we are living with his family."

The duchess did not pretend to misunderstand. "I think we are making inroads with the countess. She told me this morning that you had decent taste in evening dress."

"A concession indeed," said Sarah. "After you puffed off all my grand friends."

They exchanged ironic smiles. "People can be very superficial," said Cecelia.

"I noticed you didn't mention Charlotte."

"Sadly, a Miss Deeping would not impress your in-laws."

"And yet if any of my friends were to come here, I would most appreciate Charlotte's cutting wit."

"She would make short work of your father-in-law certainly," Cecelia agreed. "Have you seen how he always looks to the countess before settling on a facial expression?"

Sarah hadn't noticed this. She'd seen only blanket disapproval.

"We will have to see if we can elevate Charlotte to the heady heights you all are scaling," Cecelia added facetiously.

And with that teasing remark, it came to Sarah that she had risen in rank. She'd always been a mere gentleman's daughter, third in consequence among her four good friends. When Harriet became an heiress, she'd dropped to fourth and last. Now, as a married woman and wife of an earl's heir, she had surpassed Charlotte. She wasn't used to considering matters of precedence, and she cared nothing for it. But as Cecelia had pointed out, other people did. "Charlotte has sworn not to marry," she said.

"And I'm sure she will stand by that pledge right up until she meets someone who makes her want to break it."

"I can't quite imagine what sort of person that would be."

"It will be very interesting," said Cecelia.

"She thinks rank and pomp are stupid."

"They are often empty and undeserved. But sometimes they give one scope to contribute to the good of society, by which I mean everyone and not just the *haut ton*."

"You've thought about this," Sarah noted.

"Of course."

She spoke as if it was only natural, but Sarah knew it was not. Many titled people took their privileges for granted or exploited them shamelessly. She wondered if she could do good in her new position, once she settled into it. If she ever did.

Cecelia took a small notebook and pencil from her reticule and jotted down a few words. "We must remember to examine the well at Tresigan," she said when Sarah looked inquiring. "See if it looks clear and clean."

Sarah had seen her long list. This expedition was to decide the details of work to be done. "Merlin is drinking from it," she offered.

"And how very odd *that* sounds," replied the duchess.

"I don't know what else to call him."

Cecelia waved this aside. "Fine old houses should not be allowed to sink into ruin."

"Or left empty," replied Sarah. "I thought he was right about that."

"Yes."

"What will you do with him?" Sarah asked.

"I'm not sure it is up to me to *do* anything. If he wants help, we can offer some."

"What if he tries to stop work on the house? Or refuses to leave?"

Cecelia nodded, acknowledging the problem. "I did not get the sense that he would. But I might be wrong, which is another reason I wished to go back. I thought he might speak more freely to us."

"Since we are mere women."

"Precisely," said Cecelia with a sly smile.

"You are devious."

"I prefer to think of it as subtle and effective."

"Certainly that."

They reached Tresigan in good time. The coachman

and groom, along once again in case they needed reinforcements, jumped down to see to the horses. Cecelia wanted to find out about Tresigan's stables, which they hadn't observed on their previous visit. Thus, her first question when Merlin came out to meet them was about that.

"There is a barn down there behind the trees," he replied, pointing to the overgrown copse that had featured in Sarah's conversation about maenads. Her cheeks heated at the memory.

Cecelia sent the men with the carriage to look it over and continued on toward the house. She entered the open back door without asking permission, making a point, Sarah thought.

The wildly bearded resident remained outside. Out of curiosity, Sarah stayed with him. "What do you do all day?" she asked.

"Garden, walk and think, mend and cook," he answered.

"Don't you get lonely?"

"Yes." The reply was sharp and stark.

"Why stay here then?"

"Some people have nowhere to go, Mrs. Pendrennon."

It was the first time she'd been called that by a stranger. A shock ran through her.

"I am not like you, who have a great noble family to draw on."

"My family is not grand." But she could get help from them if she needed it, Sarah acknowledged.

"Yet you married Kenver Pendrennon?" Merlin stared at her from under his bushy brows. "Lord Trestan accepts only great matches."

"How do you know that?" His accent had shifted again, Sarah noticed. Whatever his antecedents, and whatever he wished to pretend, he was an educated man.

His green eyes examined her—sharp, without hesitation. "You're friends with a duchess."

Sarah simply nodded. She didn't wish to tell the story of her marriage to a stranger. A very odd stranger. Obviously Merlin was not in touch with neighborhood gossip. Changing the subject, she said, "Cecelia might help you find somewhere to go when they begin work on the house."

"To what end?" he asked.

"End?"

"Why work on it? Surely they don't intend to live here?"

"No. But they wish to preserve it even so. And then someone will have a home."

"But not me," he responded.

"Well, I don't… Perhaps you could make some arrangement." Sarah didn't know what Cecelia intended. Reliable tenants, probably.

"I wonder if they would sell the place?"

Sarah had heard Cecelia say that she didn't care to diminish the estate, but she'd also mentioned that Tresigan was far away from other Tereford holdings. "I don't know," she replied. "Would you like to buy it?"

"Oh, that is out of my reach, like so many things."

His voice was particularly precise and cutting on this phrase. Again Sarah wondered who he was. What was he doing here? It was a mystery worthy of her friends' investigative efforts, if their group had not been scattered far and wide. Might there be papers in the house bearing Merlin's true name? But she had no excuse to riffle through his things. Mere curiosity was not enough reason for that intrusion. And though some might argue that he was breaking the law by living at Tresigan, she couldn't see this as a great sin.

Cecelia emerged. "Do you have a key to the cellar?" she asked Merlin.

"No. It's always been locked."

"You haven't tried to get in?"

"It's a sturdy door, and I saw no reason to disturb the spiders."

Making an entry in her small notebook, Cecelia asked, "Have you noticed any leaks in the roof when it rains?"

"No. But then I don't venture near the roof."

"You make no effort to care for the place where you stay?"

"To what end?" he asked. He seemed fond of the phrase.

"A sense of satisfaction?"

He snorted at the idea.

Sarah left them and walked over to the vegetable garden. Merlin certainly cared for this plot of land. It was both lush and neat. She walked around it, breathing in the scents of herbs and warm earth.

A breeze stirred the ivy that draped the cliff at the back of the garden, and the strands parted like a curtain and fell back together. There was a space behind the vines, Sarah noticed. She went over and parted them, discovering a narrow, hidden pathway under an overhang, dim and green. And more than that, a few yards away, the stone gave way to a cave mouth.

Cornwall had many caves, Sarah knew. But she'd never

ventured into any until lately when they seemed to have become her fate. She slipped behind the ivy and went to look inside.

This cave was dry rather than sea girt, hardly wider than her spread arms, with a low ceiling. It seemed to be small. Sarah stepped in, rocks shifting under her shoes, and walked to the back. But here she found not an end but an abrupt turn to the right, hidden until one was upon it, a passage into darkness. She didn't dare go farther without a light. "The hollow hills," she murmured. She turned to go and tell Cecelia about her discovery, but by the time she'd passed out through the ivy, she'd decided to save this story for Kenver instead.

———————————

Kenver aimed his horse at a brushy hedge and urged him to it. Dancer gathered himself and jumped, easily clearing the bushes. The duke followed on a horse from the Poldene stables, and Kenver led him on a satisfying gallop along the lane on the other side. Men and mounts all enjoyed the vigorous exercise. Going over rather than through several gates, they passed by a number of scenic stretches of country before circling back toward the house.

They rode side by side then, and Kenver examined his companion in fleeting sideways glances. How had the man attained such effortless assurance? Yes, he was a duke, but Kenver had met men of lofty rank who were timid as mice in comparison. He'd wager that no one told Tereford what room to use in his own house or deceived him with false patches of damp. Might he have any advice? But how to ask, and why would Tereford wish to give it?

On one level, the duke was approachable, affable. But Kenver did not mistake this for an invitation to confidences. They were barely acquainted.

"Tresigan would be that way?" Tereford asked, pointing, after a stretch of silence.

"Yes. Well spotted. It is a shorter journey on horseback than in a carriage. Did you wish to go there?"

"No. Cecelia will have things well in hand."

"The duchess has an extraordinary grasp of estate management."

"Oh yes," his companion replied.

"You seem happy to leave it to her."

"Delighted, in fact."

This was interesting, even a bit unusual. "My mother is the same," Kenver said.

This brought him raised eyebrows and a puzzled glance.

"I mean, she helps manage Poldene," Kenver said. Otherwise, one could hardly compare the charming, witty duchess to his stern mother.

"Indeed."

"Did the duchess learn her skills from her family?"

This elicited a slight smile. "You could say so. But only in the sense that they threw it all onto her shoulders and walked away."

Not literally, Kenver assumed.

"Her father cares for nothing but arcane philosophies." Tereford waved a hand. "Which I know nothing about. Otherwise, he is the laziest man in creation."

"Her mother..." Kenver ventured. Perhaps the duchess had a female parent like his.

"Died when she was quite young."

"Oh, I am sorry."

"Cecelia has an extremely eccentric aunt," the duke offered like an odd compensation.

Altogether this was an odd conversation, Kenver thought. "I suppose your family was another story," he said.

The duke turned to look at him. "Story," he repeated. His tone was not promising.

Kenver didn't blame him. It had been a clumsy remark. He became conscious of a wish to gallop away. "Families... and marriage, one doesn't really know how..." To finish that sentence, Kenver thought.

"They don't always get on," the other man said. Tereford examined him. "Cecelia is good friends with your wife," the older man said. "You might speak to her."

"I don't think I could do that," Kenver replied. He did *not* need another authoritative female in his life. "There's a very fine view from that hilltop," he said. He set his heels to Dancer's sides and picked up the pace. They could ride and not talk for the rest of this outing, and everyone would be happy. Which seemed indeed to be the case.

————————

"You know, Cecelia," said the duke when the Terefords met in their suite later that day. "These missions of yours drag me into areas where I have no expertise."

She looked inquiring.

"It's all very well for you to help your friends. I commend you. But I am ill equipped to join in."

"I have no idea what you're talking about, James."

"Young Pendrennon spoke to me on our ride today."

"Yes? Well, I suppose you couldn't go through the whole outing without some conversation."

"He said something about families."

"Is he worried about his parents' treatment of Sarah?"

"Ah, perhaps that was it."

"Perhaps it should be!" She gave him a speculative look. "You do know a good deal about tyrannical parents, James."

"How to get on very badly with them," he replied, his tone gone raw.

"You came out well in the end."

He gave her an ironic bow. "Thank you."

Cecelia hesitated, examined his expression with compassion, and turned to look over some letters that had arrived from London rather than at him. "Well, you can simply avoid such conversations in the future."

Oddly, the duke found that being given what he wanted was not satisfying. "You don't think I have anything to tell him?"

"You needn't try. Don't worry, James. I will keep you out of my 'mission' for Sarah."

That was exactly what he'd requested. He ought to feel pleased. "Since you know what you're doing, and I do not," he replied.

She looked up from a letter. "Since you are not interested."

He wasn't, of course.

"Is something else wrong?" Cecelia asked.

"No."

She frowned. "If he inquires again, you could advise him to ask Sarah what she would like."

"Ask her?"

"Yes. Who else would know?"

"Indeed."

A sly smile crossed Cecelia's lovely features. "It should give him something to think about as well."

"I suppose it would." He examined her. "Perhaps you could write out a list of questions for him to use. About what wives want."

Cecelia laughed, taking it as a joke. "I'm afraid he will have to discover his own."

"But a sort of…map."

"Every marriage is different, James."

"Is it? Yes, of course it is." Feeling an uncharacteristic tremor of doubt, the duke said, "I believe you are right. I will evade the subject."

"That seems best."

She didn't mean to be patronizing. He was certain of that. But nonetheless he felt set aside as unhelpful. At a task he hadn't wanted and had complained of. So he ought to be pleased. Once again, Cecelia had gracefully given him just what he'd requested. But was it what he—and she—really wanted?

Her maid entered at this point, as it was time to dress for dinner, and the conversation had to be abandoned. Which he was glad of, the duke thought. Naturally, he was.

Eight

KENVER SEARCHED OUT HIS MOTHER FIRST THING THE next morning, before she could depart on some errand and evade him for the day. He was received in her private parlor with surprise, and he realized that he always felt like an interruption when he came to see her without being summoned. "I want Gwen to wait on Sarah," he said without preamble.

"Sarah has some complaint against Cranston?"

She wasn't startled by his request, Kenver noted. He wondered if Cranston had already spoken to her. It occurred to him that Cranston was reporting all she heard in their rooms to his mother. Of course she was. "*I* think Gwen would be a more suitable attendant."

"We did discuss this, Kenver. Gwen is not a trained lady's maid."

"Nonetheless." He was determined not to lose his temper.

"And Gwen has only been with us a year."

"So she will be well able to adjust to the way Sarah wishes to do things." He waited, ready to counter the next argument.

"Sarah might have asked me herself if she is dissatisfied with my household arrangements," complained his mother.

"I am asking," said Kenver. He concentrated on not being diverted.

"So you intend to ignore my greater experience? And wiser judgments?" Her tone was cutting.

"Not at all. I am simply making one small request regarding my wife."

"Your *wife* seems to have made you quite rude."

Kenver just barely maintained his grip on his temper. "I don't believe I am being rude, Mama. I am expressing a preference, which I can't see why you would not fulfill."

"Well, if you wish 'your wife' to be dressed by an inexperienced—"

"I do," Kenver interrupted.

His mother looked surprised. He didn't usually cut her off. No one did, really, Kenver realized. Perhaps that was part of the problem. She gave an angry shrug. "If you wish Sarah to present an odd appearance in company..."

For an instant, Kenver worried. If Gwen really didn't know how to do things properly... He pulled back from this diversion. Sarah could tell her. Sarah knew how to dress. "She won't," he answered. "Sarah always looks charming."

"Thanks to Cranston!"

It took every ounce of Kenver's control to remain silent. He had made his point. There was nothing more to say without losing ground.

His mother's face went sour. "I suppose...if you insist."

"I'll speak to Gwen right away and let her know. I believe Cranston needs to receive the news from you. If she has any questions about the change, I will send her to you."

The lids dropped over his mother's eyes. When she opened them again, she was all cordiality. "Of course," she said. "I want Sarah to be comfortable. We will make any adjustments that she may require."

Her tone did suggest that she was turning the house upside down for their convenience. But she smiled at him, brightly, warmly. Kenver left the parlor, making his way downstairs to fetch Gwen and take her to Sarah.

They found his wife in the breakfast room, and Kenver made the introductions.

Gwen, a young maid from a local family with dark hair and eyes, responded to her presentation with a ready smile. "Shall I start on your bedchamber then, ma'am?"

Sarah smiled back and gave Kenver a grateful look. "That would be fine, Gwen."

"Your first responsibility now is to your new mistress," Kenver said to the girl. "Should you have any questions about that, you may ask her, or me."

Gwen's knowing look suggested that his suspicions of Cranston were well founded. "Yes, sir. I'm very grateful for the opportunity, sir." The maid dropped a curtsy and went out.

"I think you will like Gwen," Kenver said when she was gone.

"She seemed very pleasant. Cranston really will not be back?"

"She will not."

The blazing smile she gave him heated Kenver right down to his toes. In that moment, he felt like a conquering hero who passed through great trials to win his fair maiden. He moved closer. Sarah held out a hand. And a servant came in with a fresh pot of tea.

Kenver knew he shouldn't be irritated with people who were seeing to their comfort. But sometimes it was difficult.

He filled a plate, joined Sarah at the table, and began to eat.

"There is a cave in the cliff behind Tresigan," Sarah said. "I discovered it yesterday when I visited with Cecelia."

Kenver paused with a fork full of egg. "A cave?"

"Yes, hidden behind the ivy. Perhaps it was what Merlin meant by the hollow hills? Though I suppose it can't really be an entrance into the realms of faery." She smiled to show this was a joke.

She looked happy. He'd managed that much. Kenver said, "We should go and explore it."

"Do you think we could?"

He met her sparkling blue eyes, and they shared a moment of longing for a touch of magic in their lives. "I don't see why not. I doubt the Terefords would have any objection."

"I didn't tell Cecelia about it," Sarah replied. "It's our secret."

This made Kenver think of another secret cave and a night spent in each other's arms. "I don't think she'd mind if we took a look." He didn't actually care what the duchess might think. "We can reach Tresigan much faster on horseback than by the roads."

"Shall we go over tomorrow?"

"Why not today?"

"Right now?"

She looked elated, which made Kenver think she ought to glow like that all the time. He—her husband—should be able to make it so. He would take that as a challenge, a quest.

She sat just out of reach. He would have to rise and take several steps to kiss her. Hardly any distance really. Their locked gaze went on. And on.

The Terefords appeared in the doorway and hesitated as if sensing the intense atmosphere.

"Good morning," Sarah said brightly. "They have just brought fresh tea."

The couple came in and sat down, ready as ever with cordial conversation.

It was a very good idea for them to get away on their own, Kenver thought, free from critical oversight and interruptions. The incessant, unpredictable, damnable interruptions! Marriage supposedly removed all impediments. Except that it didn't.

They set off at midmorning. At the last moment, disaster threatened when they rode past Poldene's front door and Kenver's father came out with the dogs. Papa raised a hand as if to summon them, but Kenver pretended not to see and hurried the horses on.

Sarah drew in a deep breath as they left the grounds and cantered down the lane. The pall that hung over her in the house, even after Cecelia's arrival and Cranston's rout, began to lift again, as it had when she ventured away before. If only they could live elsewhere, she thought. Surely they would do better in almost any other place.

Scudding clouds raced across the sky. The air was less active at ground level, full of the scents of late-summer plants with a whiff of the sea. Her charming mare was ready to stretch her legs. Sarah patted her neck in appreciation.

"Whitefoot likes you," said Kenver.

Sarah looked over with a smile. She'd spent her life thinking it was improper to ride out alone with a man. Now, with

Kenver, it wasn't. They could go where they liked, spend as much time at they pleased, do scandalous things. His smile was heart-stopping. He looked so very handsome in his riding dress. Why had they not done scandalous things? How did a young lady trained to avoid impropriety at all costs request them? As she'd found so often in her life, reading about a topic and speaking up were quite different things. The first was private and free-ranging, a vast freedom. The second was likely to cause raised eyebrows and shocked glances. Or worse. But she was a married woman now. She only needed to find a new voice.

Sarah urged her horse into a canter and then a gallop, venting her frustration with the rush of wind across her face and the exhilarating rhythm of her mare's hooves.

Kenver caught up with her, giving her an admiring grin as they pounded along side by side.

They rode across a field of stubble and entered a tree-lined trace too narrow and hilly for carriages. It led them into a verdant valley with a stream running along the bottom and then up to a ridge that gave them a view over the countryside.

"There is Tresigan," said Kenver, pointing.

Sarah saw that this stony ridge eventually became the cliff that backed the house. At this point, there was a zigzag path down. They took it, wound through a small wood, and came out at the entry to Tresigan's short drive. "There's a barn behind those trees," Sarah said.

"The Dionysian trees?" he asked.

"The trees where there are no orgies," replied Sarah, wanting to feel reckless.

"Yet."

She was startled into a laugh, which turned into something more heated at the look in his hazel eyes.

They found the barn and left the horses well tended. Carrying the lanterns they'd brought, they headed for the back of the house.

Merlin emerged when they rounded the building's rear corner.

"How could I have forgotten that you would be here," Kenver said. "I suppose I hoped you'd gone."

"Only Pendrennons today?" the bearded man asked. "No duke or duchess?"

Sarah thought there was something strange about the way he said the name. "No," she replied.

"Then I would think you have no right to come."

"My wife's friends are happy for us to visit," Kenver replied.

Or would be if they knew, Sarah amended silently.

"And you have no grounds to speak of rights," Kenver added.

"Since I have none?"

It seemed to Sarah that Merlin didn't like Kenver. In particular. It was not clear why, as they'd hardly spoken on the previous visit.

"More or less," said Kenver, responding to his snide tone.

This elicited a sour shrug. "Don't expect me to play host as you're poking about."

"Why would we? You are not the host," Kenver snapped.

Sarah turned toward the garden and started off.

"Where are you going?" Merlin demanded.

Sarah paused, then decided that they should tell him. Someone should know where they'd gone in case of unanticipated problems underground. But his attitude made her wish it could be someone else. Still, she said, "Into the cave."

Merlin frowned at her. "You saw that yesterday, did you?"

Sarah nodded.

"That explains the lanterns. If not the nosiness."

"Not your property, not your cave," said Kenver. "We have established that. And so, not your affair either."

With a glare at Kenver, Merlin turned and stomped back inside the house.

"He's quite angry," said Sarah.

"It's time he was moving on. I don't know why Tereford doesn't have him thrown out."

"He said he has nowhere to go."

"I don't believe he has made the least effort to find any place."

Noting that Kenver was also annoyed, Sarah led the way around the garden to the curtain of ivy that hid the cave entrance. She parted the strands and went through.

Kenver came in on her heels. "Extraordinary," he said, looking around the sheltered space.

In the filtered green light, he lit the lanterns. Sarah looped the long skirts of her riding habit over one arm. Each holding a lantern to light the way, they walked into the cave, where Sarah showed him the sharp turn that disguised the true extent of it. They turned and moved slowly along a narrow passage. There were no other openings, so no possibility of getting lost.

"Watch your footing," said Kenver. "The rocks are uneven."

Sarah lowered her lantern to check the floor. It was scattered with flakes of loose stone. She held up her light to survey the walls. "Some of this looks man-made, doesn't it?" she said. "As if the cave was widened with tools."

Kenver extended his lantern. She was right. He hadn't noticed. "Clever of you to see," he said.

They walked on along the winding passageway. Kenver became conscious of a gurgling sound, and after a bit, the walls fell back, revealing a larger darkness. Kenver held his lantern high. They'd come into a sizable chamber. A small stream running through the back corner, from one low hole in the stone to another, accounted for the noise. Sarah stepped farther inside and raised her lantern as well. With more light, the rocks came alive, streaked with bands of red, green, purple, and orange. "Oh," she exclaimed. She walked around, swinging her lantern.

Kenver did the same. The colors shifted and danced. "There must be mineral deposits in the cliff," he said.

"It looks like a chamber in the hollow hills," Sarah said.

"Where the fairies would revel and dance," Kenver replied.

"Yes."

He walked around the perimeter of the cave. "There's no other entrance. This is the full extent of it."

"You wouldn't be able to see the gateway," Sarah continued in a dreamy voice. "The stories say you'd reach a sort of veil. Or maybe a fog. A half-visible barrier of some kind.

And if you pressed through, one more step, you would be in another, magical realm."

She made it sound so real, so possible.

"I've always thought that if you found the way in, the Fair Folk would welcome you," she added. "And it would be glorious."

"Until you returned and found a hundred years had passed and everything you knew was swept away."

"That is a problem," said Sarah.

He had to laugh a little at her serious tone. "I've never understood how there could be another realm underground. There is no sun. How could anything grow?"

"Magically?"

"That is just another way of saying nobody knows."

"True." She gave the problem solemn consideration. "What if it wasn't a tunnel but rather a…portal from one location to another."

"Magical transportation."

She nodded, her smile impish in the light of her lantern.

"You have the most vivid imagination."

"This place inspires me!"

"Next you'll be talking of rock creatures stepping out of the wall."

"No, I won't!" Sarah exclaimed.

"With great clawed hands reaching for us and pointed, stony teeth."

"Kenver!" She moved closer to him. "If you are paying me back for mentioning that sea creature, well, it is too bad of you."

"Caves and monsters seem to go together." Kenver shook his head. "I prefer quests aboveground, where one can see to fight."

She gazed up at him. "Like one of Arthur's knights rather than a traveler to fairyland." The impish smile returned. "Well, you have found Merlin," she teased.

"That vagabond!"

"But is he? Have you noticed that he sometimes speaks like an educated man? Until he recalls his pose, that is."

"I didn't." Nothing seemed to escape Sarah.

"Let's look around," she said, as if responding to his thought. "There might be things in here."

"Things," he echoed in a sepulchral voice.

"Kenver!"

"Hidden treasures, you mean?"

"Perhaps."

"Merlin would have cleaned those out long ago."

They walked back and forth over the entire chamber, finding nothing but tumbled rock and dust. The water in the stream left no space to follow it. "I don't think there's anything here," Kenver said after a while.

Sarah agreed. She held up her lantern to illuminate the colorful wall. "It's beautiful," she said.

"And yet you sound disappointed."

"I suppose I hoped we'd discover some…"

"Magical doorway."

"I know there is no such thing." She swung the lantern to make the bands of color seem to dance. "And this is marvelous. One shouldn't ask for more than that."

"You can ask for whatever you want," Kenver replied with an intensity that surprised them both.

She turned to stare at him. The look seemed long and increasingly speculative. "Scandalous things?" she murmured.

"What?" Shadows jumped in the lantern light. Kenver wished he could see her face more clearly.

"Nothing."

Had she really said "scandalous things"? He was nearly certain she had. Their marriage had begun with a scandal. How long ago that furor seemed. "*What* sort of things?" he asked her.

She seemed to take this as a criticism, turning away and moving toward the path out.

He hurried to catch up with her, putting a hand on her upper arm. "Sarah."

She looked back at him. He urged her gently around to face him. "What sort of things?" he murmured again.

She hooked her free arm around his neck and pulled him down for a kiss, arching up to press close as if desperate to embrace him. Her lips were soft and sweet in the dimness. Her body was intoxicating. He pulled her even closer, drew out the kiss until he was dizzy with longing.

A scorched scent drifted on the damp air. Had he actually been set on fire by desire, Kenver wondered.

"Oh!" Sarah jerked away from him. The skirt of her riding habit had touched his lantern. A circle of the cloth was crisped brown.

"Idiot!" exclaimed Kenver.

"I didn't mean…"

"I. I am an idiot. How could I have been so careless? My God, you might have been burnt!" He was furious with himself and with every single thing in the world that seemed to conspire against them. "You are not hurt, are you?"

"No. Only my habit. Though it is my favorite."

"Are you sure?"

"Yes, because it fits so well and…"

"About the burn!"

"Oh. I just felt a bit of heat." She raised her skirt and looked. Her petticoat was barely discolored. The lantern had not reached her skin.

Kenver let out a sigh of relief, without forgiving himself for endangering her. "Come." He gave her a gentle push toward the exit.

They emerged in the green dimness behind the ivy and extinguished their lanterns. When they walked out, the daylight beyond the vines seemed very bright after the darkness underground.

"Did you find the fairies?" called Merlin from his garden as they blinked. His tone was mocking.

Kenver would have happily punched him. It wouldn't help anything, and the fellow didn't really deserve it, but it might have relieved his feelings.

"Yes, they shot a flaming elf bolt at us," said Sarah, displaying her burnt skirts.

Merlin's mouth dropped open. Kenver looked down at his wife in astonishment.

Sarah responded with a grin. Her blue eyes sparkled.

Kenver burst out laughing, his foul mood abruptly lightened.

They spread the blanket they'd brought under an oak tree near the barn and brought out the picnic basket the Poldene kitchens had provided. Merlin had retreated to the house, but Kenver thought there was a good chance he was lurking behind a bush, peering at them. Coveting their ham, perhaps.

Until his marriage, Kenver had never noticed how much of his life was overlooked. He'd felt he had privacy where none existed, it seemed.

"Should we take Merlin a sandwich?" she said.

"No. What the deuce is an elf bolt?"

She grinned again, looking mischievous. "That's what some people call the old flint arrowheads one finds now and then. I think they're actually just remains of the ancient Britons. But elf bolts sound much grander."

Merlin appeared, seemingly to carry a basket to the barn but actually to peer at their food like a hopeful dog. "I wish I had an elf bolt now," Kenver muttered.

"He has no bread," replied Sarah. "He told Cecelia he was no baker."

"He could buy some in the village. Or trade vegetables for it."

"I suppose. But we are not going to finish it all." She gathered up a selection of their viands and held it out. The blasted fellow hurried over, but instead of accepting the gift and taking himself off, he sat down at the edge of their blanket to eat.

"It was really the lantern, wasn't it?" he asked Sarah, pointing at her scorched skirt.

"You don't believe in elf bolts?"

"If there was anything uncanny hereabouts, I would have found it." He sounded regretful.

"Because you've searched?" Sarah asked.

"Oh, aye."

"Being on your own here." She looked sympathetic.

Sarah was all quicksilver sweetness and bright leaps of insight, Kenver thought. She seemed to see through things that he looked past. He could have understood that Merlin was lonely, but he hadn't bothered. The thing was: it was easier not to notice, sometimes. And he still felt the man should help himself rather than relying on his wife for company. "I'll saddle the horses," he said.

He did so. They gathered up the picnic and stowed things away. Then Kenver could only help Sarah onto her horse with lingering hands while he gazed at her with the hunger of a man seeing paradise just out of reach.

Sarah rode home in a haze of delight. They could slip up to her room as soon as they reached Poldene, she thought. There would be no Cranston to thwart them today. If they went in through the side door, they would take up from where they'd left off before the accident with the lantern. Scandalous things, she thought, flushing with heat at the thought.

But when they rode into the Poldene stable yard, a groom was sent running, and a footman came rushing back with him. "Her ladyship wishes to speak to you," the latter said to Sarah.

"To me?"

"Yes, ma'am."

This was not good news. What could Kenver's mother want?

"We will see her at dinner," replied Kenver, starting to sweep by the servant toward the door.

"She left orders that the young lady was to be brought at once, sir. As soon as she returned."

"I must change out of my riding clothes." Sarah looked down at the scorched spot. Lady Trestan would certainly notice it. She saw everything.

"Her ladyship was quite...insistent," said the footman.

Which translated as furious. What could she have done? Sarah wondered. They'd been away since breakfast.

With a muttered protest, Kenver turned toward the drawing room. Sarah followed, her mood rapidly descending.

They found both Kenver's parents sitting on a sofa, looking thunderous. Cecelia was sitting with them with the air of someone who would not be moved. The atmosphere was *not* harmonious. "You have received a letter," said Kenver's mother to Sarah. She put her hand on a sealed sheet of paper as if to hold it down.

Sarah didn't see why this should be an accusation. In the first place, it was merely correspondence. In the second, *she* hadn't sent it.

"From our daughter," the woman added. She looked outraged. Kenver's mouth fell open in surprise.

Whatever Sarah might have expected, this wasn't it. "From..."

"You did not tell us you knew Tamara," Lady Trestan added through clenched teeth.

"I don't," replied Sarah.

"Why would she write to you then?" asked Kenver's father.

"I knew you were a liar," said his mother. "What is your connection to Tamara?" Her hand closed on the letter, wrinkling the paper. Cecelia watched her as if she was a poor actor in a bad play. Sarah was certain that Lady Trestan would have opened and read the missive if the duchess had not been present.

"I have none," Sarah said. "And no notion why she has written to me. I shall be interested to see." She held out her hand for the letter.

"Did Tamara arrange Kenver's entrapment?" asked the countess as if she hadn't heard Sarah's denial. "Is this her revenge?"

"Revenge for what?" asked Kenver. "And I was not 'entrapped.'"

"How do you explain this then?" His mother tapped the page.

"Explain? Why should anyone have to…"

"*Someone* had better," she interrupted, staring at Sarah.

This was just ridiculous, Sarah thought. It *was* like a silly melodrama. Still, she was glad Cecelia was there.

"If I had to guess…" Kenver began.

"Yes?"

"I suppose my sister heard of our marriage and has written to congratulate Sarah."

"How would she have heard?" demanded his mother.

"It was rather talked of, Mama," he answered. "I suppose Tamara might have gotten the news from a local acquaintance."

"Who?" demanded the countess like a cat pouncing on a mouse.

She longed for a target in which to sink her claws, Sarah noted.

"I don't know. How would I?"

"Did Tamara grow up here at Poldene?" asked Cecelia. Her calm inquiry was like a stone dropped into a roiling stream.

The countess sat back, pressing her lips together.

"Yes," said Kenver's father.

"Then I suppose she would have friends from earlier years."

In the simmering silence that followed, Sarah stepped over and pulled the letter from under Lady Trestan's hand. The countess reached as if to snatch it back, but Sarah evaded her fingers, moving away again.

Everyone stared at Sarah. Lady Trestan looked as if she'd like to box her ears. The earl scowled. Cecelia was obviously curious. As who would not be? Did they actually imagine she was going to read it to them? Sarah turned and walked out, heading for her bedchamber. A babble broke out behind her. She ignored it.

Nine

FOR ONCE, SARAH'S BEDCHAMBER WAS A REFUGE. THERE would be no Cranston barging in, and if Gwen appeared, Sarah could dismiss her. She sat down on the bed and examined the mysterious letter.

The writer had dribbled sealing wax all across the free edge of the page. So that no one could slip a knife under a seal and wiggle it open, Sarah decided. She'd wanted tampering to be easily spotted, which said a good deal. Sarah wriggled her little finger under the edge and cracked the line of red wax. Bits scattered over the coverlet as she slid her hand along. She unfolded the letter, noticing the strong looping handwriting, and read.

To Kenver's wife,

The story of your marriage has reached me through former friends near Poldene. I expect it was hopelessly garbled. But if any parts are true, it seems to me that you will not be well treated by my parents. I decided to write and offer you my good wishes. Please be assured that if you ever need a place to go, you can come to me at the address at the bottom of this letter. I have asked *an old friend among the servants to make certain it reaches you.*

Best wishes,
Tamara Pendrennon Deane

There was a knock at the door. Sarah rose and went to look. Kenver stood in the corridor. "You don't have to tell me what she writes," he said, though he clearly wanted to know.

Sarah stepped back to invite him in. Then she handed him the note and watched him read. "So it *is* Lincolnshire," he said.

As if this was the important part. "Why would she offer me...sanctuary?" Sarah asked him.

"I don't know."

"She is your sister."

"I told you. She is twelve years older. We were never... very well acquainted."

"But still."

"And I was not told things," he continued.

"What things?"

"The things I wasn't told!" he answered, frustration clear in his tone.

"So you have no idea why your family is at odds or what happened?" Sarah couldn't keep the incredulity out of her voice. If she'd had a mysterious, missing sister, she would have moved heaven and earth to find out why. And gotten in touch with her as well! How could one not?

"It is never talked of," Kenver replied. "If Tamara's name

was even mentioned—which it scarcely ever was—everyone went quiet." He waved his hands. "It was as if a bullet had gone buzzing right past your ear."

Sarah stared at him. The image was oddly vivid.

"The subject was...frozen into oblivion," he added.

"By your parents, you mean?"

"Yes."

"But, Kenver. When you were a child, I can see you would hang back. But later on, not to insist on knowing... She is your *sister*."

"You don't understand."

But after even a short time at Poldene, Sarah had an inkling. Opposing Lady Trestan, and the earl, was difficult. If she'd lived with them all her life, trained in their ways, she might hesitate.

"I just let it be." He had begun to look puzzled. "Perhaps Tamara did something dreadful."

"What? Murder? Violent lunacy?"

Kenver gaped at her.

"She sounds quite sane in the letter. Not a person capable of nameless crimes."

"Nameless crimes?" he repeated.

"Though I must say that your mother's idea of transgressions does not coincide with mine."

He did not deny it.

"Who would know about Tamara?" Sarah asked, turning back to the mystery. "Who is this friend among the servants, do you think?" She pointed to that line in the letter.

He frowned down at the page. "What do you mean to do, Sarah?"

"Discover the truth!" The zest that had filled the investigations with her school friends was back. This was what she did, after all. She solved mysteries. The thought of digging into this one made her feel more like herself.

"To what end?"

"Well, simply to *know*, first of all." Sarah thought this self-evident. "And then we shall see. Don't you wish to find out?"

He hesitated.

"What about your quest to right wrongs? Is that only words for tenants and villagers?"

"We don't know there is a wrong."

"A girl of what, eighteen, leaves her home and is never spoken of again. On penalty of metaphorical whizzing bullets? I think that sounds wrong."

He frowned.

"We'll begin by questioning the servants," Sarah declared.

"You are allowed to speak to the staff, I suppose."

"Mama won't..."

"Your mother will never like anything I do," Sarah interrupted. "So I may as well do something useful and interesting." The way things stood at Poldene, one more disagreement scarcely mattered. Though Kenver's sister was clearly a larger issue.

"You don't really believe that."

"That I should do something useful? I certainly do!"

"No, that Mama will never like anything you do."

She hadn't wished to come between them, but really he

must see this. It was so blatant. "Your parents have made it very clear that they do not want me here and wish we had not married. They work against it every day. Particularly your mother."

"But they are adjusting."

"I've seen no sign of it, Kenver. Have you? Really?"

He started to speak, then stopped.

"I don't like to upset you." Sarah folded up the letter and put it in the pocket of her riding habit, from which it could not "disappear." It would be best to ask her questions immediately, before the countess thought to forbid all mention of her daughter. Again. "I am going to inquire," she said.

"Perhaps *you* are the fearless knight," Kenver said. "And I am…" He spread his hands.

"*Not* the damsel in distress," Sarah cut in. "Though it would be *damoiseau* actually."

"Dam…what?"

"That is the male equivalent of 'damsel.' It's French."

"How do you know that?"

"I…"

"Read it somewhere," they said in unison.

His smile was tender. Hers was sheepish.

"You are brave and chivalrous and determined," said Sarah.

"You think so?"

"Yes. I've seen it."

They faced each other beside the never-yet-marital bed. The sense of connection that had arisen in the sea cave, flamed in stolen kisses, skipped through balmy summer air, and come solidly down to earth vibrated between them. Sarah felt it, a bond woven stronger every day.

"We only need speak to those who have worked at Poldene a long time," Kenver said.

Her heart flared with gladness.

"Cook," he went on. "And the head groom. Tamara was a bruising rider."

"You know this, but not why she's gone?"

"Someone said it." Kenver shook his head.

"Perhaps you remember more than you think."

"I could hardly remember less."

The cook disavowed all knowledge of anything—sisters, letters, memories. She seemed desperate to hustle them out of her kitchen. In the stables, the head groom was the same at first. But when Kenver pressed him, he let slip that his predecessor had been "loitering about the place" yesterday.

"Benning?" asked Kenver.

The man looked annoyed at himself, but he admitted it.

"Benning worked here for thirty years," said Kenver.

"Where will we find him?" Sarah asked.

The head groom merely looked uncomfortable.

"He retired to a cottage out at the edge of the estate," Kenver replied.

"Let us go and see him."

"Now?"

"We are still dressed for riding," Sarah pointed out, indicating her scorched habit. Though it seemed that a great deal of time had passed since they returned from their picnic, it had actually been less than an hour. Even so, she couldn't help feeling that they had very little time left before someone came to thwart them.

"Horses are put away," objected the head groom.

"A thing that is easily remedied," said Kenver.

A little while later, they were riding out of the stables again, in the opposite direction from Tresigan. "I wonder if your father will set his dogs on us," Sarah remarked.

"What? Of course not."

"It won't matter if he does. They like me. That annoys him, doesn't it?"

"Yes," Kenver admitted.

"I wager he's told them they have bad taste."

Kenver choked out a laugh. Or perhaps it was a gasp. Sarah didn't care. She felt powerful and free for the first time in a long while.

After about half an hour, they came to a small thatched cottage at the edge of a woodland. Two horses grazed in a fenced field beside it. A white-haired old man came out as they dismounted. He was a little bent but clearly still strong.

"Hello, Benning."

"Mr. Kenver."

"This is my wife."

He looked curious. "Ma'am."

"We came to see you because I received a letter from Tamara Pendrennon Deane," said Sarah. "And we wondered if you might have heard something about that."

"Me, ma'am?"

His expression was bland, but Sarah noticed that his blue

eyes were twinkling under shaggy white brows. "I have heard that Tamara was a bruising rider," she added.

"She was that."

"And a friend of yours perhaps?"

"I wouldn't like to presume."

Sarah waited. She thought Benning would say more in his own time.

"Should see to your horses," he said.

He and Kenver loosened girths and put their mounts in the pasture with the others. When they were settled, the old man nodded approval and indicated a bench in front of his house. "Naught to offer you but well water or small beer," he said.

Sarah accepted the former, Kenver a glass of the latter, joining their host. They sat down together.

"Miss Tamara loved horses, and they loved her," Benning said finally. "She used to hang about the stables back when I was head groom over to Poldene. Now and then, she'd get to talking, to the air like, on account of having no one else to tell. She knew I'd listen and keep my mouth shut." He eyed Sarah.

"You kept her confidence as long as it was necessary," she said.

"Do you know what happened between her and my parents?" Kenver asked. "No one would ever tell me."

"I doubt it's my place to say anything," Benning began.

"She entrusted you with this letter to me, didn't she?" Sarah was certain of this. She pulled the page from her pocket.

He looked her over again, finally gave a nod. "When Miss Tamara was eighteen, up London way, she met a man she liked. But he weren't good enough for my lord and lady."

"What a surprise," murmured Sarah.

"They forbade her seeing him. But up there in town, with all the people about, seems they couldn't always keep them apart. According to what she told me later."

"Good," said Sarah.

"So they hauled her home."

"Of course they did."

"But the fellow followed them down here."

"Mr. Deane?" Sarah suggested, assuming it from the letter's signature.

Benning nodded. "Mr. Donald Deane, I believe it was. He came and asked his lordship's leave to marry Miss Tamara."

"Which was denied," Sarah guessed drily.

"Was he so unsuitable?" Kenver asked.

Benning shrugged, disavowing any expertise on this subject. "Miss Tamara said he was a small landholder from Lincolnshire. Well able to provide for a wife, she told me. And she liked him very well."

"But it was not a grand match," said Sarah. "And so Lord Trestan refused."

"His lordship ordered Mr. Deane off his land and then locked Miss Tamara in her room."

"What?" said Sarah and Kenver in chorus.

"She kicked up quite a fuss about it."

"Shouting and tears," Kenver murmured. "I do remember that."

"There was a deal of it," Benning agreed. "We could hear through the windows."

"I was continually being hustled out of rooms and sent away to the nursery," Kenver added.

"A regular battle, it was," Benning agreed. "Right up until Miss Tamara climbed out the window of her room and stole a horse from the stables."

His sly look made Sarah wonder if he had aided in this "theft."

"She ran off with that Deane fellow and married him."

"An elopement," murmured Kenver.

"And lived happily from that day to this, I hope," said Sarah.

Benning nodded, whether agreeing with her hope or because he knew it was the truth, Sarah did not know.

"Why did no one tell me?" Kenver asked. "Why didn't you?" he said to Benning.

"His lordship's orders were never to mention it. I was employed by him. And Miss Tamara's secrets were her own."

Kenver muttered something inaudible.

"Until now when she has written to me," Sarah said to Benning, who was no longer officially "employed," she noted.

"She gave me leave to say whatever I liked about her. In case they was locking you up, I reckon. Or worse."

"Well, that's nonsense," said Kenver.

Sarah met Benning's gaze and suspected that the old man knew a good deal about what went on at Poldene despite his retirement. "Thank you for making sure I received the letter," she said quietly. "How did you manage it?"

His face crinkled with amusement. "Miss Tamara knew if it came in the post, that butler of her ladyship's would hand it straight over to her. To end in the fire, she reckoned. So she sent it here, enclosed in a packet to me."

"You didn't simply bring the letter to me though?"

"Miss Tamara wanted it known that she'd written. She called it 'insurance' in her letter to me. You was to get it, but everyone was to see that you had. A bit tricky, that was. I hung about the place until I heard Lady Trestan was sitting with her fancy guest."

"The duchess?"

"Aye. Then I slipped the letter on a tray one of the lasses was taking up. I told her it was for the lady visitor, knowing that Liz don't read too well, and she'd just hand it over."

"A very public delivery."

Benning nodded. "I thought that would do it."

"And so it did. Thank you."

The old man's smile was a landscape of amiable wrinkles.

Kenver rose and walked over to the fence around the pasture, using the horses as an excuse to hide his muddled thoughts. An elopement was scandalous. But he knew such a slip could be mended if the couple was respectably married in the end. Particularly when they were living far away. No one in Lincolnshire would know anything about it. This was not a reason for eternal exile.

He supposed it *was* a respectable match? This Deane could be a wastrel or a blackguard or worse. Perhaps that was why Papa had rejected him. But he'd come to Poldene and presented himself to ask for Tamara's hand. The visit would have been public. A villain would not have done that. He would have tried to lure Tamara away and abandon her afterward.

His sister had told Benning this Deane fellow had a solid

background. "'Small landholder" inevitably made him think of Sarah's father. And his own marriage. And the way Sarah had been received at Poldene. Tamara did not deserve the way she'd been…removed from their family. And he had done nothing.

He saw that the sun was lowering toward the horizon. Returning to the bench, he said, "We should go back."

He fetched their mounts. When he lifted Sarah into the saddle, she felt lithe and yielding in his arms. He wanted to say something to redeem himself, but he couldn't think what.

"Your sister's arrangements, and Benning's, were very clever," she said as they rode away.

She didn't comment on why they were necessary. Would his mother have burned the letter? Yes, he believed she would.

"I am glad to have Tamara's address," Sarah added.

"I never tried to find it," Kenver admitted. "I wonder if my parents ever did."

"I can't imagine that they wouldn't have inquired."

She couldn't imagine the sort of household that had been all he knew. This incident had brought back those shouting matches from his early years. They'd been frightening. He hadn't wanted to endure anything like them again. And so, there was a hole in his family that he'd never tried to fill.

"I shall answer her letter," Sarah said, as if she thought he might object.

He acknowledged this with a nod.

"I shall take my letter to the village myself, to be certain it is sent," she added.

Did she think he would try to stop her? He would not do that. He wondered if Sarah was despising him. *She* hadn't hesitated over the letter, despite the cold reception she'd received at Poldene. Intrepid… He called her that before.

She rode a bit ahead. Was she thinking he would fail her as he'd failed Tamara? Something inside flinched at the idea. He couldn't turn away. He didn't wish to! "I shall put a letter in with yours," he said. "If I may?"

"Of course. She is your sister."

And Sarah was his wife. Quite a stirring, revolutionary wife, as it turned out. He hadn't expected that. He hadn't dreamed she would be just the…inspiration he needed. He would find a way to vanquish all opposition, for her.

They arrived home just in time to change for dinner and separated with no opportunity for further conversation. The meal was even stiffer than usual, and Kenver felt renewed appreciation for their ducal guests, who seemed able to manage anything.

"I am not sure how to respond to her," Sarah told Cecelia later that evening when they sat together well away from the others in the drawing room. Sarah had told her Tamara's story in hushed tones. "I would like to make friends," she added.

"Tell her that," Cecelia suggested. "And that you were glad to have her letter. That should be a welcome reaction from Poldene."

"Are you angry?" Sarah asked. The duchess certainly looked unusually stern.

"I am so weary of the way families oppress young women,"

she replied. "Thinking they have the right to treat them like counters in a financial game."

"Tamara escaped."

"It seems so. Things might have gone badly for her, however." Cecelia looked down at the letter, lying on the sofa between them, shielded by their skirts. "In fact, we do not know how her rebellion turned out."

"She has a home. And the authority to offer it as a refuge."

"Yes. That is a good sign."

"We were fortunate to have kind parents," Sarah said. She felt a brief stab of longing for hers. They hadn't always agreed, of course, but she'd never doubted their love.

"My father is more distracted than kind, but I certainly consider myself fortunate."

"I thought things would be so different when I was married," Sarah said. "I expected to have my own establishment. And the freedom to order it as I liked." She hadn't understood all her hopes until the reality turned out so disappointing. "I certainly did *not* imagine living among people who despise me."

The duchess's brilliant blue eyes narrowed. "Yes, we must see what can be done about that."

"I don't think Kenver's parents will change their minds about me, particularly now that I know what they did to their own daughter."

"No, they don't seem persuadable. I suppose they keep a tight hand on the purse strings as well?"

This was a touchy question. But Cecelia was a trusted friend. "Kenver's allowance is small," Sarah admitted.

"Umm." The duchess considered. "We will have to contrive."

This was kind, but Sarah didn't see what it could mean.

"We could lend you…" the duchess began.

"No." The thought was too humiliating and anyway not any sort of solution. "Are we to hang on your sleeves for years? Lord and Lady Trestan are in robust health." Sarah sighed. "Which I am glad of, really. I would not wish otherwise."

Cecelia acknowledged the difficulty with a nod.

Sarah didn't like to think of her new home as a trap, but sometimes it was hard to see it any other way. She looked over at Kenver, sitting with his parents and the duke. His expression suggested similar thoughts.

Listening to his father harangue the Duke of Tereford about the current political situation, Kenver could only admire the man's restraint. Tereford must know far more about such matters, and yet he remained affable. Kenver wondered what they would have done if Sarah's friends had not happened to visit. Their urbane company carried Poldene's little society from excruciating to tolerable. They shielded Sarah, since Mama and Papa wished to keep up appearances before them. But what was he to do when the guests departed?

He'd made up his mind to act, but resolution was easier than deciding what to actually do. He would take over the state suite when the Terefords went, with its greater space and privacy. He would move without asking. Once again a fait accompli. But was it far enough?

There were one or two empty cottages on the Poldene

estate, but they were run-down, awaiting renovation. He couldn't take Sarah to such a place, even if his father would let him have one, which he would not. Beyond the basic inconveniences, the neighborhood would explode with gossip. He suspected that his mother would add to it, blaming everything on the marriage. Sarah's father would probably come for him with a horsewhip, and Kenver wouldn't blame him.

His mother's brother might invite them to London next season. He and Kenver got along well enough. But his uncle was not in town now, and the season seemed very far off. There were Sarah's old friends. But Kenver disliked the idea of turning up to visit as more or less a beggar.

He considered his sister's unexpected letter. He couldn't ask anything of Tamara, after the way he'd let her down. Offering refuge to Sarah was not the same as welcoming them both. Tamara had not written to *him*.

He'd been searching his memories for any trace of his older sister and unearthed only a general sense of a whirlwind sweeping through the nursery, filling him with a kind of delighted anxiety. That and the shouting. It hadn't been just at the end before she ran away, he thought. There had been various episodes of shouting. Nearly continuous, it seemed. He thought he recalled—or perhaps had been told—that Tamara had gone riding in a purloined pair of breeches. He could easily imagine his mother's outrage over that. Tamara must have had nerves of steel. What was she like now at thirty-five? Should they consider going to see?

But he didn't want to run away, Kenver realized. He'd had enough ducking and weaving and evading. Sarah had shown him that. He wanted to make a home for her in this place that would be theirs eventually. He wanted her to love Poldene as much as he did, though whether she ever could after all that had happened he did not know.

"Kenver?"

The tone of his mother's voice suggested that she had addressed him more than once.

"Always with your head in the clouds," said his father.

That was not true. But in this case, he had no idea what they'd been talking about.

"I was saying that the village summer fete is next week," said Mama.

"Yes," he replied. "We provided a cow for the roast."

"I shall open the proceedings as usual," added his mother complacently.

She ought to invite Sarah to stand beside her, as the new addition to their family. But she would not. He had no doubt about that. Pressure built in Kenver's chest. He disliked quarrels. He acknowledged that he avoided them. But now he had to find a way to make things right for Sarah.

Kenver noticed that the duke was looking at him. Was he mistaken, or did he see understanding in the man's piercing blue eyes? Even sympathy? The duke gave him a slight nod. Exactly what it signified, Kenver could not tell.

Ten

UNDER CECELIA'S DIRECTION, A SWARM OF WORKMEN descended on Tresigan to begin restoring the house. "They have pulled off the ivy," she told the duke a day later. "And found some spots where mortar will need to be replaced. Nothing too dire."

"That's good."

Cecelia was sitting at the writing desk looking through a pile of correspondence that had arrived at Poldene that morning. "We've also solved the mystery of the cellar," she added.

Elegantly relaxed on a settee beside the hearth, the duke looked inquiring.

"As we could find no sign of a key, they broke the door open. It is full of…furnishings."

He groaned. "Another of Uncle Percival's rats' nests? Not like the town house, I hope."

"No, I had a look through it. It is Tresigan's fittings, stored away. Some of the pieces are very fine."

"But ruined by damp, I assume."

"Fortunately not. The cellar is quite dry. Even a carpet lasted perfectly well. Once the repairs are finished, we can bring things back up and furnish the house."

"For a tenant?" the duke asked.

Cecelia tapped her fingers on the desk. "I suppose so."

James noticed, because she was usually more decisive. "Has our resident vagabond vacated?"

"No. He lurks about outside while the workers are busy, I understand. And returns when they've left for the day."

"You don't think we should remove him? He might interfere with the repairs."

"I don't think he would dare do that." Cecelia dismissed this issue from her mind, confident that she could be rid of their trespasser as soon as she really wished it.

"Trestan is a magistrate," the duke noted.

"I would not consign anyone to the mercies of our host," Cecelia replied.

"It is true he has not shown many signs of mercies."

"No. I am surprised his son takes it so meekly."

She didn't sound approving. "Would you have him rant and rail?" asked the duke. "I never found it particularly effective."

"As a relief for your feelings?" she wondered.

He thought about this. "Not really. There was never any… denouement, you see. My father and I roared and wrangled, and then he died."

"You were only fifteen. Time might have brought…well, something different."

"Perhaps." The duke shrugged. "I thought I saw a spark of rebellion in young Pendrennon's eye the other night."

"At last!"

He raised one interrogative eyebrow.

"Would you allow your family to speak to me the way Lady Trestan does to Sarah?" she asked.

"Ah."

"Would you?"

"Not my family. Not anyone's. You may recall that I administered a sharp setdown to your own father when he belittled you."

Cecelia laughed. "And he didn't even notice because he was far more interested in his train of logic than in either of us."

The duke nodded.

"It was a masterful setdown, however. And I thank you for it."

He gave her a graceful seated bow. There was a short silence as Cecelia dealt with more correspondence. Then James spoke again. "It does occur to me that being a parent may be an extremely challenging task."

She looked up, surprised. They gazed at each other, dark-blue eyes fixed on lighter ones, a variety of emotions passing through their depths.

"You think we don't know how?" Cecelia asked in an uncharacteristically subdued voice.

He made a gesture of denial. "Your care for your friends shows otherwise. And your charitable work as well."

She looked reassured. For a little while, she gazed into the indeterminate distance as if weighing pros and cons. The duke waited.

"I will ask Sarah and her husband to show us some of the local sights," Cecelia said.

The duke blinked, frowned, drew in a breath. "Are there sights?" he asked.

"That is not the point."

"Ah, my mistake."

Hearing an odd tone in his voice, Cecelia turned to him. "It would be good for all four of us to have more time away from Poldene," she said.

"You always know best."

She examined his face, then rose from her chair and went to sit beside him. "Are you feeling neglected?" She put her arms around him.

"More receiving my just deserts," he replied, somewhat ruefully. "And finding them not entirely palatable."

"What?"

"Pay me no mind."

"Nonsense." She kissed him.

"Not in that arena, Cecelia," he began. But then she kissed him again in a way that was difficult to ignore. And her hand, resting on his knee, moved upward in a way that really could not be resisted.

———

Looking through the open door of Sarah's bedchamber, Kenver found Gwen tidying the room. The maid greeted him with a bright smile. "Do you know where I can find your mistress?" he asked her.

"She mentioned the library, sir."

"Thank you." Kenver headed downstairs, noting how pleasant it was to encounter Gwen rather than Cranston. Sarah had mentioned more than once that she liked her new attendant.

Sarah's reply to Tamara's letter had been duly dispatched. In the end, she hadn't shown it to him. She'd said she was simply thanking his sister for writing and hoping they might meet sometime soon, and he believed her. Kenver had labored a long time over the note he'd added to her packet. What was he to say to a stranger who was also his sister? A sister he'd allowed to disappear from his existence? Who must think he was a dead loss. His final product had been bland and unsatisfying. If they ever came face-to-face, they might have a frank discussion about their parents. Or perhaps not. He couldn't picture either alternative.

When he reached the library, it seemed empty. "Sarah?" he called.

"Yes?" came a disembodied voice.

"Where are you?"

Sarah's head appeared above the back of an armchair. "Here."

Kenver walked past a jutting bookshelf to discover that Sarah had made her own nest here in the library. She'd turned an armchair toward a corner, barricaded it with a small table topped by a large vase, and positioned a footstool before it. Sitting with her feet up, she was invisible from the door. Anyone glancing in would think the room empty, as he had.

Light slanting from the window illuminated the nook. It was softened with cushions and a colorful shawl. A half-empty bookshelf at the side held writing materials and an open book. The one above held the favorite volumes Sarah had brought with her. All in all, a clever arrangement.

"You've found my hiding place," said Sarah.

He didn't know how to respond to this. She shouldn't have to hide.

"Gwen helped me move the furniture. She is really quite ingenious about getting things one needs from the household."

It hadn't occurred to Kenver that this might be any sort of difficulty.

"It turns out that Cranston is *not* well liked by the staff," Sarah added. "I can't say I was surprised."

Neither was Kenver.

"Gwen says Cranston and your mother's abigail are engaged in a vicious, silent vendetta." Sarah's smile and shrug were half-guilty, half-impish. "She didn't put it just that way, but that's how it sounded."

She'd found an ally in Gwen. Sarah created such bonds whenever she had the least encouragement, Kenver realized. Look at his father's hounds. They adored her and joined Sarah at every opportunity when she went outside. Kenver thought they liked her more than they did his father, though he'd never say so aloud.

"Is anything wrong?" Sarah asked.

Only the usual things, Kenver thought. Gwen was a great improvement, but their situation at Poldene was still highly unsatisfactory. His mother had taken to leaving her bedchamber door open in the evenings when people were retiring to bed. If Kenver came near his wife's room, Mama looked out from across the corridor and made innocuous remarks. *Seemingly* innocuous.

Sarah was gazing at him. He needed a plan. He feared that

the distance between them was increasing. "The expedition tomorrow is all set up," he said.

Sarah nodded. She waited for him to go on, but he couldn't find the words he wanted. "I'll let you get back to your book," he added and left her there.

The following morning, the Terefords, Sarah, and Kenver set off to visit Tintagel. Sarah wondered if it was too odd a choice for their outing. It was the best-known "sight" near Poldene. But it was also the scene of their scandalous night in the sea cave. In the end, she shrugged this off. She didn't intend to avoid the place forever.

They went on horseback, on a bright and sultry late August day. Leaving their mounts in the shade, they made their way over to the ruins. A few others were walking about the site, all of them strangers.

"Is this place thought particularly interesting?" asked the duke as they strolled. "The ruins seem in poor condition."

"It is the connection with King Arthur," Sarah replied.

"I thought he, er, operated in Wales."

"This is where it all began." Sarah would have thought everyone had heard the tale.

"All?"

"The story comes from Geoffrey of Monmouth's *History of the Kings of Britain*," said Kenver.

Sarah plunged in. "In order for the future king—Arthur—to be...engendered, Merlin magically disguised

Uther Pendragon, King of Britain, as Duke Gorlois of
Cornwall. That way Uther could…visit Gorlois's wife,
Igraine." For specific reasons that were unmentionable but
obvious, Sarah noted.

The duke looked as if he was sorting this out. "That
sounds a bit dubious," he said after a bit.

"Merlin was fulfilling a prophecy. Of a king to save Britain
from foreign invaders," Sarah added.

"And this was the way he would…get one."

"That is the tale," said Kenver.

"The end justifying the means," replied Tereford.

"It does seem a rather underhanded thing to do, particularly from Igraine's point of view," said the duchess.

"Should Uther have agreed?" wondered Kenver. "It
doesn't seem honorable."

"He was mad with desire." The words popped out of
Sarah's mouth. She flushed when the others all looked at her.

"Ah," said the duke.

The syllable might have meant that Uther's actions were
understandable under those circumstances, or that Uther
should not have succumbed to his illicit passion. Or something else far more personal that Sarah could only hope she
had not revealed. She had no idea. It was often difficult to
know what the duke thought.

"And what was Igraine?" wondered Cecelia.

Sarah thought of that ancient queen's tumultuous
destiny—her child taken away and returned a stranger,
her reputation cast in doubt, her love for Uther tainted by
politics. Sarah noticed that Kenver was staring at her. "I

never liked Uther much," she said. "He was arrogant and intemperate."

"You speak of him as if he was an actual acquaintance," observed the duke.

"I often feel that way about people in great stories," Sarah said and then wished she hadn't. She might easily have kept that eccentricity to herself. "There was glorious Camelot," she added.

"Until Guinevere and Lancelot and Mordred brought it down," said Kenver.

"You're both very well versed in this tale," said Cecelia. "To me, Arthur's story seems to be full of sad accidents and people making mistakes."

"Rather like life then," replied Kenver.

Sarah swallowed. Did he think she was a mistake? He'd been more distant lately, since the letter arrived from his sister. Perhaps his mother had been speaking to him.

"You are a great reader," the duke said to Sarah.

Sarah nodded, setting her jaw. If the duke wished to think her odd—well, let him.

"Geoffrey of Monmouth's book is a long work, isn't it?" Cecelia asked. "I believe I have heard my father speak of it. Isn't it in Latin?"

"There is a translation. My Latin is not fluent."

"All those conjugations and declensions," said Kenver.

Did he mean that she couldn't be blamed for failing to pick it up? Or that it was just too gloriously complicated for her mind to grasp? And did everyone have to speak as if they might mean something entirely different?

"A gauntlet for schoolboys," replied the duke.

"Yes, *boys*," said Sarah. Girls who might wish to learn things were irrelevant, of course. "Come and see the cliffs, Cecelia."

Kenver watched the two ladies walk off together among the ruined walls. "I feel as if I've said something wrong," he commented. "But I don't know what it is."

The duke gave him a sympathetic look. "In past conversations, in London, I have observed that Miss…Mrs. Pendrennon objects to the unequal education offered girls and boys."

"She *wanted* to study Latin and Greek?" Kenver shook his head. "When I think of slogging through the *De bello Gallico*."

"'*De gustibus non disputandum est.*'"

"It's no use trying Latin tags on me. I've forgotten it all."

"'There is no accounting for taste,'" Tereford translated.

Kenver did actually remember that one. He ought to know more about Sarah's tastes, he thought. Her head was full of strong opinions. And like the stony ground they walked across, there was always a chance he might trip over one.

The duke went to examine one of the ruined stone walls. "So this is King Arthur's, er, point of conception?"

"Most of these walls are from a thirteenth-century castle. There's nothing left but legends from Arthur's time."

They moved through the remains of the building. Kenver pointed out various details. His mind full of Sarah, he didn't notice that the duke was contributing very little. And thus he was unusually startled when the other man said, "My father was a difficult man."

"Um. Really?" Kenver couldn't imagine the duke having trouble with anyone. It was almost as surprising as having the man suddenly confide in him.

"He, ah, specialized in harsh judgments."

It took Kenver a moment to see a connection. "Like mine." Of course the Terefords had noticed his parents' attitude toward Sarah. They simply hadn't mentioned it. Until now, apparently.

"Very like," replied Tereford. "I have been reminded."

"And your mother also?" Kenver often found Mama more prickly.

"She died when I was very young. I never really knew her."

"I'm sorry. It was just you and your father then?"

"Yes."

"And you didn't, er…"

"Get on." The duke bit off the words.

Should he commiserate? That seemed presumptuous. Kenver fumbled for a way to have a confidential conversation with this impressive man.

"He died when I was fifteen."

"I'm sorry," said Kenver again.

"I try to be more so," said the duke.

Kenver had rarely felt so awkward. The duke seemed to be feeling it too, which made things even worse. If *Tereford* was uneasy, they must be scaling the heights of unease.

"Fifteen years of seething and shouting and disputes that solved nothing. And were never resolved." The duke looked out over the sea. "Well, it can't have been quite that many years. I don't recall when I learned to talk."

Choking off a nervous laugh, Kenver said, "I don't argue very often."

"No."

Was this a criticism? Kenver couldn't tell. "There was a great deal of shouting at Poldene when I was a child. I developed a…distaste for it."

The duke took this in with what appeared to be sympathy. "I've been thinking just lately, and it seems a weighty thing to be a father."

They looked at each other—two youthful men, not much alike but newly married and likely to face fatherhood in the near future. To join a long line of fathers, Kenver thought. He'd never considered it.

"People—some people—burden their sons with vast expectations. Particularly only sons."

"You also?" Kenver asked.

"Yes." The duke made a broad gesture. "Carrying on legacies, making up for ancestral lapses. And so on."

Kenver nodded, understanding the point all too well.

"But that's no excuse to set up as petty tyrants."

This time, the laugh escaped.

Tereford smiled in response. "I learned that arguments don't convince such people. No matter how fiery. They aren't…heard."

"Not arguing isn't either," said Kenver. "Obviously." Silence could be taken for agreement.

"Both are unproductive," his companion replied.

Did he mean there was no solution? "It is affecting Sarah," Kenver blurted out. "That is what I cannot bear."

"Much harder when another person is involved. If my father had attacked Cecelia…" The duke's expression grew grim. He looked intimidating. It was a moment before he continued. "The only thing I have found helpful is to…disengage. I have had to do this within myself, since my father is gone."

As his was not, Kenver noted. How could one disengage when they were thrown together every day?

"When people are shown that their behavior is accomplishing nothing, sometimes they alter it," the duke added.

His tone suggested that "sometimes" was not often. Kenver's automatic pessimism began to surface when he was suddenly struck by a new idea. "Tresigan," he said.

The duke raised dark brows.

"Could Sarah and I live at Tresigan? Once the repairs are finished? They are, nearly, are they not?"

The other man's perplexity faded into understanding. "Ah. Hmm. Tresigan. I don't see why not." He paused as if something about the plan was amusing. "I can make arrangements," he added. "I might be quite a dab hand at arrangements."

Why he should find this funny, Kenver did not know. He did not really care as long as… Remembering a problem, he grimaced. "My allowance is not large," he said, a humiliating admission to this superior man. "I could not pay a great deal."

"Ah, well, Cecelia is always saying that careful tenants are more valuable than inflated rents." The duke smiled. Not at Kenver, but at some mysterious jest of his own. "I'm sure we can agree. Let us consider the matter settled."

Kenver felt the beginnings of relief.

"The house won't be habitable immediately," the duke added. "It is full of workmen. And our resident vagabond, of course."

"Habitable" could be a relative term, Kenver thought. He and Sarah might put up with a great deal of inconvenience to be free. Free, he thought, his spirits soaring with hope. He must find Sarah and tell her.

On the other side of the Tintagel peninsula, Sarah led Cecelia into a crevice in the rock and followed its turns and twists. "Don't slip on the pebbles," she warned. The boom of the ocean bounced off the rocky walls, and the air was damp with spray when they reached the end. "This is where we fell," she told her friend. She put her arm in front of Cecelia. "Stay back. That rock is not steady." She pointed to the opening in the cliffs below. "That is the entrance to the cave where we were trapped."

Cecelia peered over the edge. "It's fortunate you were not hurt."

"The sand is soft just there," Sarah replied. "And I landed on top of Kenver."

The duchess examined the spot. "How loud the sea is here. I suppose no one could hear you call for help over the sound of the surf."

"No. And he would not wake, so I had to drag him to shelter."

"You were quite the heroine," said Cecelia.

"That is not the term anyone used. I caused a scandal."

"You caused it together, if scandal is the word." Cecelia

gazed at the side of her friend's face. "You might have fought off the gossip. I would have invited you to come and stay until it passed if you'd told me."

Sarah remembered that Cecelia too had been the target of malicious stories. She knew how it felt. *She* had married to scotch them, however. Partly. Perhaps. Sarah didn't really know. In any case, the Terefords had been on their way to Cornwall soon after the incident. Where could Cecelia have invited Sarah to stay? Poldene? Something between a laugh and a groan escaped her. "I wanted to marry Kenver," Sarah said. After that tender night in the cave, she really had. "Before I met his parents."

"Well, I hope you will remember in future that friends wish to help you."

Meeting her concerned gaze, Sarah said, "Thank you. You *have* helped. I can hardly say how much. I don't know what I would have done without your company at Poldene." She shuddered to think of life under those circumstances.

"I was happy to help, but we cannot stay a great deal longer. The work at Tresigan will soon be done."

Sarah went still. "Tresigan," she said. "Nearly done." She put a hand on Cecelia's arm. "Could we stay there?" she asked.

Cecelia blinked.

"Things would be so much better if we did not live with Kenver's parents," Sarah went on.

"Why didn't I think of that?" wondered Cecelia. "Of course you can." She frowned. "But you know, Sarah, though we are making repairs, the place will be rather…rustic."

"I could not care less."

"Do you really understand though? There is only a hand pump in the kitchen for water and an…adequate outdoor privy."

"I don't mind inconvenience," replied Sarah. She nearly added that she would live in a hovel to escape Poldene. But that wasn't *quite* true. A worrisome snag occurred to her. "We don't have a large income. We couldn't pay much rent."

Cecelia waved this aside.

"The duke won't mind?"

"He doesn't care about such details." Cecelia assumed her planning expression. "I will urge the workmen on. We have found quite a bit of furniture in the cellar. It should be enough."

"I must tell Kenver," Sarah said, elated.

They turned away from the sea and walked out of the crevice, finding the gentlemen searching for them. Cecelia accepted her husband's offered arm and went to examine the castle ruins. Sarah ran to Kenver, who took her outstretched hands. "I have had an idea," they both said.

"What?" they both asked and then laughed.

Neither could resist going on. "To go and live at Tresigan," they caroled in unison.

They stared at each other with surprise and growing delight.

"I asked Cecelia if we might, and she agreed," Sarah said.

"I just discussed that very plan with the duke. He did too."

Their gaze held, suddenly full of hope. Kenver squeezed her hands. They were always better when it was just the two of them. Like now. He couldn't wait. "It may be a ramshackle household."

"I don't care."

"I don't know what staff we may be able to…"

"I don't care," Sarah repeated.

"I know how to roast potatoes in the ashes of a fire," he noted.

She laughed. It was the most carefree laugh he'd ever heard from her and a joy to hear. "I've read so many tales of explorers camping in the wild," she said. "I will be glad to put that knowledge to use."

Kenver was certain that her head was full of useful schemes.

———

"I've arranged for the Pendrennons to take Tresigan," James was telling Cecelia among the castle ruins.

"*You* did?"

"Yes, Cecelia, I did. Why shouldn't I? The Pendrennons' living situation is much on their minds."

"You noticed. Yes."

"The issue was rather…noticeable."

"It's just that you never take any interest…" Her voice broke off as she glimpsed a challenging look in his dark-blue eyes. "It is an odd coincidence. I just told Sarah the same thing."

"Indeed? Great minds think alike."

She looked at him. "I suppose they do."

"Can there be any doubt?"

Cecelia was more puzzled than doubtful. "I'm glad we

came to the same conclusion." Unusually, she searched for words. "They will be good tenants."

"Though paying very little, I fear."

"But bringing happiness to the house, I hope."

The duke examined her for a moment before saying, "As do I."

Their Tintagel picnic became a celebration of the new arrangement, and they rode past Tresigan on the way back to check on progress. Fortunately, the workmen had found that the structure was sound and only a few repairs were required to the roof. Some floorboards needed to be replaced, and the interior was to be freshened with new paint. But this would take days rather than weeks. Sarah and Kenver couldn't stop smiling at each other as they rode on toward Poldene.

They said nothing to Kenver's parents about their plans, not being so foolish. But as the pall of their disapproval descended over her once again, Sarah relished the idea of escape.

Eleven

By the first day of the village fete, it was clear that they would be able to move in a short time, and Kenver savored this knowledge as they set off for the opening of the celebration. He smiled at Sarah in the carriage, and she smiled back. He'd noticed that his parents were puzzled by their unshakable good humor. Sarah had been blithely unaffected by several of his mother's barbs. Kenver, reminding himself of the duke's advice to disengage, rested in the knowledge that he was getting Sarah away from them. He thought the Terefords were enjoying this too. Kenver particularly appreciated their shared secret as they prepared for their first public event since his marriage. All of them would be on show today.

But as they walked about the village square admiring examples of local crafts and husbandry, his patience wore thin. His mother acted as if Sarah wasn't there. It was always Kenver who brought Sarah forward and introduced her to any friends and neighbors she had not encountered before. Mama was losing no opportunity to slight her, Kenver thought, trying not to grind his teeth. This was different from dinner table gibes. This was public rejection and impossible to ignore.

It was too bad that the duke and duchess had not come along today. Their friendliness would have boosted Sarah's consequence. But a thick packet had arrived for them, heralding a crisis at one of the duke's other properties. They had stayed behind to prepare replies, much to the disappointment of the villagers.

Kenver paused beside one of the exhibits of handwork and let his parents go ahead. Watching Sarah praise the quality of the stitches and seeing how much her knowledgeable comments were appreciated, Kenver could not understand why his family didn't see her as a welcome addition to their ranks.

"Sarah!"

Turning at the sound of her name, Sarah saw her father and mother approaching, a surprise that ought to be delightful rather than complicated. But was not. When first married, she had asked Lady Trestan if they might invite her parents for a visit, since her old home was too far away for a call—more than two hours on horseback riding through the fields and longer by carriage. Sarah had thought it would be pleasant for the two families to be better acquainted. But Kenver's mother had put her off and made her feel she was asking for some onerous favor rather than a commonplace and kind gesture. Later, when the Pendrennons' attitude became clear, Sarah had dropped the idea. She didn't want her family to see the way she was treated at Poldene. Now the sight of them coming toward her made her heart ache. And when she was enfolded in her mother's embrace, she had to fight back the tears.

When they drew apart, her mother examined her and said, "Sarah, are you all right?"

Sarah strove to sound convincing. "Yes, Mama."

"Lady Trestan was…very cool when we asked where you were."

So they had already encountered her. Too bad. "I didn't know you were coming to the fete," Sarah answered.

"We thought we would make the drive since we had not seen you in so long."

This was a reproach. Sarah heard it and didn't know how to answer. Her mother took her arm and led her along the line of exhibits. Kenver and her father paused to examine one of them.

"Tell me how you are," said her mother in a low voice. "I know something is wrong."

She couldn't lie, but she didn't wish to reveal the truth. She looked away.

"When the earl and countess did not come to the wedding…" Sarah's mother paused, then went on. "I knew they were not pleased with the match. But now that you are married and part of the family…" Her voice trailed off.

Sarah doubted that Kenver's mother would ever see her so.

"Are they not treating you well, Sarah? You can always come home."

"And cause another scandal?" Sarah couldn't keep a hint of reproach from her tone.

"I don't care," was the fierce reply. "I won't have you mistreated."

"Thank you, Mama." Sarah blinked the tears from her eyes.

"You don't have to thank me for being your mother." They walked on, leaving most of the crowd behind. "I thought you wanted to marry him, Sarah. It seemed so to me. If I was mistaken…"

"I did."

"But if he makes you unhappy…"

"Not Kenver, Mama."

Her mother met her eyes and then looked back over her shoulder at the elder Pendrennons. "I see."

"But it's all right. We are moving into our own house in a week or so."

"Where? Nearer to us?"

"No," Sarah answered regretfully. "It is a little farther off, but we shall have our own home. We can visit." As soon as she had Tresigan in order, Sarah thought. She feared her parents wouldn't think much of the place.

"That's good."

"Don't mention it to anyone else just yet. We haven't told Kenver's parents."

This earned her an appalled look, as if things must be far worse than her mother had imagined.

"Just because we don't want arguments," Sarah added. "The house isn't quite ready."

"What sort of place is it?"

Sarah glided over any details. "It is called Tresigan. It belongs to the Duke of Tereford."

"Ah, the duchess is helping you?"

"Yes."

"I was sorry not to see her today." They had become acquainted during the London season.

"She will be sorry as well."

Kenver and Sarah's father caught up, and they silently agreed not to tell him most of this news.

"Some fine produce here," he said.

"Yes, Papa."

"Your husband tells me they promote the latest farming methods among their tenants." He gave Kenver an approving smile.

Sarah enjoyed it. She thought the two men could be friends, given the opportunity. Kenver looked from Sarah to her mother as if wondering what they had been saying.

"Shall we see the rest?" asked her father.

They walked on, and Sarah relaxed into the sensation of warm and noncritical company.

She felt the same the next day when she and Cecelia went to look over the furnishings that had been stored in the cellar at Tresigan. Fortunately the space was not damp but only dusty, and the scent of potpourri filled the air.

"Everything has been put away very carefully," Cecelia noted.

"By whom, I wonder," answered Sarah.

"According to some documents I've found, the last people to live here were two female relatives of the previous duke. They were very old when they died. I fear that means the furnishings are quite old-fashioned."

Sarah waved this aside. It was a matter of indifference to her. "They look perfectly serviceable to me," she said.

"There are bedsteads and wardrobes." Cecelia made notes. "However did they get these larger pieces down those narrow stairs?"

"With great difficulty, I imagine."

"We'll ask Merlin to help haul them out," the duchess added with a small smile.

"He won't care for that!"

"I am a bit weary of his sulking. We have not been unkind to him."

"Except by existing."

"Well, I am not willing to forego that. So there is a wash-stand, and there seem to be chairs stacked behind that dining table."

"We will have everything we need," said Sarah. "I am very grateful, Cecelia."

The duchess waved this aside. "I see no coverlets or curtains."

"Perhaps they were worried about moths."

Cecelia nodded. "We'll have to look into purchasing some. Unless…" She moved a footstool and revealed a large cedar chest. Heaving up the lid, she exposed piles of cloth. The scent of camphor wafted out. "Here we are." She lifted out a swath of drapery. "Oh."

The chintz had a wild pattern of whirling stems and blossoms in what seemed a hundred colors. "It looks as if a garden exploded onto the cloth," said Sarah.

"Now I see the kinship with Uncle Percival." The duchess drew out another panel with a different design, equally eye-popping. And then a third.

"They are not at all faded," Sarah observed.

"Unfortunately."

Sarah laughed. "They will cover the windows."

"How could you ever relax with these flowers...assaulting you?"

"They are not so very bad."

"The light is dim down here," Cecelia pointed out. "In bright sunlight, they will be blinding."

Sarah had to admit this was true.

"The attics at Poldene probably have old linens stored away," the duchess added. "I've never known a large estate that does not."

"Are you suggesting I steal them?" The idea had an appeal.

"They might be said to belong to your husband." Cecilia put the draperies back and closed the chest. "We will leave these here for now."

"Thank you, Cecelia," Sarah said again as they walked back up the stairs.

"I've done only what any friend might."

"No, you have done much more. I will never forget it."

The duchess dismissed this with a gesture.

Sarah arrived back at Poldene in a happy daze of planning to have her own home at last. In her bedchamber, she removed her hat and rang for Gwen, only to have Cranston come in response. "Where is Gwen?" Sarah asked, displeased.

"She has been dismissed," Cranston replied.

"Dismissed?"

"For immorality." Cranston's tone and expression were odiously smug.

"What?"

"She was found to be meeting a young man in secret. Lady Trestan does not tolerate such behavior."

The woman's self-satisfied smirk told Sarah that Cranston had been involved in this accusation. She was certain it was false. "I will speak to Lady Trestan," Sarah declared, turning toward the door.

"Her ladyship has gone out."

"I will see her when she returns then."

Cranston shrugged as if to indicate that the effort would be futile. "Lady Trestan will not have such a young person in her house."

"Who has accused Gwen? You?"

Cranston bridled. "I wouldn't lower myself. She's been seen by all sorts of people."

"Oh yes? Who, exactly? I would like to talk with them."

It seemed the woman had not expected close questioning. "I'm sure I wouldn't know. I don't listen to gossip."

This was patently false. Sarah was certain that Gwen's disgrace was a conspiracy between her mother-in-law and Cranston. Aimed at her. They had chosen a time when Sarah was not at home to strike.

"Shall I help you remove your riding habit, ma'am?"

"No, thank you. You may go."

"I should tidy up." Cranston looked around as if the room was a mess.

"Please go." Sarah waited until the woman departed—as slowly as could be managed without outright insolence—and then went to look for Kenver. "Have you heard about Gwen?" she asked when she finally found him walking in the gardens.

"My father told me. Apparently…"

"*Apparently* she has been a victim of malicious gossip."

"Papa said she has been sneaking out to assignations."

"Sneaking? *Gwen*?"

"It doesn't sound like the sort of thing she would do," Kenver admitted.

"Because she didn't."

"Papa said…"

"Who saw her?" Sarah demanded. "And what sort of *assignations*?"

"I don't know. Mama…"

"Dismissed Gwen because I liked her and enjoyed having her as an attendant?"

"She wouldn't—"

"Do anything to distress me?" Sarah interrupted. Her eyes snapped with emotion. "She sent Cranston back, you know."

Kenver had never seen her so agitated. "Treat a servant unfairly," he finished. But suddenly he wasn't sure. Since Sarah's arrival, his mother had said and done things he never would have expected.

"I want to see Gwen," said Sarah with narrowed eyes and a raised chin.

"I don't know whether…"

"Don't you?"

The glare that accompanied these words shook Kenver. He thought of Sarah as such a gentle person, but right now she looked fierce and…perilous.

"Will you help me? Or must I inquire for myself?"

"I suppose she went back to her family's cottage."

"You know where that is?"

"Yes."

"Good." Sarah turned and started to walk away. After a few steps, she looked back over her shoulder. "Well?"

"You want to go there now?"

"Certainly." She bit off the word.

Kenver moved to her side. He had to walk rapidly to keep up with her on the way to the stables.

They rode to a cottage on the south side of the Poldene estate. An older man emerged at the sound of hooves, and Gwen rushed out on his heels. "I didn't do anything wrong," she cried as soon as she saw Sarah.

Gwen's eyes were red with weeping.

"I was meeting my brother. Jowan!"

A young man edged out of the cottage. Tall and gangly, he shared Gwen's dark hair and eyes and general cast of features.

Gwen pulled him forward. "Jowan wants to be a footman. And he's like to have the height and all. So I been teaching him things about a grand household, so he could get a position."

Jowan kept his eyes on the ground and muttered something that might have been an apology.

"They set someone to follow me on my afternoon off," Gwen continued. "I'd swear it was Cranston, but I got no proof of that. But it was her told Lady Trestan that I was meeting a lover. She made up a story about catching us… doing something improper."

Both Gwen and Jowan grimaced in horror.

"I told her ladyship that he's my brother, but they said I was lying."

"Gwen don't lie," said the older man. "She's got an odd kick in her gallop with the joking she does, but she was always a truthful lass." He frowned. "Do you reckon Lord Trestan will take away our cottage?"

Sarah looked horrified. "He would not dare," she said.

"I will see that he doesn't," replied Kenver.

"Can you tell Lady Trestan the truth?" Gwen asked Sarah.

"I will," she answered.

"But I don't suppose I'll get my position back."

Gwen met Sarah's eyes, and they silently acknowledged that she probably could not manage this. Gwen was well aware of Sarah's position in the Poldene household. Unable to bear the disappointment in the girl's expression, Sarah took Gwen aside. "We are moving out of Poldene quite soon," she confided. "We haven't told anyone yet because…"

They exchanged another understanding look.

"But you can come and work for us in our new home. Jowan too, if he likes."

"Really, ma'am?" Relief and hope lit Gwen's face.

"Yes. Don't say anything just now. But it will be quite soon."

"Where are you going?"

"It is a house called Tresigan."

"The haunted place?" Gwen looked uncertain.

"A man who had been living there started those stories. It is a fine house. All sorts of repairs have been made."

The girl looked reassured.

"We don't want Lord and Lady Trestan to know until we are ready to depart," Sarah added.

"So I can't tell my family?"

"Not just yet. Soon."

Gwen nodded. Her bright spirit seemed to be dimmed, and Sarah was sorry to see it.

Back at Poldene, Sarah's efforts to speak to Lady Trestan were repulsed at first, but she did not give up. At last, the following day, she was admitted to the countess's private parlor. She was not asked to sit down.

"I am quite occupied this morning," said Kenver's mother. She was sitting at a writing desk with a letter in progress before her.

Sarah realized that this was the first time they'd ever been alone together. And how odd that was, considering their new relationship.

Obviously, the countess wanted Sarah to feel as she had on the two occasions when she had been called before the headmistress of her school for an infraction. Sarah refused to be cowed. "I suppose you know that I wish to speak to you about Gwen."

"Oh, is that it?"

Lady Trestan's tone was bland, uninterested. But Sarah was certain that she had known.

"I can't think that there is anything to say about such an unsavory situation," the countess added.

"The story told about her was untrue." Sarah had decided not to accuse any individual of lying. She did not want to argue that point. It was better not to bring Cranston into this. "The young man she met was her brother."

Lady Trestan looked pitying. "Such girls always have that sort of story ready when they are caught."

"I went to the family's cottage and met her brother," Sarah replied.

"I have no doubt she *has* a brother. Nor that he was primed to support her tale. Naturally he would say whatever she wished."

"They weren't like that."

"Indeed." The countess's raised eyebrows defined cool skepticism. "What were they *like*?"

"Good, honest people."

"And you knew this how?"

"I–I felt it to be true."

Lady Trestan sighed. "Really, if you are so easily duped..."

"I wasn't!"

"Then you are clearly not capable of managing a large staff. Some of them will always be lying, you know."

"I am better acquainted with Gwen than you are," Sarah declared. "She was not lying. She deserves an apology."

"I beg your pardon?" The countess sat straighter, and her eyes crackled with anger.

"She should not have been dismissed. It wasn't right." Though Sarah intended to take Gwen along to Tresigan, she wanted to help salvage the girl's reputation.

"*You* are questioning my decisions?" Lady Trestan's hand closed into a fist on the desktop.

"You were given incorrect information."

The countess stared at her for what seemed an age. "You overstep," she said finally. "You have nothing to do with Poldene affairs."

"Gwen was my..."

"Nothing here is yours!" Lady Trestan interrupted. "How could you imagine it was? A little dab of a thing like you. With no presence or dignity. No conversation, not even pretty. You will never be a proper countess, and I shudder to think of how things would decline if you took my place when I am gone."

It was as if all the criticism Sarah had received in London society was rolled into one ball and hurled at her. She couldn't help it. She flinched.

Lady Trestan saw this and enjoyed it. "However, you will *not* take my place," she continued with perfect confidence. "My son will come to his senses. You will not be able hold on to him. With what you have to offer?" She sniffed with contempt.

Sarah gathered the tatters of her self-esteem. "You don't know me."

Kenver's mother shrugged. "I know what I see—a pallid nonentity who doesn't even bring Poldene a fortune or family connections. What a waste!"

"That isn't…".

"We will have the marriage set aside," Lady Trestan continued as if Sarah hadn't tried to speak. "There is plenty of evidence that it is not a *real* union." She smiled with malicious enjoyment.

This was why she'd taken such pains to keep them apart, Sarah understood. She was plotting an annulment.

"Now go away," added the countess. She gestured as if brushing off an annoying insect.

Though she would have been willing to fight on for

Gwen's sake, difficult as that might be, Sarah saw that she would get no justice here. She stood very straight and went— out of the room and into the corridor, wondering where to turn. Cranston was haunting her bedchamber again, and she had discovered Sarah's refuge in the library as well. Orders had come to remove all the books from the shelves and clean them, leaving the room in disarray. Kenver was out on the estate with his father, unusually. Sarah might have gone to Cecelia, but whatever crisis the Terefords were handling had apparently grown larger, and Sarah didn't want to bother her. After all that Cecelia had done, Sarah felt ashamed to ask for more. Why should she need so much help?

In the end, she went outside. It was an overcast day. Rain was clearly on the way, which seemed apt, and the air was chilly. A shawl would have been welcome, and a bonnet to keep the wind from tossing her hair. But not if she had to see Cranston to get them. She strode briskly along instead, hold- ing on to her skirts and watching the flowers sway in the rising breeze. The dogs came to join her, romping along at her side.

Sarah knew she had many good qualities. Her friends had often told her so and admired her skills. But could one's friends be trusted to give an honest opinion? They wished to be kind and bolster one's confidence. Her parents were the same; they loved her.

The wider world was another matter. It seemed to agree with Lady Trestan. And what about Kenver? What did he really think of her? He was losing his home over her. They would be alone at Tresigan. What if he began to see her as only a duty and a burden?

Rain began, sweeping in from the sea like a diaphanous curtain. Sarah sheltered under a thick cedar and watched it fall. The brightness of the flowers dimmed further. The trees bent to the wind. Droplets began to trickle onto her head and shoulders, and Fingal whined as if wondering why she didn't seek better shelter. "This is ridiculous," Sarah said aloud. She was huddling here like the sort of pathetic creature Lady Trestan had accused her of being. She put back her shoulders and hurried inside, getting thoroughly wet, and faced Cranston's contempt with the appearance of indifference.

And so Sarah's world at Poldene returned to its beginnings. Cranston was more insolent than ever, disdaining Kenver as well as Sarah. It was obvious that the countess had emphasized her instructions to keep them apart, and Cranston relished her mission. She seemed to be everywhere. Sarah endured what almost amounted to persecution. She didn't tell Cecelia about this running battle. Why make the situation more awkward for a guest when they would be leaving soon?

The change made it very difficult to pack her things for the move without raising questions. It might have been impossible, except that Gwen retained some friends among the Poldene servants. The truth about her dismissal had spread among them, rousing an undercurrent of anger. Gwen recruited Elys, a kitchen maid with ambitions, who would also come along to the new household, and Elys entered into the conspiracy with relish, even though she was warned that they would have little money for wages. Sarah suspected that Elys saw them as an investment in the future and hoped she could see to it that the girl was right, though it would be some time before she could make good.

Elys gradually went off with Sarah's possessions and hid them away. She also developed a gleeful enthusiasm for pilfering the Poldene attics, seeming to view this like a treasure hunt. Sarah constantly worried that she would get caught. But it seemed Elys had a talent for larceny. She slipped about the house like a benevolent ghost. Nearly every day, she brought some small household item to Sarah's chamber as a surprise. Sarah told herself that Poldene would belong to Kenver someday and items in the attic had been more or less discarded. She also counted the hours until they could go, and though they seemed limitless, the time finally came. On Cranston's afternoon out, Sarah and Elys threw all her clothes into trunks and had two footmen friends of Elys's take them away.

Twelve

EVEN AS THE WAGON WAS LOADED, KENVER WENT TO tell his parents that they were leaving. He was actually looking forward to it. Two days ago, when Cranston had practically thrown him out of Sarah's chamber, he had lost his temper and complained to his mother. She had said, "Surely you must admit now that you have made a mistake. Sarah cannot control servants and does not know how to go on at a place like Poldene."

Whatever he said, they turned around and made it his fault, or more likely Sarah's. Their treatment of his sister had made it clear that they had no confidence in their offspring's judgment. And very little capacity to forgive. Not that Tamara required forgiveness. It was rather the other way around. Kenver felt the twinge of guilt that plagued him whenever he thought of his sister.

He knew his parents were sitting together in the drawing room. And that the Terefords were out on some business of their own. Kenver had been keeping close track of Poldene's denizens during his preparations since there were so many he and Sarah had to avoid. Making his way to the drawing room and closing its doors behind him, he stood before his parents and said, "I have come to tell you that Sarah and I are moving out."

They stared at him as if he'd spoken in a foreign language.

"To a place of our own," he added.

"How? With no funds for a lease," his father responded.

"I've made arrangements."

"What arrangements?"

"We are going to live at Tresigan."

"The Terefords know of this?" asked his mother sharply.

Kenver said nothing as the answer was obvious.

"I forbid it," his father declared, one of his favorite phrases.

"I am of age," Kenver reminded them. He'd vowed not to get angry or indeed to show any emotion.

"I can still cut off your allowance," his father declared. "How would your penniless little bride like that, eh?"

Though the insult made him clench his jaw, Kenver was ready for this threat, which had been made before. "That will make a good story for the neighborhood," he replied. "Particularly when it is perfectly reasonable for a young couple to wish to set up their own household. And not reasonable for a father to withhold funds due to the heir of Poldene. I'm sure the Rauches and the Youvilles would be surprised to hear you had done so."

His father flushed with anger. "Do you dare to threaten me?"

"I am simply telling you my plans, Papa. If you choose to make a public spectacle of our family disagreement, that is up to you."

"Wait," said his mother. The word carried such command that both men complied. "This might be a solution," she added.

Kenver frowned, unsure what she might mean.

"You can send Sarah to live at this house. The Terefords are friends of hers after all. It would make sense. We will provide an income for her while we have the marriage annulled. What a good idea, Kenver."

Kenver was speechless for a moment.

"Ah," said his father. "Yes. A fine idea, my boy."

"I would never send Sarah off to live alone." He couldn't believe he was obliged to say this.

"She could return to her parents once the marriage is dissolved," said his mother.

"In disgrace," Kenver answered before he realized that he was being pulled into discussing this as if it were an actual plan.

"Well, really, Kenver, if she had not schemed to entrap you…"

"There will be no annulment. We will not mention it again."

"But it is an elegant solution," said his father.

"To a problem that does not exist." They seemed to think of Sarah, and of him, as no more than counters in a game. "There are no grounds for an annulment," Kenver declared. He stared at them, particularly his mother. She had put every obstacle in the way of a true marriage, but she couldn't be certain that she had succeeded in keeping them physically apart. He kept his gaze stony and did not look away.

After a while, her eyes wavered. "Do you care nothing for how we feel?"

She gave him the woebegone look that had eaten at him since he was a small boy. He felt it. But he wasn't the only one involved here. He was standing in defense of his wife. "As much as you do for Sarah's feelings, Mama," he replied. "The way you treated her at the fete was deplorable."

"Kenver!"

"Yes?"

They stared at him with fuming resentment.

"Our things are packed," he added. "I have ordered a wagon to take them to Tresigan."

"I shall forbid it to go," declared his father.

"You have no power to do so. The carter is a friend of mine."

"I'll see that he…"

"A man who is not dependent on Poldene for his living," Kenver interrupted. He had made sure of that. "Should you try to make trouble for him, I will explain your petty malice to all and sundry."

"What has happened to you, Kenver?" asked his mother. Her expression was tragic. "This is all that girl's fault. She has made you hard and cold."

Could she not see that insulting Sarah did not help her case? Or that Sarah's presence in his life had done exactly the opposite? Sarah had woken him up to the coldness that surrounded him. Didn't they see it? If it was explained, wouldn't his parents want things to be different? "You treated Tamara shabbily, you know," he said. "Have you ever written her since she married? She is your daughter."

"If Tamara says…"

"I didn't write either," Kenver interrupted. "I followed your lead without thinking. But I intend to make up for that now."

"You will desert us after all we have done for you," replied his mother.

"I do not wish to be at odds," he went on. He did care about them. They were his family. "I would be happy for us to live in harmony. When you receive Sarah with respect..."

"This is all her fault," his mother repeated. "You never treated me so before you met *her*."

"What you mean is that I did not argue with you and did as I was told."

"As you should," said his father. "We know best."

"I don't see a great deal of evidence for that."

"I beg your..."

"Have you made such a success of our family life?"

"Kenver!" His mother looked shocked.

"How dare you speak to your mother this way?" His father scowled. "Don't expect to be welcomed when you come crawling back."

His mother made a cutting gesture. "Of course *you* are always welcome," she corrected.

Meaning that Sarah was not, Kenver understood. There was nothing left to do then but depart, and so they did, with a loaded wagon and two riding horses. If his father chose to make trouble about his horse, Kenver planned to create an enormous stink. The kitchen maid who had been helping Sarah rode on the wagon with the carter. Gwen and Jowan were to meet them at Tresigan.

They reached there by early afternoon. The house looked smarter and fresher without the curtains of ivy. Going in through the now-functional front door, they found the rooms much lighter, smelling of whitewash and new wood. Furniture had been brought up from the cellar, cleaned, and distributed, supervised by the enormously efficient Duchess of Tereford. There was a bed and wardrobe in each of several bedchambers, a sofa in one downstairs parlor, and a dining table and chairs in another. To Kenver the place looked bare, even a bit stark, but Sarah did not seem daunted. He wondered what it would take to daunt her.

Unfortunately, the house also contained Merlin. They had told him they were coming, hoping he would take the hint and depart. And indeed when they arrived to find his possessions gone from the kitchen, they thought he had given in. "Did you stay to say goodbye?" Kenver asked him.

"I shall live in the cave," Merlin replied. "I've shifted my things out there."

"The cave," exclaimed Sarah.

"Wouldn't you be more comfortable with some family or friends?" asked Kenver.

"I have no family or friends to turn to. The cave is better than living rough in the fields. Part of it is quite dry."

Kenver and Sarah gazed at each other. The carter offered to give Merlin a good thumping and haul him off.

Merlin bristled at the threat, looking quite ready to defend himself. "Are you going to eat my vegetables?" he asked Sarah.

"What?"

He pointed out the window to the garden. "I planted those and tended them. Are you going to eat them?"

"I suppose we are," replied Sarah.

"So I'm providing sustenance for the household."

"Yes, but…"

"I won't venture beyond the kitchen," Merlin added, gesturing upward. "The house shall be all your domain."

Elys and the driver gazed at Kenver, waiting for orders. He turned to Sarah. She looked back at him, then gave a small shake of her head. He thought she was reluctant to begin their life together here with violence. And also perhaps ruefully amused.

"I'll help carry your things in," Merlin added, heading for the cart.

The carter and Elys hesitated for a moment and then followed him.

"Should we give him a bedchamber?" asked Sarah.

"No," replied Kenver. "I don't wish to *encourage* him to stay."

"Perhaps you could find him some position. Elsewhere."

"I shall bend my mind to doing so."

Gwen and Jowan arrived on foot a few minutes later and immediately pitched in to unload the cart. With so many hands, it did not take long to empty it.

Gwen, Elys, and Jowan found places on the top floor under the slanting eaves. There were small bedchambers up there, which the duchess had sparsely furnished. Kenver and Sarah were left with the middle floor all to themselves—a circuit of nearly empty rooms of varying sizes around Tresigan's inner courtyard. The two largest had been hung with draperies that were…extremely colorful.

"We found those hangings in the cellar," Sarah said as they stood together in one of these. "They belonged to the previous inhabitants."

"Harlequins?" asked Kenver.

"Elderly ladies with a lively sense of decor."

"Or very poor eyesight."

Sarah laughed. "I suppose that could be. Or I've read that some people don't see colors properly. Perhaps it was that."

Kenver had no idea. He only knew that Tresigan did not feel homelike. Compared to Poldene, it was dreary. "This is not what I expected to provide for my wife," he said.

"If you really dislike the draperies, I can ask my parents for castoffs," Sarah began. She pressed her lips together. "Or perhaps not right away."

"You don't wish them to see your new home," Kenver said. "Your mother would be appalled."

Sarah didn't deny it. "I'll put things in better order first," she answered. "We have some fabrics from the Poldene attics."

"Old, faded hangings with outmoded patterns," Kenver said.

"Why should draperies go out of fashion? That's nonsensical. They are sound."

"You should have new things, fine things." The sort of surroundings he was accustomed to, Kenver thought. He'd never had to think about draperies or…any number of other things he suspected would become important at Tresigan.

"This is an adventure," said Sarah. "I have always longed for adventures."

She was indomitable. Kenver put an arm around her and drew her close. He was bending for a kiss when Merlin marched in with two portmanteaus and plopped them down with a thump. He did not stay, but Jowan and the carter came in right behind him with a trunk. Kenver stepped back.

"That's the last of it," said the driver. "I'll be off."

Taking the hint that he wished to be paid, Kenver walked out of the room with him.

———

"It's too bad London is so far," the Duchess of Tereford said as she and James were going down to dinner at Poldene that evening. "We could have equipped Tresigan five times over from the town house."

"That broken-down stuff?" The duke shook his head. His predecessor had been peculiar, hoarding household goods and leaving mountains of disintegrating furnishings behind.

"There were gems here and there," she replied.

"Literally. Uncle Percival was quite mad." He paused on the stair. "This meal is likely to be awkward."

Cecelia stopped beside him. "Yes."

"We've heard about the shouting." Their valet and lady's maid had made friends among the staff and kept them informed. "We are implicated in the Pendrennons' departure, as Tresigan is ours."

"Yes," she repeated.

He waited a moment before going on to see if she would say more. When she did not, he added, "We could leave now. The house is repaired and inhabited. And there is the Leicestershire problem."

Cecelia nodded. "Only..."

The duke raised an inquiring eyebrow.

"What do you think Lady Trestan will do? Say about Sarah?"

He examined her anxious face, then tucked her hand into the crook of his arm and proceeded down the stairs.

Their host and hostess looked grim as they all sat down at the dinner table. "Our son will not be joining us," said Lord Trestan.

"As you must know, since he has moved into your property," said his wife sourly.

Cecelia started to reply, but James forestalled her by saying, "Indeed."

He drew out the word, giving it an intonation that suggested Lady Trestan's remark was puzzling and possibly a bit offensive.

Only he could do so much with two syllables, Cecelia thought.

"I do not see why you allowed that," their hostess replied.

The duke raised one eyebrow. "Allowed?"

"I think you might have refused, since you must have known we wouldn't like it." She sounded petulant.

He let this remark sit in silence for a moment. Cecelia almost spoke, even though she knew nothing was going to convince the Pendrennons. But then she obeyed an instinct and waited.

"It is a common thing for young couples to set up their own households," James said.

"They had perfectly adequate quarters here," Lord Trestan snapped.

Did he really believe that, Cecelia wondered, when they had done all they could to make Sarah uncomfortable?

"Newlyweds often seem to prefer independence," said James.

"Well, we will make them sorry!"

The eyebrow came into play again. Not for the first time, Cecelia wished she could raise one brow in that intimidating way. "Sorry?" James repeated, as if the word bewildered him.

"I'll teach Kenver not to defy me!" Trestan let a fist fall on the table.

The countess looked approving. "We will tell everyone to cut them dead," she added.

James gazed at them until they moved uneasily in their chairs. "Cut them," he repeated. Once more, he made the words sound incomprehensible. "I don't understand."

"They will not be allowed to…"

"Do something that many, nay most, newly married couples do?" James interrupted.

"Against our express wishes!" declared Lady Trestan.

"Would you really expose your family to rumor and malicious gossip?" He frowned. "Over a perfectly usual occurrence?" He gazed at their hosts as if he found them bewildering. "Well, that will be a nine days' wonder and no mistake." His tone suggested they were idiots. And they clearly heard it. The earl bridled and scowled. His wife looked grim but also thoughtful.

Cecelia was surprised—not by James's conversational skills but by his willingness to intervene. He had taken the burden of their hosts' annoyance from her shoulders. He had made them reconsider their malice. And done it superbly.

He continued as dinner went on. She did her part in carrying the conversation, but he took the lead, periodically emphasizing his earlier points. The hints he dropped about how improper their outrage would look to society appeared to fall on fertile ground. By the end of the meal, the Pendrennons seemed to have dropped the idea of expressing it to all and sundry.

"Thank you," Cecelia said when they returned to their suite at the end of the evening. "That was masterful."

"That?"

"Your…handling of our hosts. I know you find my friends' problems even more tedious than estate business. But you were heroic tonight."

"You may have noticed that I have certain conversational skills."

"On numerous occasions. But you don't often bestir yourself."

"Bestir?" The duke smiled with raised eyebrows. "You make me sound like a bowl of rack punch."

"More like a god of worldly thunder," Cecelia said admiringly. "Threatening bolts of society's contempt."

He gazed at her with an expression she couldn't quite read. "I bestir myself, and always shall, for one person."

"Sarah?" asked Cecelia, puzzled.

"You, Cecelia."

She blinked. The tenderness in his deep-blue eyes made her pulse accelerate.

"You can count on that," he added. "Forever."

The last word sank in like a fish slowly descending in deep water. Since her mother's death, Cecelia had never had anyone she could absolutely count on. She realized that she found it difficult to believe in such a thing, even now.

"Do you doubt it?" he asked.

"No…I…" She couldn't find the right phrase.

His expression became wry. "Well, I shall prove it to you. While you work tirelessly on the Tereford properties, readying them to pass along to your children…"

"*Our* children."

"I certainly hope so," he joked. "I shall be just as diligent in *bestirring* myself. I'm certain you'll be convinced by the time we are sixty or so."

It was a jest, but with a slight sting. She put her arms around his neck. "I love you," she said.

"And I, you. With all my heart."

Thirteen

INFORMAL WAS A CHARITABLE TERM FOR DINNER AT Tresigan, Sarah decided. It did not convene until quite late, for one thing, after their meager household goods had been distributed from the carter's load. For another, the whole household sat down together at a dining table with no table linens and only four small candlesticks for light. They had bread and a ham. Sarah had chosen not to inquire about the several boxes of provisions that had undoubtedly been purloined from the Poldene kitchens, along with the crate that had certainly come from its wine cellar. She was certain that Kenver's mother knew nothing about these "donations" and wondered if vengeance would descend on their heads when the theft was discovered.

Looking around the group, some eating with their fingers due to a shortage of cutlery, Sarah found herself thinking "motley crew." Sturdy, blond Elys looked uneasy at the dining arrangement, perhaps worried about making a mistake before her new employers, whose kitchen she was to oversee. Siblings Gwen and Jowan seemed more at ease. Clearly, they shared a buoyant temperament as well as dark hair and eyes. Sarah suspected that sixteen-year-old Jowan saw this posting as a lark rather than an actual job. On the other side of the table, the wildly bearded Merlin was stuffing a whole slice of ham into his mouth. She'd invited him to the meal when she found him sullenly pulling radishes in the garden, unable to help herself.

With his free hand, Merlin reached for the loaf, his fingers encountering Kenver's on the same errand. Kenver frowned at him. Merlin ignored his disapproval and tore off a hunk. "Hardly ever get proper bread," he said thickly.

It was no wonder he was so thin, if he was living chiefly on vegetables, Sarah thought.

"Or earn money to pay the baker," said Kenver.

"Earn, is it?" Merlin replied. "That's what you do, eh?"

Kenver gritted his teeth. He found Merlin very irritating, Sarah knew.

"I can snare a rabbit," the hairy man added. "Can you?"

"I can," said Jowan. "Me and Dad used to…"

His voice broke off, probably because they'd been poaching, Sarah decided.

"I could go out and shoot a few birds…" Kenver began.

Sarah watched him realize that he had no way to do so. He was used to equipping himself from Poldene's sleek gunroom and walking its acres when he wanted small game. Now he had neither of these to hand. His expression suggested that he resented these lacks. Indeed, everything about the house seemed to annoy him. The idea killed her appetite.

She rose from the table, took one of the candlesticks, and went to wander through her new abode. Tresigan was not only much smaller than Poldene but also smaller than her family home. Compact, Sarah decided, refusing to be daunted.

The rooms were all arranged around the central court-yard, cleared of ivy now and looking rather bare. It must have been a garden once. Now it was tumbled earth and uneven stones. She walked along the rear of the ground floor, through the kitchen, past a pantry and a twisting staircase narrower than the front steps. A doorway led into a barely furnished parlor, the grandest room in the place. One set of the garish draperies had been hung from its windows. From there, one could pass through the entryway with its grander stair into a smaller room opposite, empty just now. Sarah had directed them to put her books here. Eventually she would have shelves, she hoped.

A closed door at the back led to the dining room. She did not return there. Instead, she went upstairs. Her footsteps echoed in the emptiness.

Four bedchambers marched around the courtyard open-ing on the upper floor—two larger at the front and a small pair in the rear. Their fireplaces lined up with the quartet below. There was an empty linen cupboard between the smaller rooms, beside the back staircase. One rather odd thing was the lack of communication between the front and rear of the house on this floor. The back stair gave access to the small bedrooms, the front stair to the larger ones. There was no passage through.

Sarah didn't go on to the attics. She already knew they were divided into six small rooms, only three of which had furnishings. Gwen Elys, and Jowan had made themselves at home in these. Looking down into the back garden, Sarah noted the privy, set well away from the vegetable planting and still adorned with a curtain of ivy, and a shed holding firewood. There seemed to be plenty of that, at least. Merlin must have been gathering it. No, more likely the duchess had procured a supply.

She went back to the largest bedchamber. The windows were black with the coming night, reflecting the light of her candle. Without the sun shining in, the place felt a bit forlorn. She set the candlestick on a trunk and pulled the wildly patterned draperies closed. The swirl of color actually seemed rather cheerful in these circumstances.

Sarah opened one of the portmanteaus. Her nightclothes were there, with her hairbrush and other necessities. She went to the other trunk and pulled out the bedsheets she had stolen from Poldene. Each member of their new household had been told to bring their own linens. She suspected that Elys had provided more than one set from the Poldene stores. She carried hers to the bed, a rather grand four-poster that had been stored in pieces in the cellar.

They had piled her luggage and Kenver's all together in this bedchamber. No one had asked for direction. They had simply assumed they would share the room.

Sarah's heart beat faster. They weren't precisely alone here at Tresigan, but at least they would face no disapproving glares. Well, except for Merlin's, but that wasn't personal. Any expectations, any rules, would be their own. She started to spread the linens over the bed.

"You don't need to do that," said Kenver's voice behind her. "I will call Gwen."

Sarah started and turned. "I want to." When he looked

uncertain, she added, "Small tasks help make a place one's own."

"I don't like to see you doing menial work."

"I don't consider the bed menial." Hearing her own words, Sarah blushed.

He stepped closer. "Shall I help you?"

Very conscious of his nearness, Sarah grew even warmer. "If you like."

He took hold of the other side of the sheet, and they pulled it over the feather mattress together. Sarah smoothed it. He mimicked her. It was a curiously intimate movement.

"You tuck in the corners like this." Sarah demonstrated a crisp fold.

He tried it, fumbled, then got it right. "That's clever."

"You've never done this before?"

"No, have you?"

Sarah nodded. "At school. We had to keep our rooms tidy."

"Ah."

He hadn't gone to school, Sarah remembered. He'd never lived anywhere but Poldene, where he'd been waited on hand and foot. And remained firmly under his mother's eye.

"It must have been grim if you had to make beds," he said.

"Oh no. It was the happiest time of my life." Meeting Kenver's gaze, Sarah realized that this had not been the most tactful thing to say. "Till now," she added. She turned back to the trunk and extracted two pillows.

"I forgot to pack any linens," Kenver said, his voice constrained. "In the...flurry of departure, I left them behind."

Flurry or fury, Sarah thought. It was no wonder

bedsheets had slipped his mind. "I didn't bring a coverlet," she answered, just noticing this. "I hope it won't be cold."

"Perhaps I could keep you warm," he said.

Sarah turned. He looked as if he was uncertain of her answer.

"Of course I know you may need time to…"

"So much time has been taken from us already," Sarah interrupted. She held out a hand.

He moved around the bed and took it.

It was odd to be shy when they had been married for weeks. She knew him better, but there was still much unresolved between them. She *was* longing for his touch. Sarah decided to throw caution to the winds. What was she thinking? She'd tossed any shred of caution to the tempest long since.

But he dropped her hand and moved away.

"Of course there is no lock on this door." Kenver tugged at one of the trunks, pulling it in front of the closed panels. "I've had enough interruptions. Far more than enough! It we don't stop him, we'll have Merlin coming up to inquire whether we have noticed the extraordinary size of his radishes."

Sarah choked on a laugh. "He promised he wouldn't intrude upstairs."

"I don't think he actually understands that concept. Nor Jowan either."

"We will have to teach him. Jowan, I mean. Merlin is…"

"Intractable. And I don't wish to talk about him right now." He straightened and came back to her, stopping so close it seemed she could feel the heat of his skin.

"What do you wish to talk about?" Sarah murmured.

"Nothing! That is, I don't wish to talk."

"What do you want to do?"

"Sarah."

She heard yearning in his voice. She could not be mistaken. She reached up and laced her arms around his neck. Their lips met in a searing kiss.

He pulled her tight against him as the kiss went on and on.

Desire blazed through Sarah, all the more urgent for having been thwarted so long. She arched up to meet him.

His hands roamed her body. She felt they ought to give off sparks, they were so enflaming.

No knock came, no nagging voice intervened to pull them apart. There was only the slight clumsiness of unfastening their clothes, and then they fell onto the sheets they had smoothed together.

"Scandalous things," Sarah murmured as her husband touched her more intimately than she'd ever been touched before.

"What?" he murmured.

She replied with a kiss, and then a moan of pleasure and surprise. They called it consummation, an errant part of her brain observed. Devoutly to be wished, Hamlet had said. But no, that was about something else entirely. And then, for perhaps the first time in Sarah's life, sensation drowned out every vestige of thought.

Kenver had learned ways to please a woman in London. He suspected that his uncle had arranged these encounters with willing older ladies for this purpose. And he was glad now that he could rouse Sarah and make her arch up for his touch and pant with desire. But he also found that this love-making was sweeter than any of those had ever been. The weeks of thwarted desire had driven him nearly mad. Yet the time had let them grow closer in other ways. He knew not only Sarah's luscious, rounded curves but so many endearing things about her. She was idolized by dogs. She had an endless store of arcane facts, many of which were fascinating. She was patient and courageous. As they—finally!—came together as man and wife, his tender feelings were as powerful as his release.

Kenver's body was hers to enjoy now, Sarah thought, as they nestled together in the aftermath of passion. She could do as she pleased. She could run her fingers down his chest so far and no farther, teasing and tantalizing. She could smooth back his dark hair. She could learn what he liked because he moaned with pleasure when she found it, which was gratifying and thrilling. It was lovely to discover this new power to enthrall. Surely now all would be well in their inadvertent marriage.

It was difficult to find a routine when each detail of life was a new challenge, Kenver thought. He'd never had to consider currycombs for his horses or shaving soap, for example, still less furniture polish and cleaning rags or utensils like mixing bowls. Householding seemed to encompass so very many small objects. Some appeared mysteriously a day or two after they had been mentioned. He suspected that Elys had a clandestine source at Poldene who sent them along, and he couldn't decide whether he was grateful or embarrassed about this. Others were more complicated, and a few seemed impossible, for now.

Some things could be settled, at least. Kenver and Sarah took their meals in the dining room. The three young servants ate in the kitchen, declaring they preferred this. Merlin hovered by the back door like a stray dog, quickly learning the best times to linger for a handout, which he was always given. Since he continued to tend the vegetable garden, from which they clearly benefited, it seemed mean to refuse him a share of their other supplies. But Kenver found his continuing presence uncomfortable.

Kenver curtailed his riding over the Poldene estate, not knowing what his father might have said about his move. But word spread, as it generally did in the country, and people from there began to come to Tresigan to speak with him, as they were accustomed to doing on his rounds. He soon set up a sort of auxiliary estate office in the small front room to receive them and deal with their requests and problems.

He made arrangements with people in the neighborhood who could supply firewood and farm products and staples. He pitched in on tasks that he'd never had to do before and admired Sarah's conviction that they were having an adventure even as he wished to give his wife more than this. She deserved an established, respected position in his family and their social circle. For all the discomfort, he had the compensation of his wife in his arms each night. At last. A joy she seemed to welcome as enthusiastically as he did. They explored the realms of physical passion together, and Kenver felt like the questing knight who had honorably won his fair maiden and was amply rewarded.

He also discovered a new delight—warm, intimate conversations in bed with Sarah tucked in the curve of his arm.

"Do you think you could take a milk cow from Poldene?" she asked him on a sultry night as September began.

"You wish me to become a cattle thief?" he asked, breathing in the flowery scent of her hair.

"But would it really be stealing? Don't heirs sometimes borrow against their future inheritances?"

"Are you speaking of post-obit bonds? A very dodgy practice, my dear Sarah. I would ask where you heard of them, but I know by now that you must have read it somewhere."

"In a novel," she replied, sounding a bit guilty.

"Aha."

"The villain was urging the hero to use them to forward his schemes."

"There you are."

"I am the villain, you mean?" Her tone was teasing.

"You know I did not." Kenver kissed the top of her head. "You could never be."

"I suppose it isn't a wise choice," she replied. "The villains' dark plots are always exposed in the end."

"In novels." Not always so neatly outside them, Kenver thought.

Sarah nodded against his shoulder. "The post-obit fellow threw himself off a cliff in the Arabian Sea and was devoured by sharks. They chewed him to pieces."

"You seem to relish the thought. I had no idea you were so bloodthirsty."

"Well, he had been extremely wicked. And it was Arabia."

"Does that make a difference?"

"It is a wild and violent place," she said.

"According to this novel? What was it called?"

"I–I don't remember." Sarah sighed. "Sometimes my brain feels like the ocean after a shipwreck. There are so many odd bits of flotsam floating about. They're often interesting but not always useful."

"I'm sure it is more organized than that," Kenver objected. "Your brain is overflowing with marvelous information."

"Some of it is," Sarah acknowledged. "And I *have* done systematic studies of a number of subjects."

"Of course you have."

"But so many other bits just bob up, not really attached to anything in particular. I tried the memory palace to put them in order, but it didn't work for me."

"What is the memory palace?"

She turned to look up at him. "You are not really interested in this."

"I am!" As Sarah eyed him, Kenver acknowledged that he was fascinated by *her* and thus ready to hear whatever she wished to say. The topic might not draw him, but the person always did.

"Well, it is a method for storing and retrieving memories," Sarah said. "You recall a familiar place, where you have actually been, one you know thoroughly. Then you move about it, in your mind, and put away things you want to remember.

In a drawer, say, or a cabinet. On a shelf. When you need that particular fact, you walk through your palace, find the right spot, and there it is."

"But I am continually forgetting where I have put things away in my actual home," Kenver said.

"And I kept getting distracted by other memories," Sarah agreed. "Things that had happened in that place that had nothing to do with what I was trying to store away. They made me recall other incidents until I'd embarked on a... memory journey. By the time it was done, I'd forgotten the one I came with."

Kenver laughed.

"Ridiculous, I know."

"Not in the least. You are never ridiculous. You are fascinating and adorable."

"You don't have to flatter me."

"I am only speaking the truth."

"But I'm not really pretty."

"What. Of course you are."

She rose on one elbow and looked down at him. "It's all right. I know I'm not a...a diamond of the first water."

"Who says so?"

"Everyone in London did. By implication if not outright. My friends Harriet and Ada are very pretty, you know. And I saw how different the season was for them."

Kenver felt a flash of anger. "I haven't met them and can have no opinion, but if they made you feel..."

"Not them!" Sarah interrupted. "Never them. But society..."

"Is narrow-minded and spiteful. We care nothing for society."

"No." She sounded doubtful.

Aware that she had reasons, he said, "The Terefords are coming for a visit tomorrow."

As he'd hoped, this made Sarah smile. "I'm looking forward to seeing Cecelia. They've been so occupied with troubles in Leicestershire."

"What happened there?"

"I haven't heard any details," Sarah said. "I do know that the previous duke left the estates in great disarray. The London town house was stuffed to the ceiling with decaying furnishings."

"How odd."

"He was, I believe." Sarah nestled closer, letting her fingers stray, and the deceased duke flew right out of Kenver's mind.

"I wanted to make certain you were comfortable," Cecelia said to Sarah the following morning. "If there is anything else you need…"

"You've done more than enough," Sarah interrupted. "We will make our own way from here."

The duchess examined her face. "You look happier, Sarah."

"I am. It has been…wonderful to be alone together here." She blushed as she saw that Cecelia understood her meaning. "But what about you? It must be uncomfortable at Poldene."

"Lady Trestan's approach is not to mention anything uncomfortable. And her lord follows her lead. But we have clearly not been forgiven."

"I'm sorry to be the cause."

"You know that you are not, Sarah. Lady Trestan creates her own difficulties. Indeed, I suspect she rather enjoys it."

"Enjoys friction?" Sarah couldn't imagine *wanting* to quarrel.

"Some people do."

If that was true, how would they ever reconcile, Sarah wondered. She had no idea, and she felt she had failed as a future countess. She and Kenver had found physical pleasure and great tenderness here, but would that be enough? Wouldn't Kenver begin to wish he'd married a grand young lady who could be accepted by his parents?

"It doesn't matter. We'll be leaving Poldene soon," Cecelia added.

"You have other urgent business."

"There is a problem in Leicestershire at an old hunting box." She shook her head. "I really cannot imagine Great-Uncle Percival atop a hunter."

"In his youth perhaps?"

"From all I can learn, his youth was much like his old age—eccentric in the extreme. The hunting box must be a relic of an earlier duke."

She said no more about the difficulties there, and Sarah didn't think it right to ask. She would miss Cecelia though.

Kenver and the duke returned from a survey of the Tresigan courtyard, and Sarah proudly served the refreshments that Elys had been rushing about to produce.

"Does that fellow Merlin always lurk out there by the cliff?" the duke asked, gazing out the window.

"He manages the garden," Kenver replied without enthusiasm.

"He's like one of those resident hermits," added Sarah. "The ones people hire to look picturesque."

"I wouldn't call him that," the duke replied.

"And isn't that usually done on large estates with a large number of visitors?" Cecelia asked.

Sarah nodded.

"I could still have him ejected," the duke offered.

"To the village?" Kenver asked "I suspect he would just come right back here."

"Like a mouse you catch and put out in the field," Sarah agreed.

Everyone looked at her.

"Is that how you treat mice?" The duke looked dubious but amused.

"My mother's cat would bring them to her before they were quite dead."

"And she didn't care to, er, make them so?"

"We thought they looked so pathetic, all mauled about," Sarah answered.

"And yet able to return."

"There was one who'd lost an ear. He came back three times."

Everyone looked at her again.

After a bit, the men went out to help Jowan ready the horses. The Terefords had ridden over rather than bring their carriage.

"We will be on our way in the next few days," the duchess said to Sarah. "I am worried what Lady Trestan will get up to if she's left without oversight."

"We must deal with that ourselves," Sarah replied. "We can't be always relying on you."

Cecelia nodded, acknowledging the truth of this.

"Kenver and I will face them together. We rely on each other now."

"Indeed."

The duchess seemed doubtful. Sarah wasn't ready to inquire too closely into why that might be. She was afraid she knew the answer—that Cecelia thought them inadequate.

Fourteen

DURING THEIR THIRD WEEK AT TRESIGAN, A POST CHAISE pulled up before the house late in the day. Sarah, sitting on the sofa in the large parlor surrounded by shoals of fabric, saw it through the front window. The vehicle was spattered with mud and looked as if it had traveled a good distance. She rose and went to the front door, opening it in time to see the traveler descend.

It was a woman of perhaps thirty-five in a neat but not particularly fashionable traveling dress. Her hair was black, her eyes hazel under straight dark brows. There was something familiar about her, Sarah thought, but she wasn't sure what it was. She didn't think they'd ever met.

The visitor strode toward her, looking Sarah up and down as if weighing her value. "Hello," she said. "I am Tamara Deane. Tamara Pendrennon that was."

"Kenver's sister?"

"That's right. Are you his new wife?"

The question was accompanied by a continuing examination, which probably found her wanting. Sarah nodded.

"Ah, how do you do? Your reply to my letter was so terse that I thought my parents might be holding you prisoner. So I came to see. But when I inquired about you, I discovered that you'd escaped."

"Is that what they said at Poldene?" Sarah tried to imagine the scene. There must have been a good deal of shouting.

The visitor threw back her head and laughed. It was a wholehearted laugh, loud and ringing and free. Sarah rather envied it. "The word is my own," Tamara said when it ended. "Benning told me you'd gone. The former head groom, you know. He's an old friend of mine."

"Yes. We spoke to him about you."

"So he said."

Sarah wondered what report the old man had given of them. She had no doubt there had been one.

"So this is where you've landed," the visitor added, surveying the house with a critical gaze.

Sarah recalled her manners. "Do come in, Mrs. Deane."

"Please call me Tamara. We are sisters now after all." The woman examined Sarah as if gauging the effect of this claim.

Sarah smiled to show she welcomed the idea. "And I am Sarah. Kenver rode into the village to see about…" She broke off her sentence. He'd gone to buy more chamber pots, but she hardly liked to say so. "We are still…putting things in order."

Tamara's smile was as beguiling as her laugh. "You must tell me all about it. But I should like to dismiss the post chaise first?"

Was she asking Sarah's permission? Did she intend to stay with them? "Of course," Sarah said.

Tamara turned to speak to the post boys. A portmanteau was removed from the back of the chaise and carried inside, payment was made, and the vehicle drove away.

Inside, Tamara looked about with an eagle eye.

Aware of the sparse furnishings and pile of drapery fabric, Sarah said, "We are not quite settled," to this first visitor in her first home. She didn't count the Terefords, who knew all about the place.

"How long have you lived here?" Tamara asked. She pulled off her bonnet and pelisse and hung them on the stair rail.

"Just three weeks." Sarah led her into the parlor. She cleared the fabric off the sofa—there was nowhere to put it except the floor—and offered her guest a seat.

"Didn't that blue brocade used to hang in the dining room at Poldene?" Tamara asked as she sat down.

As she didn't know, Sarah could only shrug. "It was put away in the attic."

"And my mother gave it to you?" The older woman sounded surprised.

"Not… We… That is… It is quite faded from the sun." Sarah showed the paler stripes on the cloth. "I don't think her ladyship would ever use it again."

"And so you stole it?" Tamara asked, her hazel eyes twinkling.

"We didn't exactly…" But they had, exactly. Unless one considered Kenver a part owner, or future owner, of everything at Poldene.

"Oh please, tell me that you did."

"Well, yes."

Tamara gave another of her ringing laughs. "Good for you! I ran off with only the clothes on my back and a few pieces of jewelry."

Sarah didn't know what to say to this.

"You've heard my sad story." Tamara seemed the antithesis of sadness.

"From Benning. Kenver couldn't really remember much."

"Well, he was only six when I left."

Her tone held no hint of reproach or suggestion that he was six no longer and might have contacted his sister, but Sarah felt moved to defend him anyway. "Your parents make a great fuss at any mention of your name. I believe they made Kenver feel…" She broke off, uncertain how to complete that sentence.

Tamara waved this aside. "I know their methods. Or Mama's, I should say. Our father does as he's told." She contemplated this sourly for a moment. "Well, I ran off to marry my despised suitor—a fine man who was kind to me and perfectly respectable, though not noble or wealthy enough for my parents. We were happy together, until he died two years ago."

"I'm sorry. We didn't know that."

"I saw no reason to inform people here." Tamara shrugged. "I knew my parents didn't care, and if they had pretended to… Or worse, congratulated me! Yes, I can imagine Mama doing that." She frowned. "Well, I am still angry at her, I suppose. I do tend to hold a grudge."

She admitted this as if it was the merest nothing. Once again, Sarah envied her brash confidence. "So you…you live in Lincolnshire?"

"Yes, I manage the Deane estate for my son, until he is of age."

"You have a son?" How could a family know so little

about one of its members, Sarah wondered. They ought to be aware of *this*, at least.

"Henry. He is ten." Tamara smiled fondly.

"Surely your parents would like to meet him," Sarah exclaimed.

"Do you think so?"

In fact, she didn't know. One expected people to welcome a grandchild. *Her* parents eagerly awaited one, or several. But Kenver's family was not like any Sarah had encountered before. "Well, *I* should like to," she replied.

Tamara smiled. "We must see that you do. He is visiting a school friend just now." She looked at Sarah more closely. "Is it true that Kenver carried you off like the young Lochinvar?" She grinned. "'So light to the croupe the fair lady he swung, So light to the saddle before her he sprung!'"

"There was nothing like that."

"I didn't think there could be. Kenver was rather a timid boy."

"He isn't timid!"

"No?"

"He is brave and honorable and kind."

Tamara's smile grew warmer. "I'm glad to hear it. I never had a chance to know him."

Sarah subsided, startled by the strength of her reaction. "What made you think of Lochinvar?"

"Oh, there are some wild stories circulating about your marriage, Sarah. That one came from a friend of mine in the neighborhood. Well, acquaintance now, I suppose, since we never see each other. But girlhood bonds can be lasting."

Thinking of her school friends, Sarah nodded.

"She is very romantical. And devoted to the works of Walter Scott. Thus, Lochinvar. I admit that curiosity overcame me. That and…"

Sarah waited, but her guest didn't finish the sentence. Instead her eyes narrowed at some inner calculation.

"So you were not swept off on horseback. I could not see how that would have happened." She made an airy gesture. "From where and why?" She leaned a little forward. "How did you come to marry into the Pendrennon family against my mother's wishes?"

"You know that she doesn't…"

"My mother made her views clear. As she does. Acquaintances of mine know friends of hers, and so the gossip travels. Yours must be a heroic tale, because I know the kind of opposition Mama can mount."

"Kenver and I…met at Tintagel," Sarah said.

"A legendary beginning!"

The story was not a secret. Many people knew the outline, and others were apparently embroidering shamelessly. Sarah told Kenver's sister about their night in the sea cave and the aftermath.

"That is nearly as thrilling as Lochinvar," Tamara said when she was done. "And has a happy ending as well. We never hear what happened to Lochinvar and his stolen bride. They might have ridden off a cliff and been killed."

"I prefer actual history."

"Do you?"

Immediately, Sarah worried that she'd sounded pedantic. Everything she had seen so far made her wish to be friends with Kenver's sister. She hoped she hadn't put her off. "Can I offer you…" Sarah remembered that they had used the last of the tea that morning. Kenver was also arranging for a delivery of provisions. But for now she had only well water. "Elys made a cake, but she ran out of sugar before it could be iced." Seeing Tamara's amused expression, Sarah realized that she'd said this out loud.

"Who is Elys?" her guest asked.

"Our cook. She worked in the kitchen at Poldene."

"Did you lure away servants as well? Oh, that must have infuriated my mother." Tamara seemed to relish the thought.

"Everything I do…" Sarah bit off this admission.

"Irritates her," Tamara finished. "I know how that is. Very well indeed! I am not hungry. I can wait for dinner."

So she did intend to stay. Sarah mentally calculated the supply of bedding.

"I can only spare a few days from home," Tamara said as if she'd read her expression.

"I'm very glad you came," Sarah assured her. "I hope we can make you comfortable."

"I feel quite at my ease already."

She seemed to be the sort of person who could be at home anywhere. Except at Poldene, of course.

The door to the kitchen creaked, reminding Sarah yet again that the hinges needed oiling. "Sarah," called Kenver.

She stood. He would have left his horse in the barn and walked up, so they hadn't heard him return.

Kenver stepped into sight holding up a chamber pot. "I found one. They are not readily available in the village." He stopped as he noticed the visitor, automatically putting the china receptacle behind his back.

"Your sister has come to see us," Sarah said.

"Tamara?"

She had also risen, and the two siblings faced each other. The resemblance was clear now that they were together. No wonder Sarah had thought Tamara looked familiar.

He set the chamber pot on the floor and came forward. "Tamara," he repeated. He stopped before her.

His sister stepped up and gave him a hug.

Kenver stiffened in surprise. Spontaneous hugs were not a feature of the Pendrennon family, and for a moment, he didn't know what to do. Then he put an arm around her.

Tamara pulled back and looked him up and down. "You've grown into a handsome man. You look a bit like our uncle Ruthven."

"I do?"

"Around the eyes I would say. Not so much in the jaw. And he is much taller, of course."

Their mother's brother was quite tall and very thin. He'd joked that he was a regular beanpole, Kenver remembered, during his stay in London.

"It is astonishing that he can eat so much and still be scrawny," Tamara added. Her smile showed that the last word was a joke.

"You have visited him?" This was another surprise.

"Yes. He doesn't always agree with Mama, you know."

He hadn't known. Apparently, there was a good deal going on in his family that he knew nothing about. Why had he never wondered or inquired? Why hadn't he become better acquainted with his uncle and learned this? Gazing at Tamara's face, Kenver found an image surfacing. "You used to have a dark-green riding habit."

"Fancy you remembering that."

"With a feather in the hat."

"Yes, I thought myself quite the fashion plate."

"And a neck-or-nothing rider," Kenver added.

His sister laughed. "In my wild youth. I am a staid and settled matron now."

"You have a nephew, Kenver," said Sarah.

He looked at his wife, then at his sister.

"My son, Henry," was her fond reply. "He is ten years old."

Kenver was assailed by a wave of shame and regret. Ten and he hadn't even known the boy existed! He'd sent no birthday or Christmas gifts. He'd offered no uncle-ish advice or support. Encountering his smiling sister's gaze, Kenver realized that his sympathy was misplaced. Henry probably had a jolly life, filled with unexpected hugs and laughter. The lonely, forlorn boy he was imagining was…himself. This felt like a body blow.

"I'm sorry I ran off and left you with our parents," said Tamara, as if she could read his thoughts. "It really seemed the only choice. And I am *not* sorry I married Donald."

"I should have written you when I was older," he managed. "I didn't know exactly where…" But that was a poor excuse. He could have found her address if he had really tried. And he had not.

"Well, I'm sure they gave you a tale that made me a villain."

He shook his head. "They would not have you spoken of at all. The slightest mention brought a tirade."

"Ah." Tamara nodded.

"But I shouldn't have gone along. I don't know why I did." Except that he hated brangling. A poor excuse.

"Because our mother can twist any set of facts to put you in the wrong. It took me years to understand that."

Kenver looked at her.

Tamara made a throwaway gesture. "If you come to Mama with some complaint or request that she doesn't wish to hear, what does she do? She throws it back at you in an outrageous form. As if you'd demanded the moon and stars instead of some perfectly reasonable thing. Thrown back on your heels, you rush to deny any such overweening ambition. Which shifts the conversation onto her ground—you defending, she accusing. Until the original topic is lost in a tangle of denials."

Kenver saw that Sarah was nodding.

"And if that doesn't put you off, she begins to moan," Tamara continued. "She wonders how a child of hers could be so cruel and ungrateful. Papa can chime in then with his reproaches and bluster. They are experts at it. Probably even worse after all these years." She cocked her head as if asking Kenver whether this was true.

Her description sent his thoughts bouncing back through the past to light on exchanges that demonstrated her point.

"I was so glad to escape them," Tamara continued. She stretched her arms as if reveling in the freedom. "But, Kenver, I don't think you should have allowed them to drive *you* out."

She looked around the room, and Kenver felt a flush of humiliation. This bare house was so different from Poldene.

"You are the heir," Tamara added. "It is your right to be there."

Of course he should be at Poldene. The estate would be his responsibility someday. And he loved it. "Things are not so simple," he replied. He didn't look at Sarah.

"They didn't want me there," Sarah said. Of course she had caught his tone.

"Ah." Tamara nodded. "And they made your life a misery. Did Mama set Cranston on you?"

"How did you…"

"Oh, she was my jailer, long ago." Tamara smiled with narrowed eyes. "Not a very imaginative one, however."

Sarah said nothing. Kenver was equally at a loss. What did one say to such forthright remarks? How deplorable? How fortunate?

"Well, let us be done with the past," his sister added. "And make a new beginning."

"I should like that," replied Kenver. Here, at least, he had no doubts.

Sarah took Tamara upstairs to get her settled in one of the spare bedchambers. Kenver went outside to walk. He strode down the overgrown lane to the road and then along it. This little-traveled thoroughfare ran through rough countryside, snaking along the bottom of the cliff, crossed by tendrils of encroaching ivy. The landscape reminded Kenver how much he missed the lush Poldene gardens, Fingal's steady companionship, and the sea. He belonged there.

And he belonged with Sarah, who had been miserable in his home. He needed a solution to that dilemma. More than merely running away. An inner voice suggested that his sister had done the same. But as she had…accused, he had responsibilities to Poldene that she did not.

Feeling frustrated, Kenver turned back.

At Tresigan, he found Merlin standing at the front of the house, mouth open as if dumbstruck. This was unlike him. The man was staring through the parlor window where Sarah and Tamara again sat. He turned when Kenver came up, even more wild-eyed than usual. "Who is that woman?" he demanded.

Kenver wondered how his sister would receive their resident oddity. From what he had seen of her so far, he imagined she would be amused.

"That's Tamara Pendrennon," Merlin said accusingly.

His impassioned tone was as surprising as the recognition.

"Or Tamara something else," he added glumly. "She's married."

"A widow now. But how do you know…"

"Widow?" The word cracked out like a whiplash.

Kenver blinked at the flare of emotion in Merlin's eyes.

"May I borrow your razor?" the man asked.

"What?" He was somewhat accustomed to Merlin's manner, but this was quite a non sequitur.

"A razor, man. I need a razor. I threw mine in the river."

He had what? "I'm not lending you my razor," Kenver replied.

Merlin grasped his bushy beard and tugged on it as if he

would pull it off. "I can't use a knife. I'd sharpen the razor for you after."

"After what?"

"Can I have some scissors at least?"

"What is the matter with you?" Kenver asked. He did not add, beyond the usual profound eccentricity.

Merlin grimaced, turned, and rushed away. Kenver watched him go, wondering if the man had gone even madder.

———

Sarah told herself that they'd coped with an unexpected visitor well enough as they sat down to dinner that evening. Elys had produced a creditable meal, and Jowan served with cheerful…informality. Or insouciance? He was more resident jester than footman. Sarah wondered what Tamara thought of their makeshift arrangements. Kenver seemed more critical of them now that they had a guest. He frowned at Jowan's antics more than once.

He and his sister began discussing mutual acquaintances in the neighborhood. Kenver described their current situations, then Tamara provided acerbic commentary on their history. Some of these made Kenver's jaw drop. Several drew a giggle from Sarah. Mostly, though, she just enjoyed watching them establish a connection.

All was going smoothly until, near the end of the meal, the door to the kitchen banged open and a man erupted into the dining room.

The stranger was somewhat above medium height and very thin, his face craggy and narrow under cropped black hair. He had on a worn cutaway coat, a knotted kerchief rather than a neckcloth, riding breeches, and scuffed top boots. "Tamara," he declared, his green eyes blazing.

It was Merlin, Sarah realized with astonishment, recognizing his voice. His long, tangled black hair had been roughly cut, and the bushy beard was gone. Even his beetling eyebrows had been trimmed. He looked younger than Sarah had estimated without all the hair, perhaps no more than midthirties.

"Yes?" said Kenver's sister. She frowned at the newcomer as if wondering who he might be.

"Have you forgotten me?" Merlin's voice trembled with some strong emotion.

"I'm sorry but I don't…"

"How could you?" He grasped his remaining hair and tugged at it.

"This is Merlin," said Sarah. "He lives in a cave behind the house."

"*This* is why you wanted my razor?" asked Kenver at the same time.

Tamara turned to stare at him and then at Sarah. "Is this some sort of prank? I am as happy to be amused as anyone, but I don't see…"

"Oliver Welden!" shouted Merlin. "The boy, man, you abandoned for some mincing coxcomb you met in London."

Tamara laughed. "I can't imagine anyone who was *less* a coxcomb than my Donald."

"You call him yours," Merlin accused.

"Of course I do. He was my husband for eleven years. And I…" Her voice wavered. "I miss him very much."

Merlin—or Oliver, apparently—moaned.

"Oliver Welden," Tamara repeated. She gazed at the transformed Merlin with a slight frown. "Welden. Oh, are you… were you the tutor at Tess Tremarthen's house?"

"You know I was," he declared fierily.

Tamara nodded. "I do remember you now." She examined him. "I hardly dare ask how you are."

"Heartbroken!" he shouted, tossing his arms.

Kenver's sister gave Sarah a sidelong glance. "Did you say he was living in a cave?" she murmured. "Is he perhaps a bit…" She gestured at her temple.

"We went riding together," the man interrupted. "We picnicked. You can't have forgotten. You kissed me!"

Sarah noticed that Merlin's rustic accent had completely disappeared and that Kenver looked shocked at this revelation.

Merlin walked over to the window and pointed outside with a stabbing gesture. "Right over there! You wanted to see the haunted house, and I brought you. I showed you the cave. You said it was deliciously mysterious. And you kissed me!"

Tamara shrugged apologetically. "I did that sort of thing, back then."

Their visitor gaped at her. "Sort of thing. Sort of thing!"

"Here and there, to annoy my mother, you know."

"Here and there," he echoed, as if he couldn't believe she'd used that phrase. "That implies…others?"

"It was a game," she added. "I meant nothing by it."

"Nothing," he repeated. "Nothing!" The fire drained out of him. He looked as if someone had landed a heavy blow that left him dazed. "You led me to believe...to hope." His eyes grew tragic. His shoulders slumped, and his arms hung at his sides.

"Are you saying I trifled with your affections?" Tamara pressed her lips together as if hiding a smile.

"Is this a joke to you?" Merlin/Oliver shouted, so loudly that Sarah winced. "Are you so cruel?"

Tamara held up a defensive hand. "I had no idea that you..." She let her hand fall and sat straighter. "I did not encourage you to think that I was in love with you."

"You played fast and loose with my heart," he replied.

Kenver's sister laughed. "That sounds so odd coming from a man. How many women have said as much?"

"And this is your answer to me? This?"

She stopped smiling. "I was taught that men would steal kisses, and more if they could, whenever an opportunity arose. Mama always said that these...attentions were empty and meaningless. A snare for foolish girls and an invitation to ruin. So I didn't imagine that you actually cared."

Their visitor mumbled something grim.

"Mama," repeated Tamara in a different tone. "I might have considered the source."

Merlin covered his face with his hands.

"I see that it was wrong of me to kiss you," Tamara continued. "I am sorry."

He let his hands drop and stared at her.

"Would you like to sit down?" Sarah asked him. "Are you hungry?"

This earned her nearly identical appalled glances from Kenver and his sister, but Sarah couldn't help pitying the man. And half their meal had come from his garden.

"Elys roasted a chicken," Merlin replied.

Trust him to know that. "Yes, she did." Sarah signaled to Jowan, who had stuck his head around the door at the first sign of shouting and listened to every word. The boy disappeared, returning a few minutes later with a loaded plate. Merlin/Oliver began shoveling in food with his usual concentrated intensity.

"Why in the world are you calling yourself Merlin?" Tamara asked him after a while.

"Like Merlin, I retreated into the wilderness and lost myself." He made a grand gesture at their surroundings, a little diminished by a forkful of potato.

"You call this a wilderness?"

"It was until *they* came and made it all…"

"Comfortable," suggested Sarah.

"I did not want to be comfortable! I had nothing to live for." He bit into a chicken leg and pulled off the meat with his teeth.

"Are you telling me you've been living in a cave for eleven years?" Tamara looked astonished.

"He broke into the house and lived here," Kenver put in.

Merlin/Oliver finished the leg and set down the bone, gazing at it on his plate. After a bit, he shook his head. "I took two other tutoring positions after the Tremarthen lads went off to school. And then I was a schoolmaster for a while." He shuddered. "That was wretched."

Sarah noted his accent grew more and more educated as he spoke about this work.

"I quit that and came back to this neighborhood where I had been happy." He shot Tamara a tragic look.

"So how long have you actually been at Tresigan?" Kenver asked.

"Two years?" His hands moved aimlessly. "I lost track."

The rest of them sat at the table as if they were not sure what to say next. Sarah felt as if she'd stumbled into a play, like those her friend Tom acted in London.

"Well, you know, Mr. Welden," Tamara began finally. "We should call you Mr. Welden now, should we not?"

"Or Oliver perhaps, since we are part of the same household," Sarah suggested, only slightly mischievously.

"No," said Kenver and Merlin at the same time, then looked at each other in unhappy surprise.

"No to Mr. Welden or..."

"I am Merlin," he declared, his face set in stubborn lines.

"Very well, Merlin," replied Tamara. "If you have really been pining after me all this time—"

"Do you call me a liar?"

"No. But I would appreciate it if you allow me to complete a sentence."

They exchanged a long, challenging look.

"You created a tale in your mind—" Tamara went on.

"A farce," said Kenver.

His sister glared at him. "Will *everyone* stop interrupting me!"

Kenver held up placating hands.

Tamara turned back to Merlin. "You must let go of that story," she continued. "It is not true. And not good for you. You should go on with your life."

"I have no life."

"Because you are making no effort…"

"And it is not for you to say what I must do." He pushed back his chair and rose. "You have said you care nothing for me. Thus, you *are* nothing to me." He strode out, slamming the door as he had when he entered.

There was a brief silence, then Tamara made a wry face. "I admit that I was sometimes a careless, self-centered girl. Nonetheless, I never said I loved him or planned to have a future with him. I do not think this is my fault."

Sarah nodded. "I think, as disappointments piled up, the tale grew in his mind as a substitute."

"I can see that, but it is not healthy."

"It's a pathetic delusion," said Kenver. "He needs to face the truth."

"That is a good thing to do," replied Tamara. "If we can see it."

"And be sure we know the whole," said Sarah.

"Always the difficulty." The two women exchanged a nod.

"Difficulty?" Kenver frowned. "It all seems quite clear to me. And a perfect opportunity for 'Merlin' to depart. I shall tell him so." He rose and followed the other man out, not noticing Sarah's upraised hand. When she turned back, she found his sister looking at her.

"I think Kenver sees things in black and white," said Tamara.

"He wants to live by the principles of honor, like a knight of old."

"I remember he had a picture book about King Arthur. He used to pore over it when he was small."

Sarah could easily imagine the little boy entranced by tales of chivalry.

"With the least bit of encouragement, he would tell the stories," Tamara continued. "If I remember correctly, it seemed that any maiden—well, noble maiden, I suppose—could appear at King Arthur's court and claim she was being oppressed. And a knight would jump up and take on the 'quest.' Which meant, I believe, that he agreed to go kill somebody at her direction. Nobody asked about the other side of the story, at least as far as I can recall."

"And then the maiden turns out to be a sorceress who has lured the knight into deadly peril in order to get revenge on Arthur for some old grievance," Sarah replied.

"Does she?"

"Well, not always. But once might have been enough."

"For them to ask more questions the next time," Tamara said.

"Yes."

"I think those knights didn't really have enough to do. All those years of training in how to kill things and so few to actually kill." Tamara made a mock sad face.

Sarah burst out laughing. "They were created to protect the realm from invaders. The Saxons and Danes and, um, Angles and Jutes."

"Jutes? Isn't that a kind of cloth?"

"Yes, but also an old Germanic tribe. That's odd, isn't it?"

Tamara smiled at her. "Perhaps they were weavers."

"I don't think... Oh, a joke."

"You're fond of strange facts."

Sarah ducked her head. "I read too much."

"I would hope you read exactly as much as you wish to," Kenver's sister responded.

She could be a real friend if only they had the chance, Sarah thought, wishing she lived closer. She said as much that night, lying in bed, entwined in Kenver's arms.

"We can visit her and have her come to Poldene," he replied.

"Henry too," she said.

"Henry?"

"Her son. Your nephew."

"Oh, of course. Henry as well."

"I suppose he'll be a grown man by then," Sarah said.

Kenver gazed down at her.

"It will be...some time before we could invite them," she added.

She meant they couldn't do so until his parents were gone, Kenver realized with a jolt. But that was...impossible. Papa and Mama would live years, decades. As they should. He didn't wish them dead! But he...they couldn't stay in this house, and away from Poldene, for all that time. This was temporary, until he found his way. Made a plan. As he had not. He turned away from her to wait for sleep. Which took its time in coming.

Fifteen

THE TEREFORDS CAME BY THE FOLLOWING MORNING TO
say farewell, driving out of their way to stop at Tresigan.
Kenver suspected that the duchess was curious about
Tamara as well. They spent a pleasant half hour together, and
he was happy to see his sister at ease in this exalted company.
When they rose to go, Sarah was clearly wistful. She and the
duchess stood together at the front door for some private
conversation while the duke went out to summon the traveling carriage.

Kenver was surprised to see Merlin emerge from the cave
and accost Tereford on his way to the barn. They conferred
for a few minutes. Finally the duke nodded. And when the
traveling carriage pulled away a little while later, Merlin was
sitting up beside the coachman on the box.

"Our resident eccentric wanted to get away," the duke
told his wife as they drove off. "There was some awkward-
ness with Mrs. Deane. He did not go into detail."

"Is that why he cut his hair?"

"I don't know. He didn't give his reasons."

"Bringing him along was well done," said Cecelia. "Two
birds with one stone and so on."

"I have no idea what I'm going to do with him."

"If you like, I can—"

"But I think I should make a push to figure it out," the duke interrupted.

Cecelia examined her handsome husband. She'd been conscious of tensions. "Because I have taken over too much?" she asked.

He looked at her.

"Yes, I have noticed that you've chafed under my... regime." She smiled to show this word was a joke.

"Not chafed," he said. "Not at all. I just found that I wished to...take a hand."

Cecelia offered him hers. He took it, and they exchanged an affectionate squeeze.

"You don't mind?" the duke asked.

"Well, I don't suppose you are planning to take over everything."

"Good God, no!" He blanched. "Unless you wish..."

"I do not. I enjoy estate work. You know that."

"Yes. It has been a boon and a joy to watch."

"Until just recently, when I became overbearing." Cecelia raised questioning brows, showing both amusement and concern.

"Never that." He squeezed her hand again.

"I hope not. I do treasure the way you allow me to be myself."

"I don't think I had any choice in that matter," he answered with a smile.

"Of course you did, and do. You might object and hamper and forbid me into misery."

"Why would I do anything so foolish?"

"To revel in your power. To 'prove' that you were right."

Their eyes met, and each knew they were thinking of the duke's tyrannical father.

"And so I never would," he said.

She nodded, her expression tender. "That is one of the many reasons I love you. To draw out another's deep self is the real gift of marriage."

"Do you say I did that? I have no idea how. No, you did it all for yourself."

Cecelia shook her head. "You made way for me. That is ideal in a husband."

Tereford seemed greatly moved. "I think, rather, that your virtues must have, er, rubbed off on me."

"So you think if we rub together enough, we will achieve a perfect balance?" she replied archly.

He laughed. "There's a capital idea." He pulled her close and kissed her. She responded with enthusiasm, and several miles passed in mutual delight. "It seems love is a complicated thing," he said. "I don't feel I will ever exhaust its nuances."

"Thankfully," his wife replied with obvious satisfaction.

They rode in silent contentment for a time, then Cecelia said, "I hope Sarah will be all right."

"They will have to find their own way of rubbing together."

"When did you become so wise?" she teased.

He gestured gallantly in her direction. "Once again, by example."

She smiled at him. "Meanwhile, there is this Leicestershire problem."

"That is worrisome. If our information is correct. I hardly think it can be."

"It was an outlandish tale."

"And a dubious source."

"You're certain you never heard of this cousin?"

"Nothing. I've listed all the relatives I can recall."

"Well, we will manage it together." She smiled at him.

"And stay long enough to get in some hunting perhaps," the duke added hopefully.

"Certainly." Cecelia looked up toward the coachman's seat. "I wonder if Merlin hunts."

A small groan escaped the duke.

━━━━━━

"I must return home soon," Tamara said at the breakfast table the following morning, as if the Terefords' farewells had inspired her. "It's several days' journey. Henry will be back from his friend's house in two weeks, and the harvest is a busy time on the land."

"I am so glad you came to see us," Sarah replied.

"Yes," said Kenver.

Tapping her fingernails on the tabletop in a staccato rhythm, Tamara gave a distracted nod. "Our parents must have heard that I am here," she said to him.

This was likely. Elys was in regular touch with the staff at Poldene, and she would have passed along such juicy news.

One of the upper servants would have thought it their duty to inform Lady Trestan.

Tamara slapped the board, making Sarah jump. "They are ignoring my presence," Kenver's sister said. "As they have ignored my existence these last ten years. It is outrageous."

There could be no argument about that, Kenver thought, with his usual brush of guilt at having done nothing himself.

Closing her hand into a fist, Tamara bared her teeth. "I shall go and see them. And tell them exactly what I think of their behavior."

That would be an epic brangle. "I doubt you'll change anything," said Kenver.

"I'm sure I won't. But I will have the satisfaction of stating my opinion once and for all." She looked at him, and a speculative gleam appeared her hazel eyes. "You should come with me."

Kenver sat back in his chair.

"We will present a united front," said his sister, nodding. "If *all* of their offspring disapprove, they must see that they are...misguided."

"I don't think they..."

"And while I am here, I should set things right for you." Her smile was almost feral. "Yes. That would be even better."

"I'll take care of that myself," Kenver replied, not liking the direction this conversation was taking.

"You should not be relegated to this." Tamara gestured at the room. "You have a rightful place at Poldene. You must reclaim it."

Something in her expression reminded Kenver of his mother.

"We are happy here," said Sarah.

"Playing house." Tamara brushed this aside.

Her tone was very like Mama's dismissive inattention, Kenver thought. The resemblance between the two seemed stronger in that moment, and he remembered how similar they looked in the portrait in Poldene's gallery.

"No proper staff," Tamara muttered. "The barest minimum of everything."

"You can leave this to me," he said more strongly.

"We will shame them into increasing your allowance," Tamara continued with rising enthusiasm. And still not listening. "Or the whole neighborhood will hear of Papa's cheese-paring ways."

"It is already aware," answered Kenver. "I don't think this is a good notion, Tamara."

She frowned at him. "But if no one objects, they will go on as they have been. Hidebound and tyrannical." She turned. "You must see that I'm right, Sarah."

Both of them gazed at her, awaiting support for their positions. Kenver could see that Sarah did not like being put between them. But if it came down to it, she would side with him. He knew this absolutely. "You have said that you tend to hold grudges," she said to Tamara. "Perhaps instead of giving vent to your…"

The moment she saw that Sarah would not support her arguments, Tamara waved this aside. She leaned forward and pointed at Kenver. "You cannot wish to stay here as time passes. Sarah deserves better."

This was a low blow. Kenver decided that Tamara had

learned a good deal from their mother during their eighteen years together. He searched for words to shift the argument.

"I am perfectly content," Sarah put in.

"Because you are a sweet, modest person," Tamara replied. "That doesn't mean it is right." She raised her eyebrows. "And I'm not certain it is even true."

"I am."

"What about the smoking chimneys?"

"That was just once. We will have it seen to."

Tamara shook her head. "No, Kenver must fight for you. It is a matter of honor."

"That isn't fair," said Sarah.

Her cry struck Kenver as nothing else had done. Perhaps he should accept an ally when it was offered. "Very well," he said. "I will go."

"Splendid!" His sister looked magnanimous in victory. She turned. "And Sarah…"

"Is *not* coming along with us," said Kenver.

Relief, and a twinge of guilt, ran through Sarah. She did not want to go. The thought of the scene at Poldene, which she could imagine all too well, made her shudder. She told herself she would have volunteered if she could have helped. But she was certain her presence would only make things worse. And the clash of Tamara and Lady Trestan promised to be acrimonious enough as it was.

"Let us go then," said Tamara, rising.

"Now?" Kenver had expected some time to prepare.

"No time like the present," his sister replied, jolly now that she had prevailed.

Kenver looked at Sarah and then away. "May as well get it over with," he muttered. He stood. "I'll help Jowan saddle the horses," he added, walking out.

"This will be grand," said Tamara, not quite rubbing her hands together. "I have waited far too long to do it."

She was practically gleeful, and Sarah didn't see how she could be, knowing the fight that was to come. Then she realized that Tamara believed she would gain satisfaction at Poldene. She could almost see the idea building in the older woman's mind. She'd begun to expect vindication. "They may not listen to you," she began.

"Don't worry. I know what I'm doing." Tamara put up a hand. "I ought to have taken better care of Kenver years ago."

"He's not a child anymore."

"Then he can take care of me," the other woman replied gaily. "And we are off to the fray. I must change." Smiling, she strode out.

Kenver brought their two riding horses up from the barn. He'd expected to wait a while, but his sister was already outside in her riding habit and ready to go. As he helped her onto Sarah's mount, she said, "Leave the talking to me."

He doubted he would have any other choice. As they rode through the lanes that led home, Kenver felt a mounting uneasiness. It would be the shouting matches of his youth all over again. How was he to make them listen to him?

They rode directly to the Poldene stables, handing the horses over to a surprised groom. At the door, Tamara pushed in without knocking, saying, "This is your home. Why would you?" Her riding crop twitched as if she wanted to strike something, or someone. One of the footmen, who had come when he heard the door open, jumped back to avoid it.

"Mama still uses the same parlor, I suppose?"

"Yes," said Kenver.

"Good. We will ambush her there."

The choice of words was not reassuring. Kenver felt that he was walking at the side of a force of nature. The trouble was, they were approaching another of equal or greater weight. What was the saying from that old Greek tale? Between Scylla and Charybdis, that was it. There'd been an illustration in the book, full of writhing tentacles and teeth. Sarah would like it.

The footman did not follow them, and so they barged into his mother's private parlor unannounced.

She was sitting at her writing desk, a pile of papers before her, and looked more annoyed than surprised at the interruption.

Tamara folded her arms, raised her chin, and said, "Hello, Mama." Her voice held a trace of triumph, possibly at the successful invasion.

Their mother said nothing. She simply stared at them, face impassive, eyes cold. She could draw out a silence until one couldn't bear it any longer.

Tamara held Mama's gaze and very slowly began to smile, as if she found her amusing.

They were like spark and tinder, Kenver decided. Any minute, there would be flames, and no evading them. He looked from one to the other. The resemblance was more marked now that they were in the same room.

Mama actually spoke first. "What are you doing here?"

"I was on a visit to Kenver, and I thought I should see my dear family," Tamara replied with falsely sweet sarcasm.

"So you've suborned Kenver, have you?"

"Suborned?" Tamara repeated mockingly. "Is someone on trial here?"

"You were always an insolent child."

"And you were always a dreadful parent."

"What would you know about it?"

Kenver blurted out, "You have a grandson, Mama."

Tamara made a slashing gesture, and he realized that she'd been saving that information as a concealed weapon. Now they were both looking at him with very similar, angry faces. He took an involuntary step back.

"You've come to beg money for the boy then?" his mother said to Tamara. "Has your weakling 'husband' come a cropper?"

He could see the fury wash over his sister. She flushed bright red. Her hands closed into fists. Her eyes glittered with rage. "I've *come* to tell you what I think of you."

Their mother shrugged. "I care nothing for your opinion."

She sounded sincere. And Kenver could see that this affected Tamara.

"It is a mistake for you to take her side, Kenver," their mother added.

"Her side in what?"

"Tamara's efforts to extort money for the product of a match we never approved."

"I don't need your money!" Tamara shouted. "I didn't ask for it. I don't want anything from you!"

But she had, Kenver noted. She'd wanted an apology or at least an admission of wrongdoing. Perhaps some vestige of affection. She was not going to get any of those things.

"Then I do not see why you are here," Mama replied without emotion.

Except for a flicker of triumph in her eyes, Kenver thought, as if she'd won a point by making Tamara lose her temper. He understood then that Mama enjoyed winning more than anything else. Anything. He moved to take Tamara's arm. "We should go," he murmured. It was a measure of his sister's defeat that she allowed him to lead her away.

"You would be advised to remember what I said to you, Kenver," their mother threw after them. "Taking her side against us is unwise."

No reply was better than anything he could think of to say.

His sister was silent until they were mounted and riding back toward Tresigan. "I'm going home," she declared. "Today if I can." She turned to gaze at him. "You understand that I have been very happy in Lincolnshire these eleven years."

"Yes," he said.

"My son does not need anything from Poldene. I shan't be 'begging' for any share of the estate." She scowled at the very idea. "Not from...*them*." She gestured back toward the house. "Nor from you later on."

Kenver thought she was owed something. The daughter of an earl should have received a substantial dowry. But he said nothing. He couldn't do anything about it now. In future, they would see.

"I pity you, that you *have* to deal with them as the heir."

He had nothing to say to that.

"But you know, you have a solid position. The title and estate come to you by law." Tamara made a face. "Papa gave that as a reason that I must marry wealth. He said his hands were tied."

"That doesn't mean much right now."

"You should speak to Figgs, find out things."

Kenver wondered if his father's solicitor would speak to him. He would probably consult Papa first, and that would cause another row.

"You can't fight them without information," Tamara added.

Was he to battle his own family? All his life, he'd wanted to fight for righteous causes and bring justice. He'd dreamed of triumphs on the field of honor. This didn't feel like that.

Tamara left for home the day after this abortive attempt. Sarah was sad to see her go, because it seemed it would be a long time before they met again. Tamara had vowed never to set foot in Cornwall as long as her parents dwelt there.

Kenver was silent on this subject. He'd said very little about the visit to Poldene, leaving the description to his sister, but clearly it had not heartened him.

Sixteen

THE DAY AFTER TAMARA'S DEPARTURE, A GROOM ARRIVED carrying a note from Poldene. Kenver's mother informed them that his father was quite unwell and wished to see his son. She added that the state suite "repairs" were now complete, and the rooms stood ready for them to occupy.

"She doesn't even mention the Terefords' stay in the suite," Sarah said to Kenver. "She makes it sound as if we moved out so that these repairs could be done." Sarah found the timing of the missive unsettling. It seemed to her that Lady Trestan was aware of what was happening at Tresigan and had waited for Tamara's departure to write.

Kenver was looking down at the crested page, his thoughts clearly elsewhere. "I wondered that Papa did not join us. I thought the servants would have told him that Tamara had come. I supposed he was out, but it seems he was ailing even then."

"Wouldn't your mama have said something?" If the illness was so serious, that would have been natural.

"She was rather occupied with raking Tamara over the coals."

"Yes."

He looked up at her tone. "What are you thinking, Sarah?"

. "It's just odd. Practically the moment Tamara is gone, we receive this news."

"And you doubt it?"

Sarah thought that the earl's illness might be feigned, because Lady Trestan wanted them back under her thumb after the scene with Tamara. But Sarah couldn't know this for certain, of course. "You must go and see him." Surely Kenver would be able to tell whether the malady was real.

"I suppose I must." Kenver folded the note. He looked reluctant.

He'd been subdued since the visit, and Sarah didn't blame him. She thought it might have opened old wounds.

"No, of course I must," he went on before she spoke.

"Give him my hearty good wishes for a quick recovery."

He took her hand. "You are always kind, Sarah."

"I hope I act so." Truthfully, some of her thoughts were not kind just now. Lady Trestan was the most difficult person she'd ever encountered. If she'd had any notion of the state of the Pendrennon family, would she have married into it? Looking up into Kenver's strained, handsome face, Sarah couldn't say no. But she could wish she saw a way toward change.

"This is not the sort of life I meant to give you," Kenver said, as if he sensed some of this in her expression. "Tamara was right. You deserve more."

He'd said this before. "What do you mean by that?"

"You shouldn't be pulling weeds in the garden or sewing draperies."

"I don't mind…"

"That's not the point! My wife should have the respect of the neighborhood and pin money to buy whatever she wants, like those books you spoke of."

This was a telling blow. Sarah had let slip her longing for some new volumes of history, but the price had been out of their reach.

"It's a matter of honor," Kenver finished.

When he said that, there was no arguing with him. Not until the subject had cooled.

"We can't stay at Tresigan forever. This is not a permanent solution."

Sarah supposed this was true. A month or so might feel like a holiday. But if it came to years away from Poldene, matters grew complicated. She knew Kenver missed his home. And she knew how that felt. And people would wonder if what might be called a honeymoon became a permanent estrangement. She had to consider Kenver's position as the future earl.

"I should go," he said.

He rode off as soon as his horse was saddled and did not return until the sun was setting.

"Papa is very ill," he told Sarah then. As if he had suspected her doubts, he added, "The doctor says he is in grave danger. My mother is worried. I think."

"You think?"

"It is difficult to tell what she is feeling sometimes." He made a wry face. "And then at other times all too easy."

"We must go back to Poldene to help," said Sarah.

"I'm not taking you back there."

The idea of living under Lady Trestan's eye again was not appealing. But it seemed to Sarah that they should act like the family they wished to be, not the one they had.

"I will go to see him each day."

"You will be always in the saddle. And hardly ever there." Sarah did not go so far as to suggest that Kenver could be a support to his mother, given all that had passed between them.

"I could stay at Poldene while you remain here," Kenver said slowly.

"I don't want that," they both responded, nearly in unison.

Kenver smiled. "What about Gwen and Elys? We promised them positions and Jowan training."

"They can stay here and watch over the house. Until matters are...clearer."

"The Terefords thought we would be doing that."

"You need to be at Poldene," Sarah replied.

"I suppose I can find another tenant if necessary." Kenver made a wry face. "One who can pay the duke a better rent." He gazed down at her. "But you..."

"*I* need to be with you."

He folded her in his arms, and they stood that way for a long time, leaning on each other.

And so the next day, they reversed their move. This time when they arrived at Poldene, they were immediately conducted to the state suite. Sarah saw that all the belongings they'd left behind had been shifted there, and the maid sent to wait on her was a young girl, not Cranston. Sarah wished she could see these gestures as olive branches and signs of a change. She suspected they were more in the nature of smoke screens, however.

But Kenver's father *was* very ill. Sarah saw that as soon as they visited his chamber to offer her good wishes for his recovery. He was flushed with fever and sweating, with a deep hacking cough and shallow, panting breaths. He seemed barely able to raise his arm when he responded to her greeting. Kenver took his father's trembling hand and pressed it. "We've come back to Poldene, Papa," he said. "I'll sit with you a while."

The earl started to respond but fell into a fit of coughing that shook his whole frame.

"It's best to keep him quiet," said the nurse the doctor had sent over. "The coughing wears him out." She brought a glass vial and teaspoon and gave the earl a dose of something. "Laudanum," she said, following this with what looked like barley water. The combination soothed the paroxysm.

"Thank you, Mrs. Dillon," said Kenver.

Sarah thought she looked calmly competent. A woman of forty or so, neatly dressed and polite, Mrs. Dillon seemed efficient. She had established herself in one corner of the room with the supplies she needed and a pile of knitting. "I'd be glad to help," Sarah told her.

"Keeping him quiet is the main thing," the nurse repeated. "He gets restless and agitated, and that makes him worse."

"I expect he is bored," Sarah said. "As well as anxious, of course."

The other two looked at her. Mrs. Dillon gave her a respectful nod.

"We must think what we can do," Sarah said to Kenver.

He squeezed her hand.

At dinner that evening, Sarah told Lady Trestan she was sorry to see the earl so depleted.

"It is a mistake to give in to these maladies," Kenver's mother replied. "Coddling oneself simply encourages them to take root."

Sarah couldn't quite believe her ears. "It is hardly Lord Trestan's fault that he is ailing."

The older woman made an impatient gesture. "A ride or two in the rain should not lay a man so low."

"Was he caught in one of those storms?" Sarah asked sympathetically. They'd had bouts of wild weather in the last two weeks.

"For a brief time." Lady Trestan seemed impatient with the topic. "Not enough to matter, I would think. But then I am never ill." She turned to Kenver. "You must ride over to Glen Farm. Wellings is complaining about the roof again."

"We should replace that thatching," Kenver replied absently, his mind clearly elsewhere.

"You will tell him it is perfectly adequate," snapped his mother.

Sarah found her tone grating, as was her attitude. If Kenver had fallen ill, she would be camped at his bedside in an agony of worry. Lady Trestan spoke of her husband's condition in the same annoyed tone she used for the tenant's complaint. And she clearly intended to leave the nursing to Mrs. Dillon. Perhaps she was well acquainted with the nurse and her capabilities, but still... How could she bear to do that? Sarah had known that the countess didn't like *her*. She had even understood that. She had been foisted on the Pendrennons willy-nilly, and she was not the sort of daughter-in-law they wanted. But she had thought Lady Trestan cared for her husband and son. Now, she wondered.

That night, as she and Kenver nestled together in the great four-poster bed of the state suite, Sarah searched for a way to inquire. "How did your parents meet?" she asked finally.

"Hmm?" He sounded surprised. "In London, during the season."

"At a ball? Or an evening party?" Perhaps they'd been drawn together dancing.

"I think my grandmother Pendrennon introduced them. She was distantly connected to Mama's family."

It sounded as if Lady Trestan had been picked out as a proper match, just as she had wished to do for her children.

"I've never heard them talk about it," Kenver added. "Why do you wish to know?"

"I just wondered," Sarah replied. Had they *wanted* to marry? Or simply been told to do so?

Kenver shifted uneasily. "Papa seems very bad, doesn't he?"

Not wanting to just agree, she said, "It may take him some time to recover."

"Yes. Recover. Yes."

"I was thinking I might offer to read to him. It would give him something to focus on. And help keep him quiet as the nurse wanted."

"That is a very kind offer, Sarah."

"It would not be a hardship for me. I enjoy reading aloud."

"As well as every other kind of reading."

She was heartened that he could tease a little. "As has been well established," she answered in the same lighter tone. "I find reading comforting."

He pulled her closer against him.

"Do you know what subjects interest your father?"

Kenver had to think. "He is not a great reader. Mostly just estate documents."

"Ah." Sarah didn't think she could manage that sort of reading. Even if Lady Trestan would provide the papers, which she would not.

"He told me once that he was impressed by Mozart. Not the music chiefly. He said he found child prodigies a mystery. I had forgotten about that."

Sarah doubted that Poldene's limited library would have anything on that subject, and when she looked the next morning, she found she was right. She settled on a history of the county instead, thinking that tales of his own familiar territory might engage the earl. The style of the volume was lively, and she knew she read aloud well.

The nurse was amenable to her plan once she understood the nature of the book. Sarah suspected she saw history as boring and likely to keep the earl quiet, if not soporific. And so Sarah arranged a chair by the side of his bed and began.

Lord Trestan showed little reaction at first. There were moments when he seemed scarcely conscious. But as she went on, he noticed her presence. It seemed to puzzle him. "It's Sarah," she said, thinking he might have forgotten they'd returned. "I've come to read to you about Cornwall."

He nodded and then drifted away again.

As time passed, Sarah thought he seemed comforted by her company and the diversion. He couldn't speak without bouts of coughing, which the nurse naturally discouraged, and so there was no conversation. This was easier for Sarah, who'd never had an easy relationship with the earl. She enjoyed the reading and of course found it far better than sitting with the countess, who did not want her. Lady Trestan was constantly busy with estate matters, often sending Kenver on errands around the land. As he fulfilled them, he resumed his customary inquiries among the people who lived on the land.

Several days passed in this manner, Sarah spending hours in the sickroom. The earl grew worse, however, and Mrs. Dillon was not encouraging. Sarah began to worry. When at last Lady Trestan came to visit, she glanced at Sarah's book as if it was ridiculous and spoke only to the attendant. "How is he?"

"In a decline," Mrs. Dillon replied. "Not likely to live, I'm sorry to say."

Sarah's mouth dropped open. She was astonished that the woman would state this so baldly with her patient lying right there. Shouldn't she be suggesting more remedies instead? Some heartening possibility? Glancing at the bed, Sarah saw that the earl had heard the pessimistic assessment. He was not always completely conscious, but this was one of the moments when intelligence gleamed in his eyes. He raised his head a little as if to speak but went off in a paroxysm of coughing instead. To Sarah's further amazement, Kenver's mother turned and walked out of the room.

"I do not think you are right," Sarah said to the nurse—loudly, so the earl could hear over his hacking. "He will recover."

"I've seen more of these cases than you," Mrs. Dillon replied. She looked sympathetic but unconvinced. Aware that Sarah was not her employer, the nurse didn't show her any particular deference. "The coughing is likely to do for him," she added.

Sarah turned her back. She saw that the earl was staring at her, his eyes wide, his expression strained. She met his gaze, held it, and gave a resolute nod. She was here, she let him know. She intended to help him fight. Anything she could do, she would. There must be something. Lord Trestan blinked back tears. And then the terrible cough took him once again. Mrs. Dillon came forward with the laudanum.

———

Kenver rode across a mown hay field, breathing deeply of the crisp air. The September sky was a glorious blue, the trees tossed in a bracing breeze. He'd resolved a dispute between two tenants to everyone's satisfaction and heard more bracing news from Stovell the schoolmaster. This was the sort of thing he was meant to do, he thought. And he'd done well.

Hoofbeats approached from behind. He turned to find one of the Poldene grooms catching up to him. "Her ladyship said you should come right away," the lad called.

"Is my father worse?"

"I don't know, sir. I was just sent to bring you."

Concerned, Kenver urged his mount to a canter. When he reached home, he started toward his father's bedchamber, but a footman diverted him to his mother's private parlor.

"Your father is dying," she said when he came in.

"What?"

"The nurse offers no hope."

"But Sarah said…"

His mother cut him off with a contemptuous gesture. "What would she know about it? The nurse is far more expert about these things."

That was probably true. Kenver's throat tightened with pain. He turned away. "I must go and see him."

"Later. We need to discuss how we will go on after you inherit."

"Surely that can wait."

"No!" She slapped a palm down on her desktop. "We will make matters entirely clear now! You will do as I tell you. I know how to manage Poldene. And I will not allow you to ruin what I've…your father and I have put in place."

"I know a good deal about…"

"Nothing!" She made a slashing gesture. "You will listen to me! And do as I say."

The cold glare in her eyes was unnerving. She must be very upset about Papa, Kenver told himself. This ferocity was a form of grief. Must be. He nodded to show that he had heard her. They would work out the sad details, if indeed it came to that, later on.

She took this for agreement and allowed him to go to his father. He found him inert and ashen. So still and pale, in fact, that he might have been gone. But his chest rose and fell with a soft wheezing sound.

Sarah sat beside his bed with a book in her lap. "The nurse gave him another dose of laudanum to ease his coughing," she told him. "He will sleep for some time."

"You really see no hope?" Kenver asked the nurse.

The woman slowly shook her head, not as if she relished the terrible news, but as if she had no doubt. Kenver sat down opposite Sarah, on the other side of the bed, took his father's limp white hand, and blinked back tears.

"We had our disagreements," Kenver murmured, speaking to the unconscious man and to Sarah at the same time. "Especially if I annoyed Mama. But when we rode out over the land together, tending to Poldene, it used to be different. *He* was different." Kenver looked into the distance. "He told me stories of his boyhood on the estate. He had them for every age—eight, eleven, fourteen. They were like mine, and unlike."

Sarah nodded, her heart aching for him.

"He showed me his secret hideaways," Kenver went on. "He said he didn't need them anymore, and they should be passed down like the house and the title. There is a huge hollow oak in a dip between three hills. Old as the Crusades, Papa said. Generations of boys have fitted it out with castoffs and treasures. I found a metal box my great-grandfather had buried in the floor. His name was scratched onto it. There was a lock of hair inside. I don't know whose."

"Kenver," Sarah whispered.

"That was when I was younger," he added. "It doesn't happen anymore."

"I'm glad he told you those things."

He looked at her. "Papa taught me to cherish this place. And he had memories of the tenants too. I used one of those recollections today when I was settling a dispute. It swayed them when nothing else had done so."

Sarah wanted to take him in her arms and comfort him. But what comfort was there?

"I wish our last days together had not been so...contentious." Kenver bent and rested his forehead on the coverlet.

Tears welled in Sarah's eyes and spilled down her cheeks. She was sorry about Lord Trestan, but she wept for Kenver. It was so hard to see him like this. She loved him, she realized, with all her heart and soul. Her accidental husband had come to mean everything to her. "He could still recover," she said.

In the corner, the nurse made a dissenting sound.

Kenver sat up. He cleared his throat and blinked rapidly. "Yes. Things may look...bad." He glanced at his inert, ashen father. "But we must not give up. You are an angel, Sarah."

The tender, trusting look in his hazel eyes tore at her. If there was anything that could be done, Sarah vowed she would find it and do it!

That afternoon when the doctor called, Sarah followed him out of the sickroom and a little way down the corridor. "How did the earl seem to you?" she asked him.

The gray-haired man merely shook his head and started to move away.

Sarah persisted. "The nurse seems to have little hope of his recovery."

"There is always hope."

"Yes," Sarah agreed. "But Mrs. Dillon told Lady Trestan that he is dying. Do you think she should have said that?"

"He is in a bad way. These lung fevers weaken the entire constitution."

"He is very weak."

The doctor nodded.

"There must be something more that can be done. How can I help?"

"Mrs. Dillon is very capable." The doctor looked paternal. "You mustn't worry."

Sarah didn't see how he could think that was reassuring. If the nurse was capable, then the earl was doomed, because that was her settled opinion. "Like Atropos cutting the thread," Sarah murmured.

"I beg your pardon?" The doctor looked bewildered.

"There must be something I can *do*."

"You've been very kind. I'm sure Lord Trestan appreciates all the time you've spent reading to him." His tone made it sound like the whim of a child. His smile as he departed was condescending.

Fuming, Sarah started back to the earl's chamber. Then she stopped, considered, gathered all her courage, and strode to Lady Trestan's private parlor instead. She walked in without knocking, because if she waited, she might lose her nerve. "I think you should consult another doctor about the earl's condition," she said as soon as she was inside.

The countess looked up from her perennial mass of papers, with her customary annoyed expression. "Why do you say that?" she asked.

"Someone with a fresh eye might notice something or have other treatments."

"Dr. Greel is known to be the best in the area. I'm sure he is doing all that can be done."

"Nobody knows everything."

"He certainly knows better than *you*," Lady Trestan said contemptuously.

Sarah's hands closed into fists at her sides. "You don't like me," she replied. "I am well aware of that. But this has nothing to do with our...incompatibility. What harm would there be in consulting another doctor?"

"There is no other competent physician available." The countess looked down at her work, a gesture of dismissal.

"So you won't even try?"

"I see no necessity. And I do not appreciate this...melodrama you are enacting."

"Don't you care?" Sarah blurted out. "Don't you love him?"

This brought Lady Trestan's head up. Her lips thinned. Her eyebrows drew together. "You are impertinent!"

"I am everything you despise. You have made that perfectly clear. So why not impertinent? I don't care. Not if I can help at all."

The countess looked surprised and perhaps slightly impressed. She set down her quill. "What do you imagine love is?"

"Greater minds than I have tried to define it," Sarah answered. She didn't try to moderate the snap in her voice. She'd lost all patience.

"Indeed. And yet you push forward your opinions." Lady Trestan straightened the pile of papers before her. "I have given my life to salvaging the legacy of a great family. I've provided the skills that are sadly…lacking in its heirs."

Sarah frowned at this seeming non sequitur. She thought it over. "That is a kind of love, you mean?"

"It is far more valuable than the bleating and whining roused by that word."

"But a legacy… It sounds so abstract. The people…"

"The land is far more important than any individual. Without land, the aristocracy is mere ghosts of fading glory."

"I don't think that's—"

"Your thoughts are of no interest to me," Lady Trestan interrupted. "You are a foolish girl and know nothing about it. That is why you are so unsuited to be a countess."

"You don't have to be an aristocrat to be a worthy individual."

"Oh, do go away. I have important matters to attend to."

"More important than your husband's health?"

Lady Trestan turned in her chair and fixed Sarah with a gimlet eye. "My husband is a weak man ill-suited to the responsibilities life gave him. And now he has succumbed to a simple chill."

"Not quite yet," Sarah replied quietly.

Kenver's mother went on as if she hadn't heard. Sarah thought she probably hadn't. "Peter was nearly the last straw for Poldene, which has suffered from a long line of poor masters." She began to tick these off on her fingers. "My husband's father made a hobby of foolish investments. He had a positive genius for losing propositions and an affinity

for swindlers." The countess shook her head in exaspera-
tion. "The man was an idiot. *His* father was a gambler and a
wastrel who wrung every penny from the estate to fund his
London debaucheries. Fortunately, he died young as a result
of overindulgence. And the earl before that was simply dull-
witted, as far as I can judge from the records. None of them
had the sense to find capable wives."

"Like you," Sarah said.

"Precisely. And if you think I will ever apologize for
taking the reins, you are a numbskull."

Sarah didn't bother replying. But she did think of Cecelia,
who did similar work with a very different spirit. Cecelia
would never speak of her husband in such terms. She obviously loved him.

"Thanks to my efforts, Kenver will inherit a healthy property and a more-than-adequate income. As long as he listens
to me, we will improve it further."

"He could do that himself."

The countess looked pained and made a derisive sound.
"Is that the sort of delusion you call love? It proves my point."

"Have you ever given him a chance?" Sarah asked quietly.
She was certain the countess knew nothing of Kenver's tending of the estate.

"Poldene cannot afford reckless experiments! When I am
gone..." Lady Trestan grimaced. "I will *not* see all my work
come to nothing. You may be sure of that. Now please go
away." She made an emphatic gesture. "And do not disturb
me again without an appointment."

After this conversation, on top of everything else, Sarah

ordered dinner in their suite that evening. She simply couldn't face another formal, tension-filled meal, and she was ready to battle any staff member who protested. Perhaps due to this combative mood, no one did.

She and Kenver needed privacy to think what to do. Sarah didn't want to pit Kenver actively against his mother, but she couldn't stand by and see the earl sink if there was any alternative. She had word about dinner sent to the countess and received silence in response.

Coming in to change after a long ride to see a fractious forester, which he had made reluctantly at his mother's insistence, Kenver discovered a table set in their sitting room. Sarah came out of the bedchamber and held out a welcoming hand. His leaden spirits lightened a little. Sarah had been heroic in her attendance on his father. She was the kindest person he'd ever known. He took her hand and kissed her as she smiled up at him. "There's no need for evening dress," she said. "We can eat as we are here."

"My father…"

"The same."

Dying, in other words. He didn't speak this aloud.

"The doctor says there is hope."

"Really?" Sarah nodded. He suspected she was just trying to cheer him. "He looks so white and feeble. This morning when I visited, he didn't know who I was."

"The fever takes him that way sometimes."

Servants came in with their meal. When they had set it out, Sarah sent them away. "Just the two of us tonight," she said. "We don't need anyone else."

"A wonderful idea."

They served themselves and began to eat. Neither of them had good appetites, Kenver noticed, even though he had been out riding all day. He pushed food around his plate. "I don't know what Poldene will be like without my father," he said.

Sarah gave him a compassionate glance.

"Mama has the...stronger personality. Papa usually followed...follows her lead." And yet Papa had been a kind of buffer, it seemed to him now. With him so ill, every conversation Kenver had with his mother was coldly abrasive. She seemed to think she had to lash out at him, as if he was a recalcitrant horse. That had been her grief, he told himself again. But he didn't quite believe it. "Things are awry with him absent. Out of balance."

"Fathers are like a bulwark," Sarah said. "Like the walls guarding a castle."

Was his? He wanted to think of him that way, though it didn't seem to fit. And if it was true, now the fortifications were collapsing.

"My papa seems so to me," Sarah went on. "He always stands ready to help with any problem that crops up."

Sarah had learned this from Mr. Moran, Kenver thought. She'd stepped forward to help his father without any question.

"We have long talks about all sorts of things. He loved hearing about what I was reading. I can always make him laugh." A reminiscent smile lit her features.

It was a beguiling picture and made Kenver realize that

his family was not prone to laughter. Tamara had an expansive laugh. Perhaps that was why she couldn't fit in? No, that was silly.

"We use to play cards in the evening," Sarah continued. "He and Mama are fierce competitors. How they would dispute over every point!"

Kenver couldn't quite imagine these scenes. Disputes in his family were...perilous.

"And then we would all laugh ourselves silly." Sarah laughed a little now.

More laughter. Hearing it and feeling the lift it brought to the room, Kenver thanked providence for his inadvertent wife. Luck had certainly been with him on the cliff at Tintagel. And more than luck. He had known somehow, that night in the sea cave, that she was the one he needed. And so it had proved.

Having eaten what they could, they left the table and went to sit together on the sofa. Kenver put his arm around Sarah and pulled her close. She nestled against him, a palpable consolation.

The servants came to clear away the dishes and close the draperies against the rising dark. When they'd gone, he pulled his wife closer. He didn't know what he would have done without her at this moment.

Sarah suddenly sat bolt upright. "Herbs!" she exclaimed.

"What?"

"My mother knows all sorts of herbal concoctions," she said. "She learned from her grandmother when she was a girl. And after she married Papa, she set up a stillroom at our house. People come to her for remedies. I should have thought of that before. How could I not?"

Perhaps because they'd seen so little of her family, Kenver did not say. He knew his mother had resisted a visit, and he suspected Sarah had been ashamed to show them Tresigan. "Won't the doctor know about those?" he asked.

"He hasn't suggested any such things." Sarah grimaced. "Women most often tend herbs, you know, and Dr. Greel seems to think a woman is only good for following his orders. Meekly."

Kenver decided not to ask what this meant. And then after a moment, he thought he knew.

"I will go and see my mother tomorrow," Sarah went on. "She will have good advice at least. And perhaps more than that."

Of course he agreed, though he couldn't muster much hope.

Seventeen

SARAH SET OFF EARLY THE NEXT MORNING ON WHAT would be a long journey for one day. Kenver had ordered the carriage, and his mother had made no objections. Sarah thought Lady Trestan was happy for her to go away for any reason whatsoever. The only thing she'd like better was for Sarah never to come back. In that, she would be disappointed.

Driving up the lane that led to her childhood house, Sarah felt a pang. This solid, unpretentious building still felt more like home than anywhere else in the world. She'd taken it for granted in her early years. Now she cherished all the indefinable things that added up to happiness. She hoped to create her own version of it someday—safe and comfortable and…joyous. Not perfect, not without disagreements and pains, but full of love.

A familiar servant let her in with a broad smile. Sarah walked through the sights and smells and sounds of memory to the sunny parlor where they always sat in the mornings.

Her mother greeted her with pleased surprise. "Sarah. How lovely. I had no word of a visit."

"I was nearly as fast as a messenger would have been," Sarah replied, taking off her bonnet and gloves.

"Come and sit. How glad I am to see you. This last year, I grew accustomed to being with my grown-up daughter, after your time away at school. Perhaps you'll stay a while? Overnight?"

"No, I can't."

"Is something wrong?"

"Yes, Mama." Sarah clasped her hands in her lap. "The nurse has told us that the earl is dying."

"Oh dear. I'm sorry. We knew he was ailing, of course. We would have come to see you..."

But they had never been welcome at Poldene, Sarah finished silently. And they were aware of it, though the matter had not been discussed. Sarah hadn't insisted on a visit. Should she have? She might have managed it, after a great fuss. But if Lady Trestan had received them as she had Sarah, with careless contempt... Sarah set her jaw. There would have been more than a shouting match, she thought. "Kenver appreciated your note," she replied.

"He must be very worried."

"He is. I can't bear to see him so sad, Mama."

"No?"

"It is breaking my heart."

Her mother actually seemed pleased with this remark, which was a little odd.

"I have to do something!" Sarah clenched her fists in frustration.

"You do?"

"Yes, of course. Anything! How could I not?"

Her mother's kind eyes were more eloquent than words. She smiled, making Sarah realize how much she had missed that loving gaze. She would visit here more often!

She reached out a hand. Her mother took it and squeezed. "I've come to you for advice," Sarah continued. "You know about herbs. You've seen many people through illnesses. I thought you might know of something."

"I will do whatever I can." Her mother looked grave. "Tell me about Lord Trestan's condition."

Sarah described the symptoms she had seen and what the nurse had done for him.

"Ah, laudanum is not so good because it prevents coughing, you see."

"But the coughs are so violent. They leave him utterly exhausted." Sarah shivered. The earl's paroxysms were painful to watch.

Her mother nodded. "Yes, but there is a reason for them. He needs to be rid of the phlegm clogging his lungs and making it difficult to breathe."

"So he must cough?" Sarah asked. It seemed a cruel fate.

"To expel the phlegm," her mother replied. "But if it is thinned out, he will make less effort, and his coughing will be more effective."

"Thinned?"

"Yes. I have a recipe for barley water with honey and ginger and peppermint that has been helpful in such cases."

"And it will cure him?"

"I can't promise you that, Sarah. I am no physician. But it will certainly not harm him and might do him good."

"We will try it."

"You would need to stop the laudanum," her mother added.

This presented a difficulty. Sarah thought of the doctor who dismissed her questions, the nurse who took orders only from him. They would not listen to her. Dr. Greel would care nothing for her mother's experience.

"They might not wish to do that," said her mother, as if she'd read Sarah's thoughts.

"The doctor and the nurse have given up on Lord Trestan," Sarah replied. "They believe he's dying." Indeed, she had the feeling that Mrs. Dillon was administering larger doses of laudanum to keep the earl quiet until he expired. "They've said so."

Her mother looked concerned. "The attitude in a sick-room can have a great effect," she said. "I have seen it more than once. But, Sarah..."

"I will talk it over with Kenver."

"And the countess, of course."

Sarah feared how that conversation would go, particularly if she was the one suggesting a change. She would not be having it. "Lady Trestan is his mother," she replied.

Her own accepted this, and they went to the stillroom to prepare the mixture. As Mama made up several bottles, Sarah noticed some small, empty vials on a shelf. They were just like those Mrs. Dillon used for laudanum. Without thinking about it too much, she slipped several of them into her pocket.

Her father returned before they were finished, and Sarah had time to talk with him over tea and cakes before she headed back to Poldene. This time together was all the more precious to her as Kenver contemplated losing his father.

Sarah reached Poldene in the evening, at an hour when Kenver and his mother were still at dinner. She did not join them but went directly to her room with the supplies she had brought and put them away.

Kenver came in sometime later. He strode over and put his arms around her. "I am so glad to see you."

Sarah held him close. He trembled a little under her hands.

"It has been a dreadful day. Papa is worse. They think he won't last much longer. A day or two perhaps. He lies there as if he'd already..." He cut off this sentence.

"Mrs. Dillon is giving him laudanum?" Sarah asked.

"She says it is all they can do and a mercy." He swallowed. "It will let him go without that awful coughing."

Sarah thought that the nurse was easing him out of the world. "My mother had another idea."

"Idea?" Kenver looked down at her. He put his hands on her shoulders and held her a little away from him so he could see her face. "What idea?"

Sarah repeated the conversation she'd had with her mother. "If his lungs could get clearer, he might improve," she finished.

"We should try it immediately," Kenver replied. "We must do anything that might help."

"They would have to stop the laudanum for it to have the proper effect."

"Fine, we will do so." He turned as if setting off to make the change.

"The doctor would need to order it. Mrs. Dillon only does as he tells her."

"I will speak to him," said Kenver. "I'll go and see him right now."

"Now?"

"He lives not far from here. It will be a relief to *do* something." He clenched his fists in emphasis. "To just sit and watch Papa fade is insupportable."

The doctor might listen to the heir to Poldene, Sarah thought, which would make matters easier.

Kenver threw on his riding clothes and went.

He returned less than an hour later, looking angry. "Dr. Greel has no patience for old wives' tales," he told Sarah and continued as if reciting a lesson. "He was surprised I would be taken in by such drivel and sorry I was given false hopes. He thinks his treatment the better course. It is a pity that not every patient can be saved, but that is the way of the world. He has told my mother as much. She was most understanding. He would be happy to speak to her again if I like."

"Was that a threat?" Sarah let slip.

"A reminder that she is in charge," Kenver answered. "I suppose she made that very clear." Some of the fire went out of him. "Obviously Dr. Greel does not appreciate any challenge to his authority. He is certain he knows best. And that I know nothing. In the end, I let him think that I agreed."

"Because it would be better if he does not speak to your mother."

"That was my thought," he said. "He may still tell Mama I was rude, after the encounter we have just had."

"I don't expect he will," Sarah replied. "You are the heir to Poldene. He won't wish to be at odds with you."

"He is," said Kenver grimly. "Whether he knows it or not. How can he refuse to try something different?"

"Some people value their own convictions over anything else."

"Including Papa's life?" He made a slashing gesture that required no answer.

"You could speak to your mother," Sarah said. "If we did not tell her that the idea came from my family..."

They looked at each other, silently admitting a great deal that had remained unsaid. Then Kenver shook his head. "I'm not certain she cares whether Papa dies."

"Kenver!"

He bowed his head. "No, I won't think that. I don't think it." He was silent for the space of two breaths. "She doesn't listen to me, however. We must find a way to do this ourselves."

Sarah put a hand on his arm. "It is only a hope, Kenver. My mother did not promise it would work."

"Dr. Greel is promising that Papa will die. Quite soon. It seems a time to try anything." He frowned. "I could barricade myself in his room and give him your potion."

Their eyes met, acknowledging the uproar this would cause. And the poor chances of success.

"I had an idea," Sarah said.

"What?"

"I have some vials like the ones Mrs. Dillon uses for laudanum. I could make up a similar-looking liquid and substitute them."

"So he gets none when she doses him?"

Sarah nodded. "Then I could give him my mother's mixture. It looks like barley water. I daresay no one would notice. It's just…"

"What?"

"Is it right to sneak?" Sarah asked him.

Kenver took a long breath and let it out. "Let us go and see Papa."

They went along the corridor to the dim bedchamber. The earl lay white and nearly as still as death.

"Sleeping," said the nurse. She scarcely looked up from her knitting. "Not long now."

"Is the laudanum really necessary?" Kenver asked. "It makes him so…" The rise and fall of his father's chest was just barely perceptible.

"It brings him peace," the nurse replied.

"Peace," repeated Kenver when they were back in the state suite. "She might as well have said 'rest in peace.' They have given up on Papa."

Sarah's worry over the size of his doses had increased. If they did nothing, the earl was unlikely to last much longer. "Mama's mixture will do no harm," she said. "And it might help."

Kenver nodded. "We'll do it."

Sarah filled her vials with a harmless liquid that mimicked those containing the laudanum. "I sit with your father while Mrs. Dillon goes for her breakfast. I can switch them then."

"I will watch at the door."

Sarah nodded.

The next morning, they carried out their plan soon after the nurse left Lord Trestan's bedchamber. Kenver put the vials of laudanum in his pocket and took them away. Sarah filled a pitcher with her mother's herbal mixture and put it on the table. It looked like the barley water that usually sat there and would rouse no questions. The earl half woke a little later, and she gave him some. Mrs. Dillon returned, administered his "laudanum," and sat down to her knitting. Sarah opened the book she'd been reading and began.

Over the next several days, this routine continued. At first, the earl's coughing increased without the laudanum. Sarah told herself this was right, based on what her mother had said, though it was hard to listen to him hack. Mrs. Dillon was puzzled and increased the dose until she said it was as much as she dared to give. But the paroxysms were less violent as time went on and produced more and more greenish phlegm.

Lord Trestan grew restless. He was periodically conscious now and knew where he was. Sarah read to him and gave him her mother's mixture as often as he would take it. She used most of what she'd brought and sent a groom for more, letting people think it was something from home for her.

The earl slowly improved. And on the autumn equinox, he finally had his first peaceful night's sleep. From that time, he began to recover, slowly, from a position of great weakness.

The doctor and nurse took credit for this "miraculous" cure, and Sarah let them. She wished she might say that laudanum had not been the best treatment, but neither she nor Kenver wanted to face the uproar this would cause. The earl's recovery was the point, and it was increasingly clear that he would pull through.

The mood at Poldene lifted. Neighbors heard the good news and called to congratulate the countess. One or two friends spent time with the earl, and if they were shocked at his ravaged appearance, they didn't allude to it.

"You saved my father's life!" Kenver said to Sarah in the evening after one of these visits. They sat together on the sofa in their rooms, and he held her close. Kenver had ordered a fire lit as a cold fog had rolled in from the sea after sunset. "You and your mother," he added. "Everyone at Poldene ought to be thanking you."

"Your eternal gratitude will be sufficient," Sarah teased.

He smiled and kissed her. "You have that. What would we have done without you?"

"Gotten on more easily perhaps," Sarah had to say. "I've caused a great deal of friction in your family."

"No."

"But if I hadn't…"

"Your presence here may have revealed conflicts. That is not the same as causing them."

"But if you had married someone your mother approved of…"

"And who would that be?"

"A noblewoman," Sarah replied. "Perhaps a duke's daughter. With a large dowry and all sorts of useful social connections."

"Who would do whatever Mama ordered," he added.

"Mmm." Sarah frowned. "You know, that might have been a challenge. The only duke's daughter I ever met was… rather accustomed to getting her own way."

Kenver shuddered at the conflicts this suggested. "I married exactly the right person."

"How can you say so when it was all so...accidental?"

"A happy accident? But perhaps it wasn't. Perhaps fate or providence or Tintagel's magic brought us together."

"Do you really believe that?" Sarah asked.

He looked down at her, at the gentle face he had learned to cherish. "I believe you have shown me what love truly is," he replied. "And I don't see how I would ever have understood it without you."

Sarah's blue eyes filmed with tears.

"You are generous and brilliant and delectable, and I love you with all my heart, Sarah."

"I love you so," she replied.

This naturally led to more kisses, which soon inspired increasingly urgent caresses, until the sofa became inadequate and a change of location seemed advisable. Arms laced about each other, they moved to the bedroom, where lips and hands enticed as they shed bits of clothing, boots, and a reckless scatter of hairpins. Tumbling into lavender-scented sheets, they did their best to drive each other wild before coming together with passion and tenderness and ecstasy that promised so much for the years that lay ahead.

Afterward, they lay nestled together while their pulses and breathing slowed. Kenver dropped small kisses on his wife's bare shoulder. "Who would have thought, when we crawled into that cave and huddled on the stone, that we would come to this?" he asked.

"This?" Sarah echoed with a smile.

"Yes. Er, marital bliss."

She laughed. "I adore scandalous things."

"I adore you."

This required a proper acknowledgment. It was some time before Sarah said, "I suppose Merlin might have thought of it."

"That Welden fellow?" Kenver looked down at her, astonished.

"No, the real Merlin, the magician. He brought Uther to Igraine at Tintagel and made a marriage."

"Well, he made a legendary hero. He didn't quite have a marriage in mind. As far as I recall. He didn't mention it in the tales I've read."

"He didn't seem to know that Gorlois was going to be killed in battle just then, did he?" asked Sarah.

"No. Apparently he was not omniscient."

"Which is disappointing."

"Is it?"

"Well, a great magician ought to foresee such a thing."

"Perhaps all of his...precognitive facilities were fixed on Arthur."

"I suppose so." Sarah's mind drifted on a cushion of physical well-being. "Our marriage will be better than Igraine's."

"Mmm." Kenver's eyelids were drooping.

Igraine's had been filled with troubles, Sarah noted. That led inevitably to the thought that *her* marriage had not gone smoothly so far. In fact, aside from Kenver, it had been difficult indeed, and the problems had not been removed by his father's recovery. Here in these rooms, wrapped in each other's arms, they were happy. In the rest of Poldene, however, problems still loomed. "Never mind," she said. They would find a way through them together. "Forget I said anything about Igraine," she added for luck.

"I do not forget anything you say," he murmured.

"Well, that could be awkward. Some things I say are just nonsense."

"Never."

Sarah decided to let him retain this pleasant illusion and simply kissed him.

———

"It is kind of you to read to me," the earl said to Sarah some days later. "Your voice is very soothing, and you find interesting things to read."

"I'm glad. If there is anything you'd particularly like to hear, I will look in the library."

"I'm content with your choices." He fell silent.

Knowing he didn't have much energy for conversation, Sarah returned to the biography she had been reading. But when the nurse left the room for a bit, Lord Trestan asked, "Why are you doing this?"

"I beg your pardon?"

Propped up with pillows, very pale and haggard, he said, "Being so ill makes a man think. And so now I am wondering why you are sitting with me. Reading to me." He gazed at her with tired eyes. "You were not made welcome when you came here. Indeed, I thought you had moved out of Poldene."

"Kenver wished to be here during your illness."

"Did he?"

"Of course."

"Of course," the earl repeated, as if examining the words. "And you came with him."

"I am his wife," she answered, with just the slightest touch of defiance.

"So you came out of duty."

Sarah hesitated. It was mostly true. She had not been eager to come. But she had felt it was right.

"But that didn't mean you had to sit with me. You've... I think I remember you've been here rather constantly."

"I wanted to help."

"Why would you wish to help me?" He seemed thoroughly puzzled. "You..." He was interrupted by a cough. He was not quite rid of it, and it shook his weakened frame. Sarah rose, poured some of her mother's mixture, and helped him drink. The liquid soothed and finally conquered the spasm.

When he had recovered, he gazed at the glass. "What is that? It's not plain barley water." He licked his lips. "There's something more in it." He licked his lips again. "I recognize the taste. You've been giving me that since I...came back from the brink."

Sarah wasn't sure what to say.

"It is...revivifying somehow. Is it something the doctor brought?"

Sarah might have let him think so. But what if he thanked Dr. Creel for the medicine? That would not go well. She checked to be sure the nurse was not coming back. "My mother made up an herbal mixture. She is known for her remedies."

"Ah." He indicated that he would like another sip, and Sarah gave it to him. "Good. So you asked her to do so?"

"Yes." She had to add, "We didn't mention it to the doctor."

The earl blinked at her tone. "He had other opinions?"

Sarah nodded and wondered if she dared tell him not to mention her mother's mixture. She decided it was better to leave it.

Lord Trestan examined her as if she was a strange exotic creature. "Why go to such trouble?" he said. "I would think you might have been glad to see me die."

Sarah was shocked. "Of course not. You are Kenver's father."

"So all was done for Kenver. For his sake."

Sarah wasn't certain how to respond. The real answer was yes. But it seemed cold to say so, after all that Lord Trestan had been through.

He spoke again before she found the words. "What else could it be?" He stared at her from weary eyes until Sarah began to feel uneasy. "Kenver is fortunate," he said then and closed them.

The nurse returned. With some relief, Sarah went back to the book she'd been reading to him.

She was nearly ready to stop for the day and return to her rooms when Lady Trestan came in, a document in her hand. "You may go," she said to the nurse. An abrupt gesture included Sarah in this command. They both rose and went out, and they both lingered outside the door. Sarah made her own dismissive motion, but when Mrs. Dillon ignored her, she said nothing. Speech would reveal her presence, and she could hardly shove the woman down the hallway. They stood there and avoided each other's eyes.

"Hello, my dear," said the earl. "You've come to see how I go on?"

"I was told you were on the mend." Lady Trestan's tone did not suggest any strong emotion about his recovery.

"Were you?"

"Of course. The doctor made regular reports."

"And you were pleased."

"Naturally I was pleased, Peter. What else could I have been?" She sounded impatient with him.

"What else indeed? You haven't been here much before, I think?"

"You know I can't bear to be around illness."

"Ah, yes. When Kenver was ailing, you left him to his nanny."

"Who knew far more about sickrooms than I."

"Yes," Lord Trestan said again.

"I've brought something for you to sign," the countess replied, as if the previous subject had been exhausted. There was a rustle of paper.

"Not now," he responded. "I can't read it. I'm too tired."

"I beg your pardon?" Kenver's mother sounded astonished. "It is important. It can't wait on your whims."

"Perhaps I can look at it tomorrow."

"There is no need for you to look at it at all. Just take the quill and sign. Here."

"Another day."

"I need it now!"

The earl began to cough. Lady Trestan exclaimed angrily. The sound of glass breaking was too much for the nurse. She rushed back in and exclaimed in dismay.

Sarah quickly moved down the corridor, well aware that her presence would be unwelcome and hoping to escape before Lady Trestan saw her.

She failed in this. The countess swept out of her husband's room before Sarah turned the corner. Ink had splashed all down the skirt of her silk gown, most likely ruining it. She looked furious, and seeing Sarah did not improve her temper. She bared her teeth like a cornered fox. "If you think you can supplant me, you are even more of a fool than I imagined," she hissed.

"What?"

"Did you think I hadn't noticed? Because I detest the smell of sickrooms?" Lady Trestan gave a little shiver. "You've been observed. I've been told how you're oiling about, taking advantage of a sick man, extending your sway over him."

Sarah was confounded. "I wasn't doing any…"

"*Pfft.* Why else would you bother with your 'reading'?"

"For Kenver," Sarah said crisply.

"Kenver asked you to do it?" The countess's eyes narrowed. "What is he plotting?"

"His father's continued existence?"

Lady Trestan looked blank for a moment. "But Kenver would…" She bit off these words, scowled, and turned away.

"You might try vinegar on that stain," Sarah said before

she could stop herself. She knew immediately it was a mistake. The information had just popped out, as bits and pieces of her reading often did.

The countess whirled and glared at her. "Do you dare to mock me?" She shook the document in Sarah's face. "This is important. It must be executed."

"I'm surprised you don't just sign for him," Sarah replied dryly.

"The bank manager knows his hand too well."

Which implied that she often did sign for him, Sarah noted. But this was none of her affair. She edged past the countess to go back to the sickroom.

"I forbid you to go in there," the older woman said.

Sarah faced her. "Who visits is up to the earl," she said, and entered.

Lady Trestan came in on her heels. She grabbed Sarah's arm and jerked. "Get out."

"Alice!" said the earl. He tried to push up from the pile of pillows. "Stop it." He fell back.

"Do not tell me—" Lady Trestan began.

"We need quiet in here," interrupted the nurse. "Or else we're likely to have a relapse on our hands."

Three pairs of eyes fixed on the countess. With something very like a snarl, she whirled and departed. To do what, Sarah wondered. Whatever it was, she didn't think it would be pleasant.

Eighteen

WHEN KENVER HEARD THAT HIS FATHER'S VALET WAS to take Sarah's place in the sickroom and that Sarah had been ordered not to show her face there again—nearly in those insulting words—he felt a flash of rage. "Who says so?" he asked Sarah.

"I received a note."

He reached out. She gave it to him. "That is Mama's hand."

"I thought it was. She came to your father's room, and we…disagreed a little. But if your father prefers to have his valet with him, that's fine."

"I doubt it." Kenver was certain that Felch would find sickroom tasks distasteful. He'd often thought personal service was an odd choice of profession for such an overly fastidious man. Felch obviously preferred clothes to living people.

"Your father did say he liked my reading."

"Of course he does. Who would not?"

"Your mother?" replied Sarah wryly.

"I will go and see Papa and find out what he wants."

Kenver found Felch hovering uneasily by his father's

bedside, under the interested eye of the nurse. He lingered in the doorway to listen.

"You have not tended me through this illness," his father was saying.

"I was given to understand that the doctor and nurse were far more skilled," Felch replied.

"So why are you here now?"

"You are much better," said the valet, as if it was something he'd learned by rote.

"Yet still bedridden," Papa pointed out.

"Her ladyship wishes it."

"I believe you are employed by me?"

"Her ladyship thinks I could be of help." Felch didn't sound enthusiastic.

Indeed, Kenver thought, there would be nothing for him to do here but straighten pillows and assist his father with personal hygiene matters, which was not Felch's forte. "She's also ordered Sarah to stay away," he said.

His father turned his head and noticed him. "What? I like her reading. She has helped me a great deal."

Meeting his father's direct gaze, Kenver realized that he knew something about how much Sarah and her mother had helped. Whether Papa realized that they had saved his life, he wasn't certain.

"Her ladyship gave orders," said Felch.

That was a fiat at Poldene. No response was expected.

"I say otherwise," declared his father.

Felch looked startled, briefly relieved, and then impassive. Kenver imagined that the same thought was going through all three of their minds. Who was to tell her so? It was not a mission anyone would want. And yet it had to be done. "I'll let her know," he said.

His father stared. Felch bowed and went out. Kenver listened to his footsteps recede down the corridor. They did not turn into the dressing room next door, as he had been concerned they might.

"Good riddance to that sourpuss," said the nurse.

Both he and his father started. Kenver had forgotten she was there. "Perhaps you would like to go downstairs and have a cup of tea," Kenver said to her.

With a shrug, Mrs. Dillon gathered her knitting and departed.

"Thank you," said his father.

Kenver knew he was referring to his earlier offer. He was surprised to find himself in an alliance with Papa, disputing his mother's wishes.

"And you'll tell Sarah to come back," Papa added.

"Yes." Kenver started to go, but something made him hesitate. "Do you remember how we used to ride out together when I was young?"

"Of course."

"You showed me the old oak tree."

His father smiled and nodded. "I haven't been down there in years."

"It is still standing, though more gnarled and shaggier than ever," said Kenver.

"I found a Roman coin in the floor there once."

Kenver moved closer to the bed. "Really?"

"When I was eight or so. I wasn't certain what it was,

though I recognized the Latin. I showed it to my tutor, and he said it came from the reign of Emperor Diocletian."

"That's amazing." Kenver sat down in the chair Sarah always used.

"He took it away from me," his father added.

"What? No!"

"He said I would be careless and lose it." Papa shrugged. "I think he just wanted it for himself. I was quite cast down."

"That's outrageous. You should have protested."

"Well, yes, I suppose. I've never cared much for brangling, you know."

"Nor do I." But somehow, this time, Kenver couldn't leave it at that. "You brangled rather well over my marriage."

His father looked guilty. "Your mother was so insistent."

"And you go along with her wishes."

There was a short, heavy silence. And then Papa surprised him by saying, "They chose her for me, you know."

"They?"

"*My* parents. They thought I didn't realize, but I overheard them talking after the engagement. Up in London, it was. They thought I was a bit dim, and Alice would set me to rights." He frowned. "Perhaps I was. I wondered if I might have just been young though. I don't know. At any rate, Alice was their answer."

"And you gave her the reins."

"Oh well, they did that really. They had the estate agent— old Yates, that was—train her up."

"They cut you out?" Kenver was appalled.

"I was there as well," his father assured him. "Heard all the same lessons. I remember them too."

"But you went along with it."

"I always have. Before."

They looked at each other. Kenver thought that a lot of history passed silently between them. "Here's the thing," he said. "I won't have Sarah bullied. Anymore."

His father nodded. "She's a taking little thing. She'd been very kind to me. I was surprised."

"She is kind to everyone, if she is allowed to be. And I *will* see that she is treated properly."

"It's different when it's someone else," Papa answered.

Kenver rather thought that he might have found it different when it was *him*. But he'd never been treated as harshly as Sarah had. Tamara, on the other hand...

"Being so ill changes your viewpoint," his father said. "World looks different from the other side of...well, death, I suppose." He looked at Kenver. "It was a near thing, wasn't it?"

Kenver nodded.

"So...what are we to do exactly?"

Papa was looking to him now, Kenver realized, rather than Mama. It felt odd.

"Your mother is..."

"Fierce," Kenver finished.

"Yes. She's done very well with Poldene, you know. She works harder than I ever did."

"She deserves our thanks and our respect," Kenver said.

"Yes."

"But not total submission."

"Ah. She does rather prefer that."

"Perhaps, together, we can make a change."

His father looked doubtful, but he nodded. Then he offered his hand. Kenver shook it.

————————

Back in their suite, Sarah was settled with a pot of tea, a buttery scone, and a pile of letters from her old school friends. The rooms were quiet. No one was likely to come in unless she rang. A steady late September rain fell outside the windows. She had left one open a crack so that she could listen to the sound and revel in the cozy feeling of being inside. A small fire crackled in the hearth. Sarah broke off a bit of scone, flaky and perfect, and ate it.

She rested her fingers on the envelopes as if they were talismans. She'd been slow about writing, but word of her marriage had reached all three of her best friends by this time. Given their far-flung locations and various attitudes toward correspondence, she was not surprised to have received all their responses at once. She suspected they would have heard from Cecelia as well. The duchess was the soul of discretion, but her opinions about Poldene had probably leaked through. Nonetheless, Sarah didn't feel a scrap of dread about the letters. Since they'd formed their friendships at the age of thirteen, the four of them had been each other's staunch supporters.

By chance, Ada's letter rested on top of the pile, and so Sarah began with that. She knew it would be extensive and expansive. They'd often joked that Ada ought to write novels, because her letters were thick, meandering narratives rife with minor characters, charming incidents, and even suspense. She'd made an epic tale of the work she and her ducal husband were doing to restore a crumbling castle in Shropshire.

Ada thought Sarah's marriage was terribly romantic and clearly mandated by Fate. The place and way it had begun showed this, because wasn't Sarah always reading myths and legends? She was only disappointed there hadn't been a buried pirate treasure in the cave. "That is your story, Ada," Sarah murmured fondly. Her friend was certain Sarah would triumph over any troubles the match had brought and that all would be well. She wished to hear much more about Kenver, and they must come for a visit as soon as may be.

Sarah smiled as she set the closely written pages aside. She could hear Ada's voice in the words—bubbling, optimistic, very happy with her duke. They *would* find a way to visit.

Harriet's much shorter letter began with worry. She had painful experience with tyrannical older relatives and so found every hint that Sarah had let drop about Kenver's parents ominous. She seemed aware of more than those hints, and Sarah suspected she had gathered more from Cecelia.

Harriet trusted that Sarah's new husband would take steps. Sarah could hear the snap of that phrase in Harriet's voice and visualize the crackling stare of her green eyes. She offered help, of whatever type and amount Sarah desired. Up to a swooping rescue by post chaise. Her new husband was in agreement, she said, and would join in the effort. Sarah was not to go quiet and stoically endure! "I won't," Sarah murmured when she read this. "We won't." Even with this stream of admonitions, Harriet's letter was softer than usual. A honeymoon daze of happiness crept in, and Sarah was glad of it. "You and your rogue earl," she said affectionately.

She braced herself a little for the last letter. Charlotte never minced words. "She doesn't even slice them," Sarah said, amusing herself as she opened it. The missive was predictably caustic at the beginning. Charlotte could not believe Sarah had not applied to her rather than allowing herself to be shoved into marriage with some stranger. Charlotte would have sent a phalanx of brothers—she had four—to pound some sense into *someone*. She still could, if Sarah would let her know immediately before the dratted fox-hunting season began. This Kenver person could have his responsibilities forcibly pointed out to him.

"A recipe for farcical disaster," Sarah muttered, though she did take a moment to imagine a troop of pugnacious Deeping brothers invading Poldene. Funny for a moment or so, then a debacle, she concluded. And she didn't want Kenver "disciplined." Nothing of the kind. Others…but no.

Sarah knew that a deep kindness lay under Charlotte's acerbic manner. She also knew that being in Leicestershire with her hunting-mad family tried her friend's patience to its admittedly narrow limits. She set the last letter aside.

It was lovely to "hear" all their voices and to feel their unwavering support. Friendship was so precious. Sarah was engulfed by a wave of memories. The four of them had learned together, consoled each other for disappointments and mistakes, celebrated triumphs, had marvelous adventures, seen three of their number married. Two very happily. And herself—that was complicated.

She would have to write back soon and reassure them, assuming she could find words to do so. Her situation descended on her again after this respite. The earl's recovery was hopeful. He seemed more sympathetic. But Lady Trestan was not. She watched Sarah with less contempt but far more calculation, as if Sarah was the sneaking sorceress who gains sway over the monarch and pulls strings from behind the throne. Only the earl was not really the monarch at Poldene, and Sarah didn't know anything about strings. Also, unfortunately, she had no sorcerous powers.

On his way back to the state suite and Sarah, Kenver heard his name called. He turned to find his mother beckoning. Felch must have reported to her right away. Of course he would have. But there was no way she could know what he and Papa had discussed after the valet left. It had only been the two of them.

"Come and sit with me for a while," she said.

As he followed her to her private parlor, Kenver had to fight an old apprehension. He was not a boy called in for a scold. Or a youth about to be burdened with some onerous task. Quite the contrary!

His mother sat down, smiling, and gestured at the armchair opposite, where his father usually sat. Kenver hesitated, then took it.

"How the years fly by," she said. "It seems only yesterday you were toddling about the nursery."

This was unlike Mama.

"There was such rejoicing when you were born healthy," she continued. "We had lost four infants before that, you know."

He had heard whispers of this, but it had never been mentioned directly before.

She heaved a great sigh. That was unlike Mama as well.

"Fingal's sire guarded your cradle, you know. He wouldn't let any stranger near you. It was as if he sensed how precious this living child was. Dogs are loyal creatures, aren't they?"

His mother never had much to do with the hounds. In fact, Kenver had sometimes thought that Fingal wasn't at all fond of her.

"You and your father have such a bond with them," she said as if reading his thoughts.

"So does Sarah," Kenver dared.

She blinked, and her lips tightened briefly. Almost before he could notice, the reaction was gone. "You used to ride on one of them when you were very small," she said.

He hadn't thought she remembered such things. "Fianna," he said.

"Yes."

"Papa named her for the old Irish war bands because she was fearless."

"Yes," Mama repeated.

Mention of Fianna brought back a host of memories. "We went on so many adventures together, chasing villains and pirates."

"You always had a great deal of imagination." She smiled.

"You gave me those books of ancient legends. One at every birthday for years." There had been good times with Mama, Kenver thought. Not rollicking fun, but solid satisfactions. He'd worked so hard to impress her, and when she praised him, it had felt like such a triumph. She didn't deal in empty compliments.

"Yes."

Something in the way she said it this time made Kenver wonder if she really remembered those gifts. She had always handed them over, tied with ribbons. He realized he couldn't quite see her tying those bows. The picture wouldn't come.

Mama shifted in her chair, straightened a bit. Kenver recognized the movements and understood that the conversation so far had been preliminaries. Now they were over. Some of the cordiality drained out of him.

"You know, Kenver, your father's illness made me realize that it is important for us think about the future."

Kenver simply looked inquiring.

"It seemed for a time that we would lose him."

He nodded.

"And the sickness weakened him so. Indeed, I fear it may have affected his wits."

This was a surprise. "I've seen no sign of that."

His mother gave him a sympathetic smile. "I know him better than you. I expect he hides it in your presence so that you will not lose respect for him. That would wound him deeply."

The picture she'd begun to paint was affecting. But it

wasn't right. "There's no danger of that. We just had a long talk. He seemed very sharp."

Mama frowned. She shifted in her chair again. "I worry that his constitution has been irretrievably shaken. And that he will soon be ill again."

"We must take good care of him."

"Of course. Though the mere fact that we must exert ourselves to do so…" She put a hand on some papers on the desk beside her. "I've had Figgs draw up a document for you and your father to sign."

Wondering what the solicitor had to do with his father's health, Kenver held out his hand for it.

She didn't give it to him.

"I am always thinking of the good of Poldene, you know," she said instead.

"I know you are, Mama." The good of the people living here seemed a separate issue for her. Far less important.

"I'm glad you agree with me, Kenver. We will work very well together, I think."

As if his father was already gone. "I can't agree with anything until I've read the document," Kenver pointed out.

His mother waved a careless hand. "It is convoluted. These lawyers scarcely write English, do they? 'Herewith'… What a word!"

"I will endeavor to puzzle through it." Kenver was proud of his tone. He felt he'd almost achieved the Duke of Tereford's languid sarcasm. He held out his hand again.

She picked up the pages, slowly. Finally she gave them to him. Kenver began to read. The document *was* stuffed with legal jargon, and his mother's intense stare was a distraction, but he pushed on.

"Really, Kenver," she began after a while.

"You must let me get to the end, Mama."

The verbiage seemed endless. The tension in the room cranked higher. But Kenver concentrated all his faculties, and at last, he finished. "This appears to limit my power to make decisions about the estate. Rather severely. And it stipulates that Sarah will never have any say, no matter what the circumstances." He met her eyes and continued with purposeful starkness. "Even if every other member of the family has dropped dead."

"I wouldn't put it..."

"Figgs more or less did," Kenver interrupted, tapping the page with one finger.

"You exaggerate."

"No, Mama, I don't."

She leaned forward. Her eyes burned with the fervor of a fanatic. "The most important thing is to keep a great estate intact and thriving."

Setting aside the fact that other things in the world were more crucial, Kenver said, "And you think, in our case, that only you can do that."

"I am the one who has!" she exclaimed.

"I know you have done well. Papa does too."

She looked gratified. "Well then."

"But that doesn't mean no one else can manage."

"Your father is a fool."

"You know, I don't think he is, Mama."

"And so are you. Not to mention that girl you..."

"It would be better if you did not—" Kenver cut in.

His mother clenched her fists. "If you think you can set me aside after all I have given to this place." She bared her teeth in fury and...fear.

Kenver wasn't sure he'd ever seen her afraid before. Perhaps he'd simply never recognized it. He saw it now. And understood. His father was the Earl of Trestan. He was the heir. In the view of the world, they were the powers at Poldene. His mother had no standing unless she could convince or intimidate. And she hated this, with a bitterness that spilled over into every part of her life.

"Do you want to see your heritage fall into ruin?" she hissed.

Pity and resentment made an uncomfortable mixture, Kenver noted. They roiled together in the stomach. He rose. "I will keep this document and go over it with Papa."

His mother reached out. "No! Give it back."

"We will give it due consideration," Kenver replied. Which was none, he added silently. That was all it was due.

"You will be sorry if you oppose me!"

He was already sorry, for a number of things. Though not that one. Kenver left his mother's parlor. This was not a matter he could solve alone.

———

"We are going to have to speak to Mama together," Kenver said to his father and Sarah later that day. He'd gathered them in the earl's bedchamber when the nurse had gone for her dinner and his mother was dressing for theirs.

His father was clearly uneasy, Sarah thought. She had not wanted to come. She'd seen the document Lady Trestan had prepared. It was insulting to her, but hardly a surprise after all that had passed between them. Dealing with it seemed a matter for the Pendrennons.

"You are to be carried down to the drawing room tomorrow, Papa," said Kenver. It was to be the earl's first foray from his room. "We will do it then."

"So soon?" His father grimaced. "I'm still feeling poorly, you know. I wonder if I can go downstairs after all."

Sarah understood his response. She didn't want to face Lady Trestan's wrath either.

"Won't it be better to get it over?" Kenver asked.

"I suppose." This sounded more like a question than a statement.

"Before Mama thinks of some other scheme?"

Sarah saw that hit home. Lord Trestan sighed.

"I am prepared to take the lead, Papa. You need only stand by me."

"She gets so very angry," his father replied.

"She will be angry at me."

The earl looked unconvinced.

"I don't see why I should come," Sarah began.

"I hope you will," Kenver responded.

"He is doing this for your sake," his father unexpectedly told Sarah. "He would never have dared otherwise."

Sarah met Kenver's hazel eyes and saw that this was true. He was facing the anxieties of a lifetime because he loved her. She felt the strength of that bond stretching between them, woven by laughter and daily challenges, interests that inter-twined, and tender caresses in the dark. Her heart swelled. If he could dare for her, she could do as much for him, even though she was afraid. She nodded.

"You do things for each other," said the earl. He looked at Sarah. "You got the medicine for me because you care for Kenver."

It seemed unkind to agree, so Sarah said nothing.

"I am happy to see it." Lord Trestan sounded wistful, which made Sarah notice how pale and shaky he remained. His chin slowly came up. "I can do as much for my son. I can play my part."

Kenver looked moved. He nodded to both of them. "So, Mama will see that we are agreed and cannot be separated out and persuaded. That is the only way this will be settled once and for all."

"I am going to order dinner in our rooms," Sarah declared. "I cannot sit in the dining room tonight."

The following morning, once the earl was settled in the drawing room, they sent a footman to invite Kenver's mother to join them. She had not bothered to see the earl carried down, and Sarah wondered if she would come. But after an interval to show that she would not be peremptorily summoned, she did.

"What is this?" she asked when she entered. Clearly she had not expected to see Sarah.

"We wanted to have a family talk, Mama," said Kenver.

"A what?"

"I do not feel that the document Figgs prepared is in the best interests of Poldene," Kenver went on.

"*You* do not?" His mother waved this away. "You are a green boy."

"No, I am not."

She turned to the earl. "Will you allow him to speak to me this way, Peter?"

"I thought he was polite," said Lord Trestan.

"Polite!" She spit the word as if it was offensive.

"And he's right about the document."

Lady Trestan reared back, apparently stunned.

"We appreciate your dedication to Poldene," said Kenver. "But we won't be superseded anymore."

"Superseded! Hoity-toity."

"We can work together…"

"You don't know what work means!" she interrupted.

"I believe that I do. And what I do not, I can learn. I am rather good at that, Mama."

The countess's glare swept the group, lingering a bit longer on Sarah as if she blamed her for this scene. "So you are all against me. Perhaps you think I have mismanaged the estate. You will accuse me of embezzlement perhaps?"

"No, Mama. And you are changing the subject."

"Perhaps I should go to the gun room for a pistol and put a period to my existence," Lady Trestan said.

A frightened exclamation escaped Sarah.

The countess pounced on it. "Everything has gone wrong at Poldene since you came here, you sneaking little…"

"Stop it, Mama. I will not have Sarah bullied."

Kenver's mother bridled. "Do you dare tell your elders how to behave?"

"I regret that I have to. I don't like being disappointed in you."

This got a reaction. For once, Lady Trestan didn't seem to know what to say.

"I've never seen you treat anyone as you did Sarah on her arrival," Kenver went on. "A girl of nineteen!" He frowned. "Well, except for Tamara, I suppose. But I don't really remember that."

"Her name is not to be mentioned," declared his mother dramatically.

"It *will* be mentioned. Quite often."

Lady Trestan looked startled at this calmly implacable response.

"In fact I intend to invite Tamara and her son to visit," Kenver added.

"Son?" said his father.

"You have a grandson," said Sarah. "Didn't Lady Trestan tell you?"

"She did not." The earl frowned.

"How can you side with this stranger over your own family?" the countess asked Kenver.

"Sarah is my family now."

"She rather than me?" She gestured at her husband. "Us?"

"Not 'rather than.'"

Sarah admired the way Kenver was staying calm and measured. She wasn't sure how he was managing it. She was trembling.

"But additionally and providentially, I must say. Sarah has shown me what love is."

A tremor of emotion crossed Lady Trestan's face. "I am to be nothing then. Rejected, reviled…"

"No, Mama. Nothing of the kind. We are simply making

some changes in our…arrangements. I have made a list." He offered her a sheet of paper.

Sarah knew the list included a rise in Kenver's allowance, gestures of reconciliation with Tamara, the return of Gwen and Elys to their old positions, and assurance that Sarah would be treated with public respect at the least.

Lady Trestan took the page, glanced at it, tore it in pieces, and scattered them on the carpet. Then she glared like a defiant child.

"I have a copy," Kenver said dryly. "And Papa has already agreed. Perhaps I will just tell you…"

"Don't bother," she replied. "As I no longer matter." She half turned as if to leave. But she didn't actually go.

"This is not all or nothing," Kenver said. "Things are almost never a case of all or nothing, Mama."

She stood still. It seemed she had finally run out of words.

"You know more about managing Poldene than anyone," Kenver continued. "We cannot give that up."

"No, indeed," said the earl.

Lady Trestan grew alert. Sarah was reminded of Fingal when he scented a rabbit.

"I will learn at your side," Kenver said. "You will show me all the ins and outs of estate business."

"I'm to be your tutor?"

Kenver made a face. "I prefer to say colleague."

"I wouldn't spare you work."

"I would not wish you to."

Her expression grew speculative. "You will tire of it in a month."

"I don't think I will, Mama."

She was already plotting new stratagems, Sarah saw. She underestimated Kenver's determination, as well as the efforts he had already made. And more importantly, the earl's readiness to support him. That would make the difference. Would he be steadfast? Sarah looked down at the older man, leaning back in his chair.

"A grandson, eh?" he murmured. "I should like more of those. Granddaughters too."

Sarah blushed.

It was agreed that Kenver and the countess would meet each morning to review the tasks of the day. The estate agent, solicitor, and others were to be notified of his new position. Consulted about details, Lady Trestan gradually seemed to accept, if not embrace, the new system.

"You are a hero," Sarah said as she and Kenver returned to their suite later that morning.

"Only because I was inspired by you," he replied. "No wonder all those knights of old tried so hard in their jousts and on their quests. They wanted to demonstrate their love for the fair maidens."

"I don't want to be just a spectator waving the hero on."

"You shall be whatever you wish, my dearest love."

"No," Sarah replied sadly.

"Why not? I will see to it."

"You can't."

"You don't know what I can do." He gestured grandly.

"But I would really like to be a mighty sorceress with a host of arcane powers."

Kenver laughed and pulled her into his arms.

Epilogue

"Too expensive," said Kenver's mother as the two of them sat together in her parlor two months later. She flipped the top page of the plans he had presented with one contemptuous fingernail. "We can't fling money about. You are naive and irresponsible."

Kenver kept a strong rein on his temper. "Slate roofs last three or four times longer than thatch," he replied.

She looked surprised, as she always did when Kenver showed a good grasp of some business matter. Still.

"They'll hold up better in the storms from the sea as well."

"Slates can be blown off. There will be repairs."

"Yes, Mama. As with any sort of building at all."

She bent to look again at the drawings. Her face creased as if she was swallowing unpalatable medicine. "It's possible that your idea has *some* merit."

"Slate roofs will be solid when my great-grandchildren are managing Poldene."

She blinked, gazing at him.

"Same as the oaks we planted for replacement beams," he added.

At last he had reached her. They bent over the document together and began to dissect its details.

Kenver had found that if they could move past her habitual way of responding to any hint of disagreement, his mother was actually open to new ideas. Her habit was just so engrained that an attack always came first. If she got no reaction, she tried again. It was like descending stairs from insulting to irritable to grumpy and then finally to reasonable.

It was wearisome. Kenver had nearly snapped more than once. But then Sarah had suggested that it was like re-educating a horse who was an inveterate biter. A trainer who calmly kept at it could change the animal. The comparison had made him laugh, and it gave him something to cling to when Mama was particularly recalcitrant. Kenver really didn't know what he would have done without Sarah. His life would have narrowed down to nothing. He suppressed a shudder.

As usual in their discussions, his mother's long experience with the Poldene lands was useful. "That's a good point," he told her along the way. He noted a change on the plans.

When he looked up again, she was staring at him. "I should not have said irresponsible," she said. "That was…an exaggeration." She swallowed. "No, it was untrue."

Yes, it was, Kenver did not say. She so rarely admitted as much.

"I'm sorry," she added.

It was difficult to keep his jaw from dropping. Mama had apologized. Sincerely. To him! He tried to remember another time this had happened. He could not. Thinking that anything he might say would disturb this fragile new balance, he simply nodded. Mama would never be easy, but he felt a touch of hope.

His mother avoided his eyes. She snatched up a bill from the pile of papers before them. "Now this is highway robbery. You must tell Hicks we will not pay so much."

Reading upside down, as he had lately become proficient in doing, Kenver saw that it was the charge for repairs to the state suite. Allowing a tinge of irony to enter his tone, he said, "Hicks did work very quickly. When you asked."

Realizing she had made a tactical error, Mama dropped the page.

They moved on to other matters, jousting every step of the way. Sarah had suggested that a certain amount of friction could be productive, producing better solutions in the end. She was right, though that didn't make the process any more pleasant. But after the unprecedented apology, Kenver dared to hope that it might be, as time went by.

Their business finished, he made his way to the library. This room had become Sarah's undisputed domain, as his mother's parlor was hers. Sarah had decorated it to her own taste, and it was now the most welcoming chamber at Poldene, in Kenver's opinion. Packets of new books also arrived with some regularity. He found his father there with his wife, sipping an herbal tonic. "Has your mother been here?" Kenver asked Sarah. "I'm sorry to have missed her."

"No, I made it myself," Sarah replied. She had set up a stillroom near the kitchen. Mrs. Moran was a frequent visitor, training Sarah in its uses. Kenver sat down beside her and felt peace and contentment wash over him.

"Tastes like the elixir of youth," said his father and smacked his lips.

"You promised you wouldn't say such things," Sarah replied.

"That's how it makes me feel."

"My mother is very strict about this. We do not claim miracle cures."

"She is a lovely lady." He drank again. "I gave Alice some of this. She said it filled her with energy."

"You had better not tell her I made it," Sarah joked.

"I didn't. At first."

"You have now?" Kenver asked, curious about his mother's reaction.

Papa nodded. "She allowed as how you knew what you were doing," he said to Sarah.

"She did not!"

"Yes, she did. Well, once I reminded her of all the good things she'd already said about the drink. She couldn't deny that, eh?"

"What makes you think so?" Kenver wondered. His mother was perfectly capable of changing her position without warning.

"Well, she could have. But I don't think she wanted to."

Sarah raised her eyebrows.

"She knows you saved my life," Kenver's father told her. "Took her a while to face up to it, but she did. You managed something she couldn't do."

"She was almost cordial at dinner the other night," Sarah acknowledged.

"Shall we call it grudging respect?" Kenver asked.

"Tamara learned to hold a grudge from her," his father

mused, picking up on the word. "But I think Alice can learn to let one go from you."

Sarah looked surprised and touched. "Thank you."

"No, thank *you*."

Kenver met his wife's blue eyes. They smiled, and he felt all his remaining tension relax.

His father dug a piece of paper from his coat pocket. "Letter from Henry," he told them. "I must say a grandson seems like a fine thing. Pure enjoyment and no worries."

His father preferred that, Kenver had concluded. He and Sarah had come to agree with his mother on this topic. Papa actually wasn't a great estate manager. Poldene had benefited from Mama's fierce qualities. Which was not to say her methods were the only ones.

"Need any help with your mother?" Papa asked, as if reading his thoughts.

"No, I can handle her." Kenver thought of mentioning the apology and decided to save that for Sarah alone.

"Well, if you should need me…"

"You are better as a distant, silent threat."

His father grew sheepish, acknowledging the hollowness of this idea. "No chance of tripping over my tongue in that case."

The look he gave Kenver said everything. He was glad his son had taken over—admiring and grateful and proud—things Kenver had wished for all his life.

"We must have Henry down for a visit," Sarah said.

"Could we, do you think?"

"Yes," answered Kenver without qualification.

His father looked delighted. "I'll show him the old oak. Did I ever tell you about the Roman coin I found buried beneath it?"

He had, but Kenver didn't care. He saw that Sarah felt the same.

Papa ran on, full of anecdotes and expressions of love for the land. Finally, though, he noticed the slowing of responses. "I should run along and give you youngsters some privacy," he said then.

He clearly wanted to linger. On the other hand, Kenver wanted to sit with his wife, so he didn't urge him to stay.

"Don't forget what I said about a ball," Papa added as he rose. "We ought to introduce Sarah to the neighborhood properly."

He seemed able to forget the slights they'd offered her in the beginning. Not for the first time, Kenver wondered if Papa's illness had weakened his memory.

With a jaunty wave, his father went out, leaving the door slightly ajar.

Kenver pulled Sarah closer. "Do you want a ball?"

"I'd rather have a greenhouse for growing herbs."

He laughed.

Tess the deerhound pushed into the room. She carried a squirming puppy by the nape of its neck. She put it down near Sarah's feet and went out. A few minutes later, she brought another. This process was repeated three more times.

"She brings them to you wherever you are?" Kenver asked.

"Whenever she can reach me."

"I've never seen her do anything like that before."

"She may feel a kinship."

"Eh?"

Sarah put her hand on her midsection. "Next year, your father will get his wish for another grandchild."

"Oh, my love!" Kenver drew her into his arms, then pulled back. "You feel well?"

"Perfectly. Mama says all is as it should be."

Once again Kenver felt grateful for Mrs. Moran's wisdom.

"I do hope it will be a boy," said Sarah.

"It doesn't matter."

"Your mother said…"

"We have agreed that much of what Mama says is nonsense."

"Yes, but the earldom requires an heir."

"A daughter would be delightful," Kenver insisted.

"If it is, I suppose we can simply try again," Sarah conceded.

"Oh yes, we can do that," he replied, kissing her with all the love in his heart.

Keep reading for an excerpt of the first
book in the Duke's Estates series

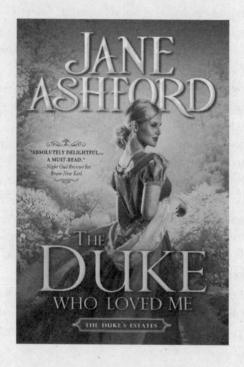

One

THREE DAYS AFTER HE INHERITED THE TITLE DUKE OF Tereford, James Cantrell set off to visit the ducal town house just off London's Berkeley Square. He walked from his rooms, as the distance was short and the April day pleasant. He hoped to make this first encounter cordially brief and be off riding before the sunlight faded.

He had just entered the square when a shouted greeting turned his head. Henry Deeping was approaching, an unknown young man beside him.

"Have you met my friend Cantrell?" Henry asked his companion when they reached James. "Sorry. Tereford, I should say. He's just become a duke. Stephan Kandler, meet the newest peer of the realm as well as the handsomest man in London."

As they exchanged bows James silently cursed whatever idiot had saddled him with that label. He'd inherited his powerful frame, black hair, and blue eyes from his father. It was nothing to do with him. "That's nonsense," he said.

"Yes, Your Grace." Henry's teasing tone had changed recently. It held the slightest trace of envy.

James had heard it from others since he'd come into his inheritance. His cronies were young men who shared his interest in sport, met while boxing or fencing, on the hunting field, or perhaps clipping a wafer at Manton's shooting gallery, where Henry Deeping had an uncanny ability. They were generally not plump in the pocket. Some lived on allowances from their fathers and would inherit as James had; others would have a moderate income all their lives. All of them preferred vigorous activity to smoky gaming hells or drunken revels.

They'd been more or less equals. But now circumstances had pulled James away, into the peerage and wealth, and he was feeling the distance. One old man's death, and his life was changed. Which was particularly hard with Henry. They'd known each since they were uneasy twelve-year-olds arriving at school.

"We're headed over to Manton's if you'd care to come," Henry said. He sounded repentant.

"I can't just now," James replied. He didn't want to mention that he was headed to Tereford House. It was just another measure of the distance from Henry. He saw that Henry noticed the vagueness of his reply.

"Another time perhaps," said Henry's companion in a Germanic accent.

James gave a noncommittal reply, wondering where Henry had met the fellow. His friend was considering the diplomatic corps as a means to make his way in the world. Perhaps this Kandler had something to do with that.

They separated. James walked across the square and into the narrow street containing Tereford House.

The massive stone building, of no particular architectural distinction, loomed over the cobbles. Its walls showed signs of neglect, and the windows on the upper floors were all shuttered. There was no funerary hatchment above the door. Owing to the eccentricities of his great-uncle, the recently deceased sixth duke, James had never been inside. His every approach had been rebuffed.

He walked up to the door and plied the tarnished knocker. When that brought no response, he rapped on the door with the knob of his cane. He had sent word ahead, of course, and expected a better reception than this. At last the door opened, and he strolled inside—to be immediately assailed by a wave of stale mustiness. The odor was heavy rather than sharp, but it insinuated itself into the nostrils like an unwanted guest. James suspected that it would swiftly permeate his clothes and hair. His dark brows drew together. The atmosphere in the dim entryway, with closed doors on each side and at the back next to a curving stair, was oppressive. It seemed almost threatening.

One older female servant stood before him. She dropped a curtsy. "Your Grace," she said, as if the phrase was unfamiliar.

"Where is the rest of the staff?" They really ought to have lined up to receive him. He had given them a time for his visit.

"There's only me. Your Grace."

"What?"

"Keys is there." She pointed to a small side table. A ring of old-fashioned keys lay on it.

James noticed a small portmanteau sitting at her feet.

She followed his eyes. "I'll be going then. Your Grace." Before James could reply, she picked up the case and marched through the still-open front door.

Her footsteps faded, leaving behind a dismal silence. The smell seemed to crowd closer, pressing on him. The light dimmed briefly as a carriage passed outside. James suppressed a desire to flee. He had a pleasant set of rooms in Hill Street where he had, for some years, been living a life that suited him quite well. He might own this house now, but that didn't mean he had to live here. Or perhaps he did. A duke had duties. It occurred to him that the servant might have walked off with some valuable items. He shrugged. Her bag had been too small to contain much.

He walked over to the closed door on the right and turned the knob. The door opened a few inches and then hit some sort of obstacle. He pushed harder. It remained stuck. James had to put his shoulder to the panels and shove with the strength developed in Gentleman Jackson's boxing saloon before it gave way, with a crash of some largish object falling inside. He forced his way through but managed only one step before he was brought up short, his jaw dropping. The chamber—a well-proportioned parlor with high ceilings and elaborate moldings—was stuffed to bursting with a mad jumble of objects. Furniture of varying eras teetered in haphazard stacks—sofas, chairs, tables, cabinets. Paintings and other ornaments were pushed into every available crevice. Folds and swathes of fabric that might have been draperies or bedclothes drooped over the mass, which towered far above his head. There was no room to move. "Good God!" The stale odor was much worse here, and a scurrying sound did not bode well.

James backed hastily out. He thought of the shuttered

rooms on the upper floors. Were they all…? But perhaps only this one was a mare's nest. He walked across the entry-way and tried the door on the left. It concealed a larger room in the same wretched condition. His heart, which had not been precisely singing, sank. He'd assumed that his new position would require a good deal of tedious effort, but he hadn't expected chaos.

The click of footsteps approached from outside. The front door was still open, and now a fashionably dressed young lady walked through it. She was accompanied by a maid and a footman. The latter started to shut the door behind them. "Don't," commanded James. The young servant shied like a nervous horse.

"What is that smell?" the lady inquired, putting a gloved hand to her nose.

"What are you doing here?" James asked the bane of his existence.

"You mentioned that you were going to look over the house today."

"And in what way is this your concern?"

"I was so curious. There are all sorts of rumors about this place. No one has been inside for years." She went over to one of the parlor doors and peered around it. "Oh!" She crossed to look into the other side. "Good heavens!"

"Indeed."

"Well, this is going to be a great deal of work." She smiled. "You won't like that."

"You have no idea what I…" James had to stop, because he knew that she had a very good idea.

"I know more about your affairs than you do," she added.

It was nearly true. Once, it certainly had been. That admission took him back thirteen years to his first meeting with Cecelia Vainsmede. He'd been just fifteen, recently orphaned, and in the midst of a blazing row with his new trustee. Blazing on his side, at any rate. Nigel Vainsmede had been pained and evasive and clearly just wishing James would go away. They'd fallen into one of their infuriating bouts of pushing in and fending off, insisting and eluding. James had understood by that time that his trustee might agree to a point simply to be rid of him, but he would never carry through with any action. Vainsmede would forget— willfully, it seemed to James. Insultingly.

And then a small blond girl had marched into her father's library and ordered them to stop at once. Even at nine years old, Cecelia had been a determined character with a glare far beyond her years. James had been surprised into silence. Vainsmede had actually looked grateful. And on that day they had established the routine that allowed them to function for the next ten years—speaking to each other only through Cecelia. James would approach her with "Please tell your father." And she would manage the matter, whatever it was. James didn't have to plead, which he hated, and Nigel Vainsmede didn't have to do anything at all, which was his main hope in life as far as James could tell.

James and Cecelia had worked together all through their youth. Cecelia was not a friend, and not family, but some indefinable other sort of close connection. And she did know a great deal about him. More than he knew about her.

Although he had observed, along with the rest of the *haut ton*, that she had grown up to be a very pretty young lady. Today in a walking dress of sprig muslin and a straw bonnet decorated with matching blue ribbons, she was lithely lovely. Her hair was less golden than it had been at nine but far better cut. She had the face of a renaissance Madonna except for the rather too lush lips. And her luminous blue eyes missed very little, as he had cause to know. Not that any of this was relevant at the moment. "Your father has not been my trustee for three years," James pointed out.

"And you have done nothing much since then."

He would have denied it, but what did it matter? Instead he said, "I never could understand why my father appointed *your* father as my trustee."

"It was odd," she said.

"They were just barely friends, I would say."

"Hardly that," she replied. "Papa was astonished when he heard."

"As was I." James remembered the bewildered outrage of his fifteen-year-old self when told that he would be under the thumb of a stranger until he reached the age of twenty-five. "And, begging your pardon, but your father is hardly a pattern card of wisdom."

"No. He is indolent and self-centered. Almost as much as you are."

"Why, Miss Vainsmede!" He rarely called her that. They had dropped formalities and begun using first names when she was twelve. "I am not the least indolent."

She hid a smile. "Only if you count various forms of sport.

Which I do not. I have thought about the trusteeship, however. From what I've learned of your father—I did not know him of course—I think he preferred to be in charge."

A crack of laughter escaped James. "Preferred! An extreme understatement. He had the soul of an autocrat and the temper of a frustrated tyrant."

She frowned at him. "Yes. Well. Having heard something of that, I came to the conclusion that your father chose mine because he was confident Papa would do nothing in particular."

"What?"

"I think that your father disliked the idea of not being... present to oversee your upbringing, and he couldn't bear the idea of anyone *doing* anything about that."

James frowned as he worked through this convoluted sentence.

"And so he chose my father because he was confident Papa wouldn't...bestir himself and try to make changes in the arrangements."

Surprise kept James silent for a long moment. "You know that is the best theory I have heard. It might even be right."

"You needn't sound so astonished," Cecelia replied. "I often have quite good ideas."

"What a crackbrained notion!"

"I beg your pardon?"

"My father's, not yours." James shook his head. "You think he drove me nearly to distraction just to fend off change?"

"If he had lived..." she began.

"Oh, that would have been far worse. A never-ending battle of wills."

"You don't know that. I was often annoyed with my father when I was younger, but we get along well now."

"Because he lets you be as scandalous as you please, Cecelia."

"Oh nonsense."

James raised one dark brow.

"I *wish* I could learn to do that," exclaimed his pretty visitor. "You are said to have the most killing sneer in the *ton*, you know."

He was not going to tell her that he had spent much of a summer before the mirror when he was sixteen perfecting the gesture.

"And it was *not* scandalous for me to attend one ball without a chaperone. I was surrounded by friends and acquaintances. What could happen to me in such a crowd?" She shook her head. "At any rate, I am quite on the shelf at twenty-two. So it doesn't matter."

"Don't be stupid." James knew, from the laments of young gentleman acquaintances, that Cecelia had refused several offers. She was anything but "on the shelf."

"I am never stupid," she replied coldly.

He was about to make an acid retort when he recalled that Cecelia was a positive glutton for work. She'd also learned a great deal about estate management and business as her father pushed tasks off on her, his only offspring. She'd come to manage much of Vainsmede's affairs as well as the trust. Indeed, she'd taken to it as James never had. He thought of the challenge confronting him. Could he cajole her into taking some of it on?

She'd gone to open the door at the rear of the entryway. "There is just barely room to edge along the hall here," she said. "Why would anyone keep all these newspapers? There must be years of them. Do you suppose the whole house is like this?"

"I have a sinking feeling that it may be worse. The sole servant ran off as if she was conscious of her failure."

"One servant couldn't care for such a large house even if it hadn't been…"

"A rubbish collection? I think Uncle Percival must have actually been mad. People called him eccentric, but this is…" James peered down the cluttered hallway. "No wonder he refused all my visits."

"Did you try to visit him?" Cecelia asked.

"Of course."

"Huh."

"Is that so surprising?" asked James.

"Well, yes, because you don't care for anyone but yourself."

"Don't start up this old refrain."

"It's the truth."

"More a matter of opinion and definition," James replied.

She waved this aside. "You will have to do better now that you are the head of your family."

"A meaningless label. I shall have to bring some order." He grimaced at the stacks of newspapers. "But no more than that."

"A great deal more," said Cecelia. "You have a duty…"

"As Uncle Percival did?" James gestured at their surroundings.

"His failure is all the more reason for you to shoulder your responsibilities."

"I don't think so."

Cecelia put her hands on her hips, just as she had done at nine years old. "Under our system the bulk of the money and all of the property in the great families passes to one man, in this case you. You are obliged to manage it for the good of the whole." She looked doubtful suddenly. "If there is any money."

"There is," he replied. This had been a continual sore point during the years of the trust. And after, in fact. His father had not left a fortune. "Quite a bit of it seemingly. I had a visit from a rather sour banker. Uncle Percival was a miser as well as a..." James gestured at the mess. "A connoisseur of detritus. But if you think I will tolerate the whining of indigent relatives, you are deluded." He had made do when he was far from wealthy. Others could follow suit.

"You must take care of your people."

She was interrupted by a rustle of newsprint. "I daresay there are rats," James said.

"Do you think to frighten me? You never could."

This was true. And he had really tried a few times in his youth.

"I am consumed by morbid curiosity," Cecelia added as she slipped down the hall. James followed. Her attendants came straggling after, the maid looking uneasy at the thought of rodents.

They found other rooms as jumbled as the first two. Indeed, the muddle seemed to worsen toward the rear of the house. "Is that a spinning wheel?" Cecelia exclaimed at one point. "Why would a duke want such a thing?"

"It appears he was unable to resist acquiring any object that he came across," replied James.

"But where would he come across a spinning wheel?"

"In a tenant's cottage?"

"Do you suppose he bought it from them?"

"I have no idea." James pushed aside a hanging swag of cloth. Dust billowed out and set them all coughing. He stifled a curse.

At last they came into what might have been a library. James thought he could see bookshelves behind the piles of refuse. There was a desk, he realized, with a chair pulled up to it. He hadn't noticed at first because it was buried under mountains of documents. At one side sat a large wicker basket brimming with correspondence.

Cecelia picked up a sheaf of pages from the desk, glanced over it, and set it down again. She rummaged in the basket. "These are all letters," she said.

"Wonderful."

"May I?"

James gestured his permission, and she opened one from the top. "Oh, this is bad. Your cousin Elvira needs help."

"I have no knowledge of a cousin Elvira."

"Oh, I suppose she must have been your uncle Percival's cousin. She sounds rather desperate."

"Well, that is the point of a begging letter, is it not? The effect is diminished if one doesn't sound desperate."

"Yes, but James…"

"My God, do you suppose they're all like that?" The basket was as long as his arm and nearly as deep. It was mounded with correspondence.

Cecelia dug deeper. "They all seem to be personal letters. Just thrown in here. I suppose they go back for months."

"Years," James guessed. Dust lay over them, as it did everything here.

"You must read them."

"I don't think so. For once I approve of Uncle Percival's methods. I would say throw them in the fire, if lighting a fire in this place wasn't an act of madness."

"Have you no family feeling?"

"None. You read them if you're so interested."

She shuffled through the upper layer. "Here's one from your grandmother."

"Which one?"

"Lady Wilton."

"Oh no."

Cecelia opened the sheet and read. "She seems to have misplaced an earl."

"What?"

"A long-lost heir has gone missing."

"Who? No, never mind. I don't care." The enormity of the task facing him descended on James, looming like the piles of objects leaning over his head. He looked up. One wrong move, and all that would fall about his ears. He wanted none of it.

A flicker of movement diverted him. A rat had emerged from a crevice between a gilded chair leg and a hideous outsized vase. The creature stared down at him, insolent, seeming to know that it was well out of reach. "Wonderful," murmured James.

Cecelia looked up. "What?"

He started to point out the animal, to make her jump, then bit back the words as an idea recurred. He, and her father, had taken advantage of her energetic capabilities over the years. He knew it. He was fairly certain she knew it. Her father had probably never noticed. But Cecelia hadn't minded. She'd said once that the things she'd learned and done had given her a more interesting life than most young ladies were allowed. Might his current plight not intrigue her? So instead of mentioning the rodent, he offered his most charming smile. "Perhaps you would like to have that basket," he suggested. "It must be full of compelling stories."

Her blue eyes glinted as if she understood exactly what he was up to. "No, James. This mare's nest is all yours. I think, actually, that you deserve it."

"How can you say so?"

"It is like those old Greek stories, where the thing one tries hardest to avoid fatefully descends."

"Thing?" said James, gazing at the looming piles of *things*.

"You loathe organizational tasks. And this one is monumental."

"You have always been the most annoying girl," said James.

"Oh, I shall enjoy watching you dig out." Cecelia turned away. "My curiosity is satisfied. I'll be on my way."

"It isn't like you to avoid work."

She looked over her shoulder at him. "*Your* work. And as you've pointed out, our...collaboration ended three years ago. We will call this visit a final farewell to those days."

She edged her way out, leaving James in his wreck of an inheritance. He was conscious of a sharp pang of regret. He put it down to resentment over her refusal to help him.

About the Author

Jane Ashford discovered Georgette Heyer in junior high school and was captivated by the glittering world and witty language of Regency England. That delight was part of what led her to study English literature and travel widely. Her books have been published all over Europe as well as in the United States. Jane was nominated for a Career Achievement Award by *RT Book Reviews*. Born in Ohio, she is now somewhat nomadic. Find her on the web at janeashford.com and on Facebook at facebook.com/janeashfordwriter, where you can sign up for her monthly newsletter.